The Ghosts of Chateau du Chasse

Also by J. J. Zerr

Guerilla Bride War Stories
The Junior Officer Bunkroom The Happy
Life of Preston Katt Noble Deeds
Sundown Town Duty Station The Ensign Locker

The Ghosts of Chateau du Chasse

—A NOVEL—

J. J. ZERR

Primix Publishing
11620 Wilshire Blvd
Suite 900, West Wilshire Center, Los Angeles, CA, 90025
www.primixpublishing.com
Phone: 1-800-538-5788

Published by Primix Publishing   10/07/2021

ISBN: 978-1-955177-45-0(sc)
ISBN: 978-1-955177-46-7(hc)
ISBN: 978-1-955177-47-4(e)

Library of Congress Control Number: 2021920715

Thanks: to my writing buddies of Coffee and Critique and the editors at iUniverse.

To the memory of US Army General John Galvin,
And to his right-hand man, George.

Contents

Prologue ix

One 1
Two 10
Three 19
Four 24
Five 29
Six 36
Seven 46
Eight 53
Nine 63
Ten 72
Eleven 77
Twelve 86
Thirteen 99
Fourteen 106
Fifteen 113
Sixteen 121

Seventeen 127
Eighteen 137
Nineteen 146
Twenty 152
Twenty-One 160
Twenty-Two 167
Twenty-Three 176
Twenty-Four 184
Twenty-Five 191
Twenty-Six 198
Twenty-Seven 205
Twenty-Eight 214
Twenty-Nine 223
Thirty 234

Prologue

Following Sunday Mass and the post-service social at her parish Henrietta Defonce drove home to the family farm. The farm was located ten kilometers northwest of Mons, Belgium. Her son Rene occupied the passenger seat. It was a joyful experience to travel by car with her boy. Her boy was forty-five. Rarely were their trips together longer than the one to Mons. It didn't matter. In their precious moments together, they floated above the dirt as the body of the auto cocooned them from the hurt aprowl outside.

She stopped next to the backyard and the steps climbing to the rear door of the two-hundred-year-old farmhouse. No regrets over the short duration of the trip. There'd be others.

Rene smiled a thank-you and extricated himself from the car. He closed the door gently.

She drove on and parked in the machine shed, next to the barn, and also next to her brother's car.

Both cars were old. Not so the gleaming plowing, planting, cultivating, and reaping implements parked like soldiers on dress parade. She, as others in the village of Toussaint did, wondered where the money came from to buy such equipment. The other farmers in Hainaut province squeezed a living out of ancient machinery and muscles and sweat, and sometimes blood.

She asked her brother Louis about it many times.

"I work hard for what *we* have."

He always said "we have." *To make me an accomplice in possessing the money.*

She reached the back steps of the house, stopped, turned, and looked across a kilometer of stubble field to *Chateau du Chasse.* It belonged to the Belgian royal family and should have been of no concern to a commoner farmer. But the mansion did concern Henrietta. It, and what happened to her in the basement of the castle, had haunted her for almost fifty years.

She saw the grand royal building every day. Every day the sight of it tormented her. A ghost inhabited the chateau. The ghost was not a soul that, for one reason or another, after departing a body, could not leave earth for either heaven or hell. Rather, it was the ghost of what had happened to her in August 1944.

She had never heard of an *event* creating a spiritual entity. She knew, though, the evil inflicted on her body and soul lived on in the chateau. It may not have been the proper term for it, but ghost was the only word she could conjure.

She crossed herself. Then she thanked the Lord for his great goodness. For, from that awful and evil deed, a miracle, something wondrous had sprung.

The chateau and the ghost were there, a comfortable kilometer away. At least it was comfortable when she remembered to keep God in her heart. The structure, unoccupied now for a number of years, was cold. It had been a hotel for two decades. People living inside warmed the place, rendered it comfortable.

Then she entered the house to prepare Sunday dinner for her heathen brother and angelic son.

One

THIS MONDAY AND SAN DIEGO morning, Kate Marshall's eyes did not, as the first order of business, in the bathroom mirror, seek out the three gray strands corrupting her raven hair. This morning, waves of elation coursed through her body shoved the gray hair counting ritual aside, made her hands shake, and stopped her effort with the curling iron lest she brand herself. Her green eyes sparkled. After years and years of subordinating her wants and needs to those of her husband Bill, the US Navy, and her children, she was being allowed to pursue a dream of her own.

She took a deep breath, held it, then expelled the giddy tension muddling her thoughts and firing spastic nerve impulses, just as she did before serving a tennis ace.

Her boss had offered a partnership in Claire Daley's jury consulting business. Last night, she and Bill had talked about the future.

"I can't take the job if the Navy is going to move us to D.C.," Kate said.

"It's a great opportunity, Mr. Obvious points out. What if you accept the offer, stay here with the kids, and I'll do the Pentagon tour. It's just for two years."

"No. The last decade was one sea duty assignment after another. It's 1990, we will not begin the new decade with more separation. The job is not as important as keeping our family together."

Just before 9 p.m., after they'd hashed over every pro and every con tied to taking the job and not taking the job, Bill told her she had to accept Claire's offer. "You've taken a back seat for twenty-five years supporting me in my navy career. You've been the one who held us together. They'll never promote me to admiral. I—Bill checked for the absence of children—pissed off too many of them. I'll put in my letter of resignation. We'll stay here. Take the offer, Kate."

"Bill!" It was all she'd been able to say.

So many years, the only thing that mattered was what Bill wanted, what the navy required, what their children needed, and now, she could do what *she wanted*. It was an alien thought.

"Call Claire," Bill had said.

"It's too late."

"Call her."

She did, and Claire had been pleased, in a mature businesswoman way.

Now, in the midst of her morning bathroom procedure, Kate's image reflected the jubilation again boiling up inside her.

This is the happiest day of my life!

Catholic guilt, or her guardian angel wielding a tennis racket, smacked the sinful, selfish thought out of her head like a vicious service return.

When the nurse laid Heather, her first born, across her chest, and she made skin-to-skin contact with her baby, that had been the best day. Eleven years ago. That marked the happiest day of her life.

The births of Sally and JR—William, Junior—were happiest days, too.

Kate acknowledged that, until Heather's birth date, she'd always counted the day she fell in love with Bill as the happiest day of her life. Their college speech class. Bill had been assigned the task of defending the proposition that women's suffrage should be repealed. A preposterous notion. But as Bill spoke, Kate fell in love with the blond, trim-waist, six-foot Wyoming cowboy. Never mind the words coming out of his mouth.

As happened at times, the image in the mirror became Kate's guardian angel. Guardian angels were concerned with saving the souls of their humans. Saving bodies and lives counted for little compared to the worth of souls.

Are you happy now? Kate inquired of her angel. She had relegated this day to fifth happiest. No! Her guardian suggested that First Communion and Confirmation Days should count higher than a day of personal gratification.

Enough!

Kate unplugged the curling iron. Her image smiled at her. There was more than enough happiness in the fifth happiest day of her life.

From downstairs, JR screamed as if a demon from Hell was stabbing him with a pitchfork of fire.

Kate ripped the bathroom door open. Then JR laughed. Which meant there was no blood, and no broken glass.

JR and Heather. They loved to antagonize each other. They were responsible for her three gray hairs. After that scream, a fourth was probable.

⁓⁓⁓

Kate dropped the children off at Sacred Heart Catholic School, crossed the bridge from Coronado to San Diego, parked in the garage beneath the office building, and took the elevator to the sixth floor. Until last night, Kate had been office manager for jury consultant Claire Daley. Her duties included opening the office by 8 a.m.

The elevator slowed, stopped, dinged, and the doors opened. Kate's jaw dropped. The sign on the door read: "Daley and Marshall." Yesterday afternoon, when Kate had closed the office, the sign read, "Claire Daley." She must have had a sign painter on standby. What a wonderful sur—

Kate stuck her arm out to keep the elevator doors from closing and stepped out of the car. She smiled at the sign. Then she looked up and down the corridor. *Good.* No one had seen her standing there grinning like an asylum escapee.

Behind her, the elevator car began its journey to a lower level. Kate shook her head as she stared at her name on the door. The grin returned. She was powerless to stop it.

Katie girl!

Her dad's voice, telling her to, "Get a move on." She was still the office manager until Claire, until she and Claire, hired a new one. Kate dug the office keys out of her purse and unlocked the dead bolt.

Then it was as if her heart pumped in a slug of ice water. When she walked through that door, so much more would be expected of her. She was no longer the office manager, but partner. She was expected to perform just as Claire did. And she'd dressed as she did every morning.

Why didn't I wear the black suit? I'm dressed like an office manager.

"God help me," Kate mumbled with her hand on the doorknob.

A moment before, her spirit effervesced euphoria. Now, it oozed inadequacy.

Open the bloody door, Katie girl: her father's voice again.

Deep breath. Exhale. Open the door. As she fumbled for the switch, the lights came on.

"Surprise!"

It was a surprise all right. Just short of a heart attack. The others were never in early unless they had an active case, and, that morning, they didn't.

Claire was there with her reserved smile. Steve, the square jawed, steel-wool-gray-haired, retired-police- detective investigator, flashed a grin beneath his grizzled moustache.   Thirty-year-old, black-hair-in-a-boy's- haircut, pierced, and tattooed data analyst, Annabel, shrugged. A black woman nodded pleasantly. She had temped for the office a few times. Her name was Loretta.

There was a cake. "Congratulations Partner," in blue icing. The cake contained a hideous amount of sugar. Never mind.

There was champagne. Steve handed Kate a glass.

"Cake and champagne. The real breakfast of champions," Steve proclaimed as he raised a glass. "To the new partner."

"To the partner."

They all sipped. Kate tried not to wrinkle her nose.

Claire said to Kate, "You remember Loretta. She'll be our new office manager. If you approve."

Kate did remember her, and resisted the impulse to tell Claire she approved on the spot. Loretta had done a good job as their temp. Kate shook Loretta's hand and told her they'd talk after the hoop-de-rah was finished.

"Your husband is a chief aviation boatswain mate on the *Constellation*, right?" Kate asked.

Claire liked to hire the wives of senior navy officers and enlisted men. She'd told Kate, navy wives knew how to deal with mindless bureaucracy, knew how to get things done without making enemies, knew how to size people up, to figure out who can be counted on, and who can't. "And you are accustomed to subordinating what you want for your husband's career. When you get a job you can sink your teeth into, you pour your heart into it."

Loretta nodded and handed Kate a slice of cake on a paper plate.

Kate liked Loretta, and she thought, Loretta approved of her, too.

"I," Annabel said, "would like to propose a toast. To the not old, but former, office manager, and to the new one."

"Here, here."

"When I met Loretta this morning," Annabel said, "she told me if I was a book, she would not buy me because of my front cover, but she sure as hell would pick me up to see what they wrote about me on the back. When I met Kate three years ago, she didn't say those words, but she was thinking them."

"So she's an open book?" Steve asked.

Annabel rolled her eyes. "You'll see, Loretta. Aside from being a man, Steve isn't a bad sort."

Claire related how, a year past, she decided to take office manager Kate along on a jury selection, so that Kate could see what her boss did. "I did not expect my employee to be showing me how to do my job, but that's exactly what happened. The lawyer I was working for had just questioned a prospective juror, and I looked down to make notes on a pad of paper. I wrote 'accept.' Kate grabbed my hand and shook her head no. Tell them what happened, Kate."

Kate shrugged. "While Claire wrote her notes, a look of pure disgust and hostility passed over the juror's face. I was sure the man was thinking the lawyer's suit cost as much as his Ford, or Chevy, out in the parking lot."

"So," Claire picked up the narrative, "I signaled the lawyer to reject that juror. I learned that, in our business, two sets of eyes are better than one. I learned that I had gotten complacent and needed Kate to nudge me into paying better attention. She and I have done a dozen jury selections, and trials, together this past year. Kate and I make a great team. I became convinced that we could expand the business, take on a few more clients on an annual basis.

"Thank you, Kate, for agreeing to be our partner and giving us the wherewithal to expand."

"Here, here."

⁓⁓∘⌒⌯⦾⌯⌒∘⁓⁓

Steve upended the champagne bottle in the bucket, re-congratulated Kate, re-welcomed Loretta, and said he had to be going.

"Take some cake," Claire offered. A lot of sheet cake remained.

"Already had my annual sugar intake. Gotta watch my girlish figure." Steve patted his flat stomach. He wore a golf shirt under a tan sport coat. He'd told Kate he wore the sport coat for the pockets, not to make a fashion statement. It also concealed, to an extent, his belt pistol.

Steve and Annabel departed.

Claire handed Kate a lawyer's business card. "Mr. Green will be here at one to talk about hiring us. I'd like you to take the lead in the discussion. There are two files on my desk. One is on the lawyer and covers past cases I worked for him. The other is on his client and what he is charged with. I will be out the rest of the morning. Why don't you give Loretta a refresher on how we operate, then review those files?" She grabbed her purse.

Kate stopped her. "The sign. When the elevator door opened and I saw my name, it overwhelmed me. I just stood there with my mouth hanging open. The elevator doors almost closed on me and took me back down to the garage. Thank you so much, for that, for everything."

"We are going to do great things together."

In the silence that followed Claire's departure, Kate stared at the closed office door. The enormity of the partnership with her former boss was still a blossoming awareness. She smiled at Loretta.

"Sorry. I still haven't totally absorbed … this."

Loretta's smile was filled with understanding and empathy. "I liked you all when I temped here. My impression was that you are the opposite of that saying, *it's not personal, it's business.* You seemed more like family than business."

"We are, in a sense, family. I have been here three years, but Claire and Steve and Annabel have been together twice as long. We work well together. But we are a real business. Our financial margin is comfortable, but only because we work at it. The only full-time employees are you, Claire, and me. And if you want the job, it's yours."

"I do."

"Then by the power vested in me, I welcome you to the family."

"Thank you."

"All right then. First thing is Steve and Annabel both take other jobs. The company pays for their health insurance, which gives us first claim, but not exclusive claim, on their time. When you temped with us, you saw us in the middle of a case. Both Steve and Annabel can bring on extra help if they need it. As office manager, you will be responsible for keeping the hours-worked records up to date. And none of us have a private office. We all operate here."

Kate swept her hand around the large room equipped with eight desks, filing cabinets, and book cases.

"Down there, you may recall, is the bathroom, complete with a shower. There are cots. During a case, quite often, we go twenty-four hours a day. If privacy is required, or to meet with a client, there is a conference room. Outside the office door, and down the hall to the left.

"The other thing is communications. Everyone has a pager. Claire has a cellular phone in her car. The office keeps a spare. One of your jobs will be to make sure the phone battery is charged."

"Phones in cars," Loretta said. "What'll they think of next?"

"Claire says this office lives on reading people, on data, and on time. We can get access to vital information, but if we don't get it to our lawyer in a timely fashion, it does neither his client, nor us, any good."

Kate showed Loretta how to log onto the office computer system and how to transfer a call to Claire's cellular telephone.

"Now, unless you have questions, I'm going to turn the office over to you. I will be right over there studying the files on our prospective client."

Kate took the desk next to Claire's.

The folder on attorney Gordon Green was thick. The lawyer had used Claire three times. The folder contained the history of each of the cases, the assessment of strengths and weaknesses of the prosecutor's evidence, the going- in-strategy the defense used, and how the strategy was altered during the course of the trial.

She turned a page and it hit her. She hadn't called her mother. For the past week, Kate had called her as soon as she entered the office.

Three weeks prior, her mother had suffered a ruptured appendix. The rupture was encapsulated, which masked the symptoms for days. Kate began to check on her every day. "I," Louella Mary O'Reilly declared, "have a touch of the flu. I am not going to the hospital." But she looked paler, more drawn with each passing day, and Kate had gotten her to the ER, finally, " just in time." Her mother stayed in the hospital for a week. She was home now, but not snapping back as Kate expected her to.

Kate dialed and the phone rang and rang and rang. Her mother did not believe in answering machines. Bill's suggestion that she take a cordless phone with her into the bathroom appalled her.

With concern mounting, she called Bill's office. Busy.

The phone on Loretta's desk rang. She answered; then said, "Your husband."

"Listen Kate—"

Bad news. The tone in his voice told her that.

"I have to fly back to D.C. right away. I am at the naval air station. They are holding a plane for me. I'll call you this evening. Love you."

"Bill."

"Gotta go, Hon. Sorry."

"Wait!"

He hung up.

Two

BILL HAD TOLD HIS WIFE to accept Claire's offer. Captain Bill Marshall had told her he'd resign from the United States Navy. He'd gone in early to get the letter written as the first thing he did that day. But now sitting at his desk, the enormity of what he was about to do hit him like a kick in the stomach. It could take some time for the letter to be approved. He had no idea how it worked. *I never resigned before.*

The letter stared back at him from the computer screen. He sat absolutely still but his brain fired frantic impulses, as if he were drowning and his brain thought his stupid body wasn't working near hard enough to save them.

When Bill turned that letter in, he would no longer be a naval officer. More importantly, he would no longer be a fighter pilot.

He thought about twelve years prior. At that time, he was a test pilot. All his reports were written long hand and a yeoman typed them up. On mimeograph masters. It took forever to get a report done without a typo. He'd proofread a page, find one typo, and the page would be redone with the mistake corrected but three new errors glaring at him. Now he could type his own letters more quickly than doing it long hand. Progress. Now, when he wanted things to go slow, somebody had figured out how to make them go very, very fast.

He thought of that day in May 1972. That day, Lieutenant (junior grade) Bill Marshall had been assigned to fly his first combat hop over North Vietnam. An all- consuming passion to be a fighter pilot, to fly combat missions, had propelled him through navy flight training. In each phase of training, he'd knocked down top grades and proved himself to be a natural stick and throttle jockey and a cool-headed decision maker. He'd been afraid the war would end before he got there. But then he was there, on the flight deck, waiting for the crew to come and start his F-8 fighter for his first mission in the enemy's skies, and he was afraid of something else. *I don't want to die!* screamed inside his head, petrified him. Twenty years later, sitting at his desk, he could still feel how his legs shook. He wasn't sure he'd be able to manage his brakes. But he must have. He could not remember taxiing to the catapult on the bow. He could not remember the launch itself. God must have flown the plane for him. Once the violence of the catapult shot ended, it was as if he woke to find himself flying. *Raise the gear* a voice told him. He raised them. *Rendezvous.* So he flew to overhead the carrier and joined with the other thirty-five airplanes.

He remembered thinking all his flight training had been aimed at his hands, so they would know what to do without him having to think to tell them which button to push, which way to move the control stick. As he flew, he left the memory of the fear he'd felt on the flight deck a thousand miles behind him. His hands flew the plane and his mind drove his eyes to scan the sky for MiGs, missiles, and flak.

The three dozen planes attacked a railroad marshalling yard south of Hanoi, and as they headed back for the safety of the coast, Bill saw two MiGs chasing two A-4 bomber planes. He attacked one of the enemy fighters and shot it down. The other one ran away. When he returned to the carrier, Bill was a hero. He'd shot down a

MiG on his first combat hop. No one ever knew how frightened he'd been before the catapult shot. He'd never told anyone, even Kate.

He didn't like to think about that fear, but he thought about it then, with his letter on the computer screen. And it was very like *I don't want to die!* except now it was *I won't be a fighter pilot anymore.* Just then, dying did not seem as bad as not being a fighter pilot.

You promised Kate. Print the damned the letter.

He printed it. He signed it. He took it to the admiral's chief of staff.

"You sure about this, Bill?"

Hell no! but he said he was.

Walking back to his office, he felt as if the devil had a special corkscrew that he'd used to pull his soul out of him. He thought he could feel the Evil One's claw-tipped fingers gripping the arm of his soul and dragging it to hell. If he wasn't a fighter pilot, was he anything? He had a wife. He had children. But what did they have? An empty shell with no man inside.

Before he could sit down at his desk, the phone rang.

"Captain Marshall, sir."

"Get your butt over here." The caller, Admiral Early, his boss, hung up.

Admiral Early had never called him directly before. Always his aide, or secretary, or chief of staff called with, "The admiral wants to see you."

Back to where he'd just come from. He did not think the admiral wanted to see him about his letter. That was just routine paperwork. The admiral called his briefcase his RCC (Routine Crap Container). That sort of material he dealt with after a civilized dinner with his wife and with a civilized dollop of Scotch over two ice cubes in his hand.

When he entered the admiral's outer office, the aide jumped up, opened the door for Bill, and closed it behind him.

The admiral was on the phone. Bill stopped just inside the door. Admiral Early waved a *Get the hell over here* at him.

"He's here, general," Early said. "I'm putting you on speaker."

To Bill: "General Sampson, SACEUR."

"Captain Marshall, what do you know about NATO, SHAPE, and SACEUR?" the general asked.

Bill frowned.

Admiral Early jabbed his finger in the direction of the phone. *Answer the damned general.*

"Well, sir, even a west coast puke like me has heard of NATO. I don't know what shape is. SACEUR, Supreme Allied Commander, Europe. SACEUR is the commander of NATO's military forces. Such as they are," Bill replied.

Frosty silence filled the room and persisted for a long moment. During the moment, Bill winced and wondered why the Sam Hill he'd appended the last phrase to his response. Then General Sampson chuckled. "Well, Fudd, you warned me."

Vice Admiral Elmer Early's call sign had been Fudd when he flew US Navy fighters.

"Such as they are. Tell me what you mean by that, Captain," the general said.

"First, Bill, why don't you pull your foot out of your mouth, then answer the man," Admiral Early said.

Admiral Early peered up at Bill through the eyeholes of his poker player mask.

Bill cleared his throat. "It's NATO general. Sixteen sovereign nations. Two of them, the UK and France are ready to go to war over the right to claim who invented hubris. Germany would be in the fray as well, but they need to log a couple more decades as pacifists. The Italians don't care who invented hubris, they just wish they had some. You have the hot-blooded Spanish and Portuguese and cooler headed Norwegians and Danish who probably say "Let's wait a bit more and see how this plays out," which the ever-practical Dutch would go along with without having to say so out loud. The Greeks and the Turks, they are concerned primarily with not allowing anything good to come to the other. So, for the NATO military to do anything, you need consensus out of that political dog's breakfast."

"You don't think much of politicians?"

"General, we have to have structure to our society. Structure means we have to have politics and politicians."

"And they have to do their best to sort out the *dog's breakfast* of competing, in NATO's case, competing national interests. That it?"

"That's one thing they should be doing, sir."

"What do you think of the Chairman of the Joint Chiefs?"

"General Powell. Based on what I read, for a soldier, he's a heck of a politician."

"What do you think of him as a soldier, as a warfighter?"

"Sir. I have never worked for, with, or even near him. I can't answer the question."

"Fudd," the general said, "I'm ready to hire this captain of yours based on the phone call, but can you fly him back to Andrews? Today? And get him here before 1800 east coast time?"

"Wait just a damn minute," Bill said. "What the hell are you guys talking about? Hire him? Are you talking about me? I put in my letter of resignation this morning."

"You mean this?" Admiral Early held up an 8 and1/2 by 11 sheet and tore it in half and the halves in half.

"Admiral. Kate has a great job offer. I promised her, it was … just ten hours ago, that I'd resign, that after all the times she let me do what I wanted, now she could do what she wanted. I promised her."

"She'll get over it," the admiral said.

"She'll get over it! Says the man on his third wife."

"Bill, goddammit. This is not an argument. You took an oath to obey the orders of the officers appointed over you. This. Is. An order. You are going to take the job working for General Sampson. If he wants a shoots-his- mouth off mental pissant, that is." Admiral Early pointed at the door. "Get your ass home. Pack for a week, and get back to the air station. Hop to it."

Bill's chin sunk onto his chest. *Here I am again.* Except this time, it was different. This time he derived no power from the conviction that he was right and everyone else was wrong. The other times, when everyone else hated him, Kate stuck with him, propped him up. This time she would hate him.

"Captain Marshall!"

Bill put his hat on, snapped to attention, saluted, performed an about face, and marched toward the door.

"He going to be okay, Fudd?" General Sampson asked.

"Yes, sir," Admiral Early replied. "I'll send my aide with him to make sure he doesn't commit seppuku with his Swiss Army Knife."

Bill paused with his hand on the doorknob. He and Vice Admiral Early weren't friends. But they respected each other. But now the admiral was laughing at him. Congealing out of the cloud of white hot anger was the thought, *Well, dumb-shit, you probably shouldn't have goaded him about his wives.*

As Bill drove home, Admiral Early's aide followed him. In the condo, Bill threw uniforms into a suitcase. The aide suggested he take a business suit as well.

Bill was not in the mood to hear a suggestion, or anything else, from a kid naval officer. Early's aide was, as was the norm for aides, a tall, trim, athletic figure come to life from a recruiting poster. He'd done a great job as a junior officer in his first assignments, or he would not have been selected to be an admiral's aide. He almost tore into the kid, but Bill considered senior officers, who in the midst of a bad day, take out their frustrations on subordinates as the worst kind of leader. He kept his mouth shut and packed a suit.

Then the kid drove the two of them back to the naval air station. Bill knew the aide wasn't a kid. He was in his thirties and in his fourth navy job.

"I'm sorry, Captain," the aide said, "about having to break the promise to your wife."

"How do you know about that?"

"You were pretty loud, sir."

Bill frowned. "You married?"

"Yes, sir. Just over a year."

They rode the rest of the way without speaking. There was

no need to voice what they were both thinking. *The only thing the young bride has seen of navy life is as the wife of an admiral's aide.* For a moment, Bill's mind leaped at the opportunity to feel sorry for the rude lessons ahead of the aide's wife. It took him away from thinking about calling Kate before he boarded the airplane. He had no idea how to tell her he was breaking his promise to her.

When he did get her on the phone, he could not bring himself to tell her. He could only say he had to fly to D.C. and that he would call her from there. The flight to Andrews Air Force Base took five and a half hours. Bill Marshall the coward hoped that during the flight, he'd come up with the courage to tell Kate what he'd done to her.

In the passenger terminal at Andrews, Bill called Kate's office. It was 1600 west coast time. The office stayed open until 1700. No answer.

Oh God! Maybe they closed early, to celebrate Kate's promotion. God!

He called home. The answering machine clicked on and beeped. "Kate, Admiral Early is sending me on a trip to Europe. I am flying out of Andrews shortly. I will call as soon as I can to explain what is going on." He sighed. "I love you."

He hung up before he said any more words utterly devoid of meaning and truth.

SACEUR had his own airplane. It wasn't Air Force One. Just business jet sized, but equipped with an impressive communications suite, based on the antennas festooning the exterior. Inside the passenger compartment, Bill sat at the small table in the passenger compartment across from General Sampson.

The general was about five-ten. Probably had to keep his clothes and shoes on to weigh one fifty. He had white hair and looked like a grandfather more than an army general or a warrior. Except for the eyes. The soul looking out of those dark brown eyes was hard and ruthless. Abruptly, softness suffused the eyes.

"The promise you made your wife, you know you promised something you should not have, don't you?"

"Yes, General. In hindsight. I thought the navy would be happy to be rid of me. I've made enemies. The way my detailer explained it to me, if I wanted to resign, it would be no problem. If I wanted to stay in for two more years, there was a job in the Pentagon he could send me to." Bill looked into those soft brown eyes. "I didn't think I was promising more than I could give. The last thing I wanted was to betray my wife. It doesn't matter that Admiral Early ordered me to come here. It doesn't matter if you hire me or not. That's what I've done. I betrayed my wife."

"I won't tell you Kate will get over it, but I will put money on the two of you working it out. Eventually."

The general turned around and beckoned. Three men sat farther back in the compartment. One of the three was the aide. He answered the summons.

"Carl, say hello to Captain Marshall. He's joining our staff."

Carl was a lieutenant colonel. And a hulk. His face looked like it didn't quite know how to pull off a smile. He stuck out a paw. Bill shook it.

SACEUR's plane took off. Besides the aide, the pilot and copilot, the other two were army enlisted personnel, a communications specialist and a cabin attendant. The attendant brought the general a glass of red wine and Bill the Jack Daniels on the rocks he ordered.

General Sampson said, "Here's my cut on eastern Europe. The Berlin Wall came down, the Soviet Union and Yugoslavia are coming apart. Some think it is wonderful, that we just won the cold war, that we can get rid of NATO, but with all this political disintegration, the possibility for chaos and anarchy are significant. I think we might need NATO as much as we did coming out of World War II."

"You need a new strategy," Bill said. "In the past, it was easy to see the Soviets as the threat. Hell, they made it easy. But now the threat, the reason for NATO's existence, has disintegrated. At least the press says it has."

General Sampson smiled. "Admiral Early said you are quick to see the big picture."

As Bill and the general ate dinner, they continued their discussion. The aide had a notebook open next to his plate. He did more writing than eating. An hour after dinner, the general retired to the aft-most compartment. In there, a couch could be transformed into a bed Carl told Bill. Sometime later, Bill was reading a folder filled with the military capabilities of the NATO nations when the comm specialist handed a message to the aide. Carl read it, glanced at Bill, then turned and entered the sleeping compartment. Shortly, the general emerged wearing pajama pants and a tee shirt. He sat by Bill.

"I'm sorry, Bill. Your wife's mother passed away. Admiral Early found out and sent the message."

Bill looked away from Grandfather Sampson and out the window. To the outer darkness. Where he was. And God wasn't.

Three

G ENERAL SAMPSON WENT BACK TO sleep. The others in the main compartment slept. Bill could not. If he closed his eyes, his soul shouted to his mind: *You betrayed her. When she needed you most, you were gone. Again!*

To avoid his conscience, Bill found a pad of paper and went to work identifying the new threat NATO and SHAPE faced in eastern Europe.

He laid out his rudimentary understanding of prevailing conditions in the countries around the Baltic Sea, south through eastern Europe, and into the Adriatic and Mediterranean Seas. There were many details and many facts to run down before he had a clear and concise statement of the threat, but by the time General Sampson woke for breakfast, Bill had a start to step one of formulating the new strategy. In his notes, Bill also drew a parallel to the situation at the end of World War II and the need for the Marshall Plan. He also noted the development of air cavalry tactics during Vietnam as possibly holding lessons for current NATO forces.

Over a cup of coffee, General Sampson read over the ten pages

Bill had written. On the last one, he looked up, and said, "Huh. The Marshall Plan."

The General didn't say whether he liked Bill's paper or disliked it. He asked his aide if he had arranged to get Captain Marshall back to the states for his mother-in- law's funeral.

"Yes, sir," Carl reported.

⁓◦◦❦◦◦⁓

The plane touched down in Belgium. SACEUR and his aide deplaned. After the crew refueled the aircraft, it took off for a short flight to Ramstein Air Force Base in Germany. There, a car transported Bill to the passenger terminal. By 1100, he was in a massive C-5 cargo jet and crossing the Atlantic in the other direction.

Bill had trouble sleeping in airplanes. That another man was flying the craft, a man who could not possibly be as good a pilot as he was, bothered him. On top of his other soul troubles, it kept him awake despite his fatigue. Finally, somewhere over the ocean, sleep overwhelmed his anguish and claimed him.

When the pilot reduced the throttles to begin descending, Bill vaulted from deep sleep to heart pounding panic. *The plane lost power! We're going to crash!*

The other passengers, twenty-five of them, mostly air force enlisted personnel, dozed or played cards. They were as calm as he was panicked.

He always woke like that after sleeping on a plane. Always when he woke like that, he thought, *That took ten years off my life!* Which, had it been true, would mean Bill Marshall would have been dead for twenty years. It happened often enough.

Another car took Bill to the BOQ. He called home. Answering Machine answered. At Claire's office, a woman responded with, "Daley and Marshall, this is Evelyn."

Bill asked for Kate.

Kate was out dealing with a death in the family. Evelyn was a temporary office manager. The regular manager was out assisting Ms. Marshall.

After he identified himself, Evelyn told him Loretta had a cellular phone in her car. She gave him the number. No answer there either.

He was relieved at first. He dreaded hearing Kate on the other end of a phone. He didn't know what she would say, but he knew it would be bad. At the same time, he knew he had to get it over with, and the longer it took, the worse it would be when it happened.

Bill brushed his teeth, shaved, brushed his teeth again, and stood under the shower with the water as hot as he could stand it for as long as he could stand it. An army major—he was in charge of SACEUR's office in the Pentagon—showed up to drive Bill to Dulles Airport. Bill asked the major to convey to Carl, General Sampson's aide, that Bill was so very grateful for all the travel arrangements he'd set up for a no-account navy captain. "Tell him the BOQ room at Andrews saved my life," Bill said.

I wish Carl knew how to save my marriage.

Admiral Early's aide met Bill at baggage claim at the San Diego airport.

As they waited for the luggage, the aide said, "I haven't spoken to Mrs. Marshall, Captain. I did speak with a woman named Loretta, from your wife's office. Loretta was going to meet you here, but I told her I'd pick you up and bring you home.

"Loretta, I think is doing a great job supporting your family. She told me they have preliminary funeral arrangements set up."

For a moment, Bill appreciated Claire Daley putting her office manager to work supporting Kate, but then he recognized it as more hard evidence he had failed in his duty as husband.

"Admiral Early, by the way," the aide said, "did speak to Mrs. Marshall earlier today. He had the sense that if he told her he'd ripped up your letter of resignation it would not have helped. It would have made it worse. So, he just said he was sorry for her loss."

The luggage arrived. The aide grabbed it and wheeled it outside where the admiral's car and driver waited. The driver held the door for Bill and the aide climbed in the other side of the rear seat. The car pulled away from the terminal.

Bill turned and found the aide staring at him. "What?"

"General Sampson called. He asked me to see if I thought you could handle doing a few minutes work on the way home."

"Give it."

The aide popped open his brief case and handed Bill two sheets paper from a fax.

It was his strategy. Gussied up to a fare-thee-well. He frowned. The way it was written was all wrong.

He turned the paper over and wrote on the back:

This is not like the Marshall Plan. It IS the Marshall Plan, part two. General, you want a NATO plan. You want the Europeans to push this themselves. I didn't think of this, last night, if that's when it was, but you need a general from a European nation to push this for you.

He listed the sixteen nations on the sheet and drew a line through each nation that would not be suitable. After a moment, every country had been struck except the UK.

"Send this back to General Sampson," Bill said.

He leaned back in the seat. Two days ago, he was a west coast sailor intent on resigning his commission. Now, he was up to his ears in European politics. It was a bit like on an aircraft carrier. Half the crew was assigned to the airwing, responsible for the planes. The other half was assigned to the ship. Between the two factions there was more than a little animosity. Bill had seen both sailors and officers transfer from an airwing job to be part of the ship's company, and overnight, by some form of spiritual osmosis, the former airwing guy became a member of the crew. And, overnight, he began to detest the airwing, wingnuts they called them. If nothing else, the navy taught a person to be adaptable.

Then Europe faded and Kate loomed in front of him with a lot more animosity than that between ship guys and plane guys on a carrier.

He opened the door of their condo, and Heather and JR squealed and swarmed him. Bill knelt on a knee and took his oldest in one arm and the youngest with the other. He looked up and found Sally next to her mother. She let go her mother's hand and walked to him and squeezed between her siblings.

"It is good to have you home, Father," Sally said.

Sally so reserved, restrained, and mature. Especially compared to Heather and JR.

Sally returned to stand by Kate. Bill stood and shooed the other two into the room ahead of him. He walked to Kate. He opened his arms and embraced her. It was like embracing a polar bear who'd just crawled out of an ice cave after having her nap interrupted.

He never touched his wife again over the next few days in San Diego, during the trip to and stay in Green River, Wyoming, for the funeral, or the return to San Diego.

On Sunday after the funeral, JR howled, "Don't leave, Daddy."

Heather said, "Do you have to go?"

Sally said, "I'll miss you, Daddy."

They all rode the elevator to the parking garage under the condos. The children sat in back. Bill drove. At the airport, he parked at the curb in front of the terminal and pulled his luggage from the trunk. Kate gave him a sisterly hug; then she said, "The children and I will come to Belgium after school lets out."

Bill clamped down hard on his emotions. It would not do to let them bust loose. He had to let things proceed at a pace and a manner determined by Kate.

But it meant they had hit bottom, and that, now, things were getting better between them.

God, please don't let me screw this up.

Four

Monday, after the funeral, the elevator car lurched into motion, and for a moment, Kate had the sensation she was outside herself, curiously watching a strange, yet familiar, woman ride to the sixth floor. For a moment, she thought it was ten days ago as she watched the woman levitate on a cloud of euphoria congealed out of one of the best days of her life. But she knew, too, that one of the best days had transmogrified into the absolute worst day.

The elevator stopped with a ding. Kate held her breath. The doors opened. She saw the sign on the office door. "Daley and Marshall." Kate exhaled.

The sign hadn't changed. Kate had half expected to find her name removed. By all rights, Claire should have removed it. Still, it would have been yet another betrayal. Kate shook her head. In a corner of her mind, she was disappointed. Disappointed she had been prevented from wallowing in more victimhood.

Katie girl! the cigarette-smoke-cured vocal cords of her father growled.

Inhale. Exhale. She turned the knob.

All the desks were occupied with men and women on phones, writing, or typing words into a computer. Loretta was on the phone and making notes on a legal pad. She looked up, saw Kate, and sympathy and concern spilled over her face.

Kate clamped her teeth together, forced control to push back on all the emotion expanding inside her like a balloon ready to burst. *Breathe.* She breathed. *Hold it together.* She held it.

"Loretta, finish the call," Kate said.

From across the room, Claire's eyes met Kate's. Control stretched again to the popping point. Again, the power of Kate's will, just sufficient.

Claire stood and motioned for Kate to go into the hallway. Kate did. Claire exited the office and led the way to the conference room. In the room, they found Annabel asleep atop the table. Snoring.

Claire moved to wake her.

"Let her sleep," Kate said.

The two women regarded each other. Kate read understanding in Claire. Claire knew what her partner was dealing with. Something entirely different from anything she'd experienced before. The death of a squadron pilot in a plane crash, the loss of a squadron member's spouse or child through an illness or a car crash, in those instances, the others in the unit all pulled together and each lifted a small sliver of grief from the soul of the bereaved, making the burden just a little lighter. In Kate's case, though, if anyone lifted some of her burden, her control would tumble like a house of cards. At the core of herself, it was anger at Bill that propped her fragile mastery of her emotions.

"How are the children?" Claire asked.

On the table, Annabel smacked her lips. Her mouth opened. The snoring ceased. On another day, Kate would have smiled.

She took a moment. "Bill, you know, came back for the funeral. He—it was hard to get the rest out—helped with the children. He … took care of them, helped them through it all. He flew back to Belgium yesterday. The kids are back in school this morning, and glad to be there."

Claire had her arms crossed across her chest. "When you called last night about coming in today, I thought it was a mistake. Are you sure you want to do this?"

"I need to work. I cannot go back to our place and be there alone all day. And I can't deal with my mother's apartment just yet. I need to work. I will hold up my end. Let me run the office. Loretta can go with you to jury selection. She can be your second set of eyes."

"You're sure the children are okay?"

"Yes. And thanks so much for having Loretta help me after I found my mother. I could not have managed without her. And, you know, one good thing has come of this. You know how we look at people and our minds register things automatically like skin color? After a few days with Loretta and I working things together, I found myself looking at her and no longer seeing the color of her skin. My mind stopped caring about that. Minds are funny things, and it was a blessing to find that in mine."

"Would it be okay if I hug you?"

"I think I can handle it now. I think it's time to find out."

Kate allowed a few seconds of embrace; then she stepped back. She'd handled it. And she would handle managing the office.

The next morning, Claire took Kate to the conference room again and asked first about the children and then about her mother's illness.

The children were following the same path they followed before to adjust to their father's absence.

"Mother was always so full of life. And she and Father loved each other very much. The only thing they argued about, as far as I knew, was about me. Father worried she mollycoddled me. She worried Father was trying to turn me into a boy. When Father died of lung cancer … they also fought over his cigarettes. Anyway, I worried Mother would be devastated. But she surprised me with how she handled his death. We brought her to San Diego to live with us for a while. We thought she'd go back to Green River, Wyoming. But she loved being near the ocean and being near to her grandchildren. So, she stayed.

"And everything was fine until the appendicitis. She started to look bad, but more importantly, her spirit started to decline as much as she did physically. I should have gotten her to hospital sooner."

"Your mother was opinionated and headstrong, right?"

Kate nodded.

The next morning in the conference room, Claire wanted to know about the days immediately following the discovery of her mother's body.

The day after that, Claire asked about the funeral.

The next day, Claire again took Kate to the conference room.

"You know how navy fighter pilots are, Kate."

Claire's husband had been killed in 1972 when a Surface to Air Missile struck his F-4 Phantom over North Vietnam.

"I am sure Bill sees things the same way my husband did. My Hank told me a fighter pilot had to think about priorities and have them set in his head. Things pop up that require instantaneous decisions. Not just in the air. If you haven't thought about it, you will probably screw it up. Make the wrong moral decision. 'My priorities are God, country, navy, family, self.'"

"Claire Daley! I see what you've done. You worked me like you and a lawyer work a jury. You think I should forgive Bill."

Claire smiled ... *like a teacher at a dense student who has finally had the lightbulb come on.*

Claire walked out of the conference room. Kate went to the window. The window afforded a view of the carrier pier at North Island Naval Air Station. Two carriers were tied up there with the battleship *Missouri* sandwiched between them.

The navy was going to have the battleship towed to Pearl Harbor and berth it near the USS *Arizona* Memorial.

"You know what that will be when the *Missouri* is there in Pearl?" Bill had asked. He didn't wait for her to guess. "The memorial fairly shouts *the Day which will live in infamy* next to the vessel on whose deck the Japanese surrendered. It is a symbol of *Don't Tread on Me*." Bill.

Claire had developed a sound strategy, executed an effective campaign, and delivered a good closing argument.

Still, if Kate was a juror, she would not vote to acquit, even if the other eleven did and put all kinds of pressure on her to do so, too. Bill was guilty.

But the tiny voice in the dark rear corner of her mind whispered. *But not as guilty as he was.*

Five

Captain Bill Marshall slumped back in his chair behind his desk at SHAPE. His head buzzed like an overloaded transformer. His eyes felt ready to pop. That had come to mean it's midnight. He checked. Midnight.

Two weeks ago, he reported to NATO's military headquarters and eagerly picked up the job of formulating SACEUR's new strategy. After initial progress, now, all he was doing was beating his head against a reinforced concrete wall. The strategy was not moving forward. The impediments to progress were numerous.

SACEUR wanted Bill to work on the strategy by himself, without a lot of fanfare. When General Sampson considered the concept mature enough, he'd begin making it public, begin selling it to the member nations. In the meantime, though, the SHAPE staff and especially the other eight officers in the Planning Division had looked on Bill's efforts at first with amusement, then annoyed tolerance, and now with indifference. Disdain in one case. The senior officer in the planning group was a German Army colonel. That afternoon, Bill had asked the colonel for help in gaining access to Germany's assessment of developments in East Germany. SHAPE intelligence had their own assessment based on inputs from the member nations, including Germany, but Bill knew each nation had things they kept exclusively for themselves, and did not share readily. Sometimes a specific request could spring an additional level of detail beyond that shared with NATO. And Bill wanted one specific area of the new threat covered in some detail, to give the strategy a solid footing. He thought dealing with East Germany, if he get enough detailed information from West Germany, held the most promise for what he wanted to do.

"Herr Hauptmann," the colonel had sneered in front of the rest of the planning group. *Hauptmann* was an insult. The colonel had used the term for an army captain, three ranks lower than his and Bill's. He probably thought the American wouldn't even know he'd been belittled.

"Why do you need this? I have assigned no task to you where you would need this information. In fact, I have assigned no task to you at all. Do you know, *Captain* Marshall, what your fellow American naval officers call you? West coast puke they call you. They say you know a little bit about Japan, a little bit about the Philippines, and nothing at all about Europe.

"How do you Americans say it? Ah, yes. Don't call me. I call you."

Over the last ten years, Bill had been in that exact spot a number of times, in front of a superior's desk while he was being humiliated. He had come to see it as a necessary step in pushing new and important concepts through entrenched go-along-to-get-along bureaucrats.

"Are you waiting for a formal dismissal? Very well, you are dismissed, Captain Midnight."

European NATO officers had a saying. "Two Americans are stranded on a desert island. In a week, one of them is working nights."

Bill had nothing to go home to except Jack Daniels, and Jack had enough allure without spending more time with him. Bill worked the night shift after working days. They ridiculed him for doing so.

Bill looked at his smug boss and smiled. "Oh, no, sir. That's not what I was doing. I think German Army officers have most attractive uniforms. I was admiring it."

Sitting at his desk at … seven past midnight, he recalled the encounter with the colonel. He'd had practice absorbing humiliation and not letting it show. Even if he hid it, it rankled deep and wide and stank like a rotten egg. It would take some Jack Daniels to cut that stink.

No! This has gone on long enough. Those bastards will learn. Don't mess with Captain Midnight.

He knew what he would do in the morning.

When he was not on travel, General Sampson reliably arrived at his office at 0645. As Bill waited for him, he had second thoughts at pushing SACEUR. The man could, after all, fire him a lot easier than hiring him. And, Bill admitted to himself, it would pull out a piece of his heart if he could no longer work on the strategy.

Maybe, Bill Marshall, you should not rock the boat this time.

But he had to. It looked absolutely necessary last night, and with as much objectivity as he could muster against the survival and self-preservation instinct, in the light of day, it appeared even more necessary.

Into the valley of death—

Bill mumbled, "Oh for Christ sake!"

"Talking to yourself already, Captain?"

Bill was sitting in a chair at Warrant Officer Herb Lang's desk. Lang's title was Administration Officer. His desk sat in the Admin Office, but he did little in the way of administrative duties. What he really did, according to some, was, as SACEUR dealt with high level issues, Herb ran Europe from the base of the clouds to the ninth level of hell. The general's aide, Carl, told Bill, "If you are in a position to have to piss off either General Sampson or Herb, piss off the general, not Herb."

Herb looked at Bill with a deadpan expression and said with

the same kind of intonation, "Generally, it takes a full month for SHAPE to get sailors talking to themselves."

Bill sat up straight. "What can I say, Warrant Officer Lang? I'm a quick study."

Through the warrant's window, they saw SACEUR's car drive by. "Go on in, Captain."

Bill entered from the Admin side as the general walked in from his private entrance. The aide was with him carrying a brief case. Carl pulled a folder from the case and laid it on the front edge of the desk. It was the desk General Eisenhower had used when SHAPE had been established in Paris. As desks went, it was not an impressive piece of furniture, but Bill always sensed the spirit of the first Supreme Commander resident in the obviously cared for and well-tended antique.

Bill picked up the folder. Inside was the strategy paper the general had marked up overnight. General Sampson had a group of senior US Army officers that he had formed into an informal think tank, and every night, they critiqued what Bill produced during the day. Bill flipped through the pages quickly taking in the red marks. He closed the folder.

Big inhale. Exhale. "Here's where I think we are with this thing, General.

"First. For the last couple of nights, I send you home with the latest version of the strategy. The next morning you come back with every place I said *happy*, you and your cronies have changed to glad. The next day you want the *happies* back. The top-level stuff is 97% as good as we can make it.

"Second. Aside from you and me, nobody on this staff sees the need for a new strategy. Most of them think, *Hey. We just won the cold war. Why are you ranting on so, Yank?* As a sailor, I am outnumbered fourteen to one by army and air force officers. They absolutely cannot and will not see that any new strategy, if we can even get them to admit we need one, will have to have a stronger naval element to it.

"Third. I think the strategy is ready for you to take forward if we get one more element nailed down. We need to develop a detailed statement of the threat we see in a specific area of Eastern Europe. Then we need to formulate a detailed plan to counter that threat. That will be the blue print to extrapolate from the Baltic to the Mediterranean.

"Fourth. I think we should focus first on East Germany. If we do, we can avoid the navy issue with this overwhelmingly army and air force organization of yours. Plus, if we get Germany on board, it's my opinion, we'll pull the other nations along without too much struggle.

"Fifth. We need to do something about the leadership of the Planning Group in operations. They are stone walling every request I make for information and intelligence. I think you should fire the German Army colonel running the group."

"Five points. That it?"

"It's all the fingers you have, General."

General Sampson sat and scowled up at Bill.

Bill couldn't figure out if he'd offended the man or walked into the office with his fly down.

The general rubbed his hand over the wood next to the green felt blotter. "Get the exec and Herb in here now."

Bill went to fetch them. General Sampson's executive assistant was Brigadier General Rob Hastings. Not many generals rated a brigadier exec. Off the top of his head, Bill thought the Chairman of the Joint Chiefs might be the only other one.

The exec was two inches taller than Bill and stick thin and stick straight. Herb was two inches shorter, beefy, and he reminded Bill of blacksmiths in western movies.

The three of them stood in front of the Eisenhower desk.

"Our navy captain here wants to fire a German army colonel in planning group. Rob, tell him what will happen if we do that."

"In the first place, sir—"

"Tell him."

"In the first place, Bill, you will piss off all three of the other four-star generals on the staff at SHAPE. A US Air Force, A German

Army, and a Brit Army general. They will all come gunning for you because they will know you went around them. They will know where the suggestion came from."

"Does that change your mind, Bill?"

"No, sir. It's what needs to be done."

"Damn the torpedoes, eh, Captain?"

"There's a time to damn the torpedoes, General."

General Sampson stood up and all three of them snapped to attention.

"At ease, goddammit," the general barked.

"Bill, how many hours a day are you working?"

"Uh—"

"He's in to work before you are and goes home after midnight, General," Herb reported.

"What other sins is he committing, Herb?"

"Sir. I know he is not getting any exercise. I'll bet a month's pay he's drinking too much."

"Rob, get this navy captain into racquet ball."

"Bill, your family will be over here in a month. Do you have a house for them?"

"I'm on the list, sir."

"List my ass! Herb, fix this." General Sampson sat back down. "Now then, Captain, we are not going to fire the German colonel. We are going to fire the entire planning staff. Each and every bloody one of them. Rob, you call the four stars and tell them this comes from me. Tell them also, that my navy captain is going to come to them for help, and that they will give it, or they'll be on the way home next.

"Rob, have Carl take Bill shopping for racquet ball gear. After you finish with your phone calls, kick navy's ass on the court. If you don't kick his, I'll kick yours."

It took two towels to mop up Bill's whiskey sweat. And he did have his butt kicked. Thoroughly. Back in the office, Herb showed Bill a picture of the house he and his family would live in.

"What the hell is this?" Bill asked. "How the hell can I pay for that?"

That night Bill turned out the lights in his office at 2345, and fifteen minutes later, he turned them on in his apartment. After a long hot shower, he poured a drink and wrote a note to JR. Tomorrow night would be Heather's turn. With his second drink, he wrote to Kate. He hadn't gotten a letter from her yet. He was getting mail from the kids.

Dearest Kate,

He always began her letter that way. Since he'd been in Belgium, the next lines read "I love you more than air. I am sorry I broke my promise to you." That night he wrote:

I love you more than bacon. I am sorry I broke my promise to you.

Before that night, he hadn't written, or mentioned during their phone calls, anything about his job. That night he laid out some aspects of it. In restrained tones. It was time Kate began to understand the importance of what he was doing. It was time they began to heal the Cold War of their relationship.

He decided not to tell about the house. Not right away. She'd pester for details, pictures. He wanted the house to be a surprise.

Bill finished the letter and dumped out the remaining half of his second drink. Tomorrow, he decided he wouldn't have even one drink. Well, maybe just one. *Rome was not built in a day.*

He went to bed. There he slept the sleep of a baby angel.

Six

Louis Defonce took pleasure from Sundays.

Forty years ago, as he reclaimed the fields, and rebuilt the house and buildings, he ended each day exhausted but supremely pleased with what he'd accomplished with his muscles and sweat. He used to say, "Well, Tuesday, we got some work done today, eh?"

He still did all those same chores Monday through Saturday. But he no longer talked to the days of week, and they no longer gave him pleasure from his labors and sweat. Somewhere over the decades that had died.

At age 64, 183 centimeters, and ninety sturdy kilograms, he was still strong and vigorous. Mondays through Saturdays he worked his fields, tended his animals, delivered products from his farm to Mons, thirteen kilometers to the southeast, and bought supplies there. He still had time to maintain his fences, the barn, the outbuildings, the house and property so it was a showplace. His neighbors, he knew, envied the appearance of the Defonce farm.

Louis sold cow, sheep, and horse carcasses, at a very good price, to the butcher in *Toussaint*, a tiny *ville* two kilometers east of his place on *Rue Le Grand George*. The butcher knew the owner of the café, of course, and thus, the butcher knew what Louis's neighbors talked about in the café. Alonzo, Thad, and Charles always crowed about how their kilograms per hectare were higher than Louis's fields yielded. One of them would say something like, "That Louis paints fences. We grow crops."

It was Sunday, and Louis stood at the counter in the kitchen of his two-hundred-year-old farm house and cranked the handle of the coffee grinder. He smiled thinking about Alonzo and Thad and the others. Let them wallow in their self-deceit. Year after year, Louis's acres out-yielded theirs. Sometimes by thirty percent. Louis knew. It wasn't hard to learn how much the others produced. All a man had to do was to ask the quay master. He weighed the wagons before and after a farmer's grain was loaded onto a barge at the edge of the canal. He knew how many kilos each farmer sold. Just ask him about anyone, and he'd tell the number. And everyone knew how many hectares each farmer planted in which crop.

Louis asked. Because he wanted to know. The others did not ask. The truth would have prevented them from enjoying their coffee at the *Toussaint* Cafe.

Wasn't that the way of things? If you can't stand the truth, make up a new one and get three other people to agree to it. *Voila!* Truth a man can live with.

His neighbors might be happy with manufactured truth, but not Louis. He analyzed his soil, treated it appropriately, and his farmland produced for him.

Henrietta said to him, "Alonzo and Thad and the others, they are friends with each other. The only friend you have is your dirt."

His sister's quip came, as they usually did, with thorns sticking out of her words. But this particular barb did not bother him as her others did. His land *was* like a friend to him. They worked together to manage the vagaries of weather. Too much rain for the seeds, not enough rain for the sprouts, too much wind and hail just before the harvest. The best thing about his land, though, was he didn't have to talk to it. If he were friends with Alonzo and the others, they would ask questions. They would want to know things, about Henrietta, and about the boy, Rene.

Louis scowled as he dumped grounds into the coffee maker and took it to the new electric stove and turned on a burner. Henrietta, his sister, hated this appliance. He thought she'd be delighted with it. Didn't she always complain he spent money on the latest and best farm equipment, but never spent a penny to make her life easier?

Once it was, "Everyone else has the indoor plumbing. We still have an outhouse. Rene and I have to empty your chamber pot."

He hired a carpenter and a plumber. They installed a bathroom on the ground floor and another on the first floor.

Then it was the electric wiring. "If I have the radio and lights on and the refrigerator motor starts up, it blows a fuse."

Puh. Rewiring the whole house had been expensive. Next, she wanted a television. Henrietta and the boy sat before the flickering screen as the box spewed inane drivel every night. It did however, occupy them, especially Henrietta. It gave her something to do besides find things to go on about.

When he bought her the stove, he thought she'd be pleased. He'd given her something new and modern *even though she hadn't complained about the old one.* He had it installed while she and the boy were shopping. She'd loved it when she first saw it, and said, "Oh, Louis," in a way that came very close to unseemly for a woman to say to her brother. But then she'd cooked with it, or tried to, and burned the stew so badly it ruined the pot. Now she hated it.

"Why did you buy this … contraption without asking me?"

The coffee pot gurgled a happy tune.

"You are a fine stove," Louis told the gleaming white enamel covered box. "As long as Henrietta stays away from you."

Sundays were pleasant with Henrietta and the boy away at Mass, but even Sundays could slide away if he didn't work at holding onto the finer feelings.

He poured a cup of coffee and took it to the table and sat and stirred in sugar. He sipped. Ahhh.

Then, as he did on Sundays, he gazed down at the tabletop. Smoothed over gouges and burn marks scarred one corner, but the rest of the oak top glowed with a dark reddish golden patina redolent of age and history and family. His grandfather had felled the trees, aged the wood, sawed it, shaped the legs, and built the table. Then he asked Grandmamma to marry him. And she did. Grandpapa gave his bride the table. The newlyweds moved in to the downstairs bedroom. Great Grandmamma got rid of her old table to make room for her daughter-in-law's new one.

Grandpapa had two older brothers. They chided their younger sibling. "Most men give their fiancé a diamond ring. You give yours lumber!" The two brothers laughed. Briefly.

Then Grandmamma, in her mother-in-law's house, in her mother-in-law's presence addressed her brothers- in-law, "I cannot imagine how disappointed your mother must be in you."

The truth in those words hit the brothers like a slaughterhouse sledge. They were a disappointment to their mother, but even more to their father. Locked into bachelorhood, they would never produce a son to take over and preserve the Defonce farm. Family lore had it that the two unmarried men tiptoed around their sister-in-law as if walking on eggs the rest of their lives. Lore also had it Grandmamma had gotten along very well with Great Grandmamma, even before she bore the son who became Louis' papa.

He rubbed his hand over the table, almost as if he were summoning a genie from the magic lamp. The family back to great grandparents were in that table, grandmamma's engagement lumber.

The ground floor of the farmhouse contained the kitchen, the hallway to the door fronting on *Rue George le Grand*, with the parlor to one side of the hall and the ground f loor bedroom on the other. The ground floor bedroom housed, over the years, grandparents or newlyweds, but it hadn't had an occupant since 1939 when Louis's grandfather died, and ten days later, Grandmamma followed her beloved table-maker.

The table and the house. If the devil pulled those things out of his soul, Louis thought there would be nothing left of him, not even an empty shell.

He sighed. So many paths to darkness slithered off his family history.

History, though, is always important, but it is especially important to someone with no future. Louis knew this for truth.

He poured a second cup of coffee and returned to the table. And the happy time. The years before the Second War.

Without the leaves, the table seated six. On Sundays, during the happy time, the leaves were inserted and all sixteen chairs occupied. Grandparents, parents, Louis and Henrietta, Uncle Guilliaume and Aunt Marie—they had no children and despaired over the fact—and Uncle Marcel and Aunt Lorrie who had six children and were burdened by their fact. Until dinner was served. Then the happy and unrestrained laughter from the children's end of the table lifted the entire family to where worry over weather and crops, enough business for the uncle's trucking company, no children, or too many, all of it just faded. And all of them, Defonces all, reveled at being at that table with Grandpapa at one end and Grandmamma at the other with the children. It was the finest place on earth to be. Louis never considered that it might not go on forever. And he didn't think of it as the happy time until it no longer was that kind of time.

Louis placed his hand on the table as if pressing the *happy time* back down into the wood, so it would be there again next Sunday. He stood and took his cup and saucer to the sink. Henrietta could place them in the *machine a laver la vaisselle. Puh!* A machine to wash the dishes.

Louis walked out the rear door and descended the three stone steps. He crossed the gravel driveway and stood on the grass. A kilometer to the west stood *Chateau du Chasse.* The mansion belonged to the Belgian royal family. Since 1830 it belonged to them. The immediately preceding forty years, a time prior to the establishment of the Belgian monarchy, might not be important to many Belgians, but it was very important to Louis.

He heard the story from Grandpapa the first time Louis sat with the men after Sunday dinner rather than run with the barbarians, as Grandpapa called the young ones. Papa took over the telling after Grandpapa died, even though the uncles were older. They had a business in Mons. Papa ran the farm.

The story:

A French nobleman built the chateau during the revolution. He wanted a place away from the turmoil, but not too far. He had hopes of reclaiming his holdings in Normandy after the madness subsided. When the chateau was completed and work had started on the moat, the nobleman moved in with his wife, Twyla, and his daughter, Sophie.

At the same time, a two-meter tall prince, George the Tall, had reason to leave his native Swabia. Besides being extraordinarily tall, George was extraordinarily ugly, with a visage considerably more porcine than humanoid. George's father arranged a marriage for him. His fiancé, rather than marry *The Pig*, slit both her wrists while in her bathtub. The girl's distraught father blamed George and his ugliness and sent his son to challenge George to a duel. The son was a notable swordsman.

George fled, headed for Paris. On the way, he heard stories of what happened to noblemen there, and changed his destination to Brussels. Stopping for the night at an inn in Mons, as he ate dinner, he overheard a group of men at the bar talking.

The men, six of them, as commoners did, bemoaned their lot in life. It was hard, they said, to keep track of to whom they owed allegiance. Always, some empire or other conquered them. Then they had to learn Spanish, or a snooty form of French, or an east European language.

At this point in the story, both Grandpapa and Papa inserted dialogue. Now, when Louis told the story aloud, his only audience was the boy, Rene, across the table from him. Henrietta was always there in the kitchen at the sink cleaning up after dinner. But at this point in the story, she rattled the pots and pans, protesting, without verbalizing, that she was sick of hearing the family history. But she didn't stop the narration or tell her son to go in the parlor and watch the television. Rene loved the story and especially loved the dialogue part, which had become his part to say.

In that inn in Mons, George the Tall listened to the men at the bar. In the narration of the Defonce history, each of those at the bar had a line to say. Rene's face beamed an angelic smile and an aura, like around the head of a saint on an icon, and he counted off the speakers on his fingers.

Rene stuck up a thumb, and said, "Language isn't the issue. There is no Belgian language."

Louis inserted, "Which stirred up no small amount of mumbling, half in French and half in Dutch, into tankards of beer."

Rene held up the thumb and one finger. "The issue is, Belgians should be able to determine for themselves who their ruler should be."

Another finger: "What?"

And another: "God appoints princes and kings."

The full set of digits: "Then why doesn't God appoint one for Belgium?"

Again, Louis inserted a line. "George the Tall sat up straight."

The thumb on Rene's second hand raised out of his closed fist: "Obviously, God didn't send the French nobleman to us."

Rene beamed more brightly when he completed the last line of dialogue.

Louis standing next to his driveway, looking off at the *chateau*, muttered "Puh!"

Rene, the keeper of the Defonce family history! He'd probably die before Louis. Many persons with Down's Syndrome did not live to be forty-five. Rene was forty- five and still, seemingly, healthy, but that could change quickly.

Rene and Louis. What a pair they were. The end of the Defonce line.

White haired, white bearded, barrel-chested Louis stood with his sturdy legs spread, his back to his stone walled two-story farmhouse, looking across one of his fields to the grand two-story royal dwelling. History chained the royal residence, what had been a royal hunting lodge in the early years of the monarchy, to his common abode.

Members of the royal family would huff and turn their noses up at the suggestion of a connection to common farmers.

Grandpapa, when he told the story, occasionally inserted a bit of his philosophy. Once he said, "History in not stories of men fighting men. At the base of it is angels and devils fighting for mastery of the greatest number of souls." Another time, "History is a living place. Its inhabitants are ghosts." And, "History is like a lake. 00When you look at it, you can't tell if it is five centimeters deep or fifty meters. The first Louis Defonce, your namesake—Grandpapa had placed a hand on Louis' shoulder—organized the 'Belgium for Belgians' locals to follow George's leadership. They captured the chateau from the French nobleman, and George used it as his castle to secure the southern border of what eventually became our country. Also, George the Tall and his vassals fought against Napoleon at Waterloo. That was how they came to name a road after him. People remember him, not the Louis Defonces of 0the world."

Grandpapa said sometimes truth and history are the same thing. But not always. What he'd just told was five- centimeters deep history. Deeper in the lake, where not much light reaches, and it's colder, that's where the truth resides.

After 1790 Louis and his friends had grumbled a while in the inn in Mons, they began muttering goodbyes because none of them had money for more beer. A giant of a man sauntered up to them. The men as a group stared open-mouthed. The size of the man astounded them, as did his resemblance to a pig. But then he bought them a round of beer. And introduced himself as Prince George from Swabia, a region much fought over just like Belgium.

1790 Louis considered it a miracle from God. A prince bought beer for him and his friends! And he had splashed an eager empathy for their cause around and over their company.

As they drank his second round, the prince asked about the French nobleman and his *chateau*. They described the size of the building, the partially completed ditch for the moat in the rear, and the high stone fence with a gate in front.

"The Frenchman has twenty armed men inside," 1790 Louis said.

"He keeps one man on guard in front and another in the rear. And he can summon another twenty men farming the land to the north, east, and west of his castle. To the south is a great forest."

"Does this Frenchman have alliances with other nobles near here?" George asked.

"I do not think so," 1790 Louis said. "When we went to him with our cause, he told us we were common. God ordained that some men be noble and others like us. We should go to church with ashes on our heads and ask God to forgive us for fighting against His holy order. He looked down his nose at us and said, 'Belgium for Belgians!' He called us barbarians. He said if we came back, his men would slaughter us and leave our bodies in the forest for the wild pigs.'"

George the Tall bought another round with the last of his coins. Then he said, "I have a plan."

Late the next afternoon, George appeared at the hinged iron grate in the stone wall before *Chateau du Chasse.* Blood streamed from a gash on his forehead. His left sleeve was slashed from shoulder to elbow, and more blood soaked his jacket and shirt sleeves.

The front guard summoned the French nobleman. George explained he was a prince from southern Germany, on his way to Brussels on a diplomatic mission, and traveling without a retinue to avoid attracting attention. The Frenchman's eyebrows rais0ed and looked up at the pig face towering above him.

"I made the mistake of allowing some common trash to see my purse at an inn in Mons last night," George said. "Six of them waylaid me this morning. They thought I was dead. I thought I was dead."

"Mon Dieu!"

"Dear God, indeed," George replied. "Some of the French commoners' rebellious attitudes have migrated to southern Germany. My father wants to establish alliances to combat this … this devil-spawned revolution."

At this point, George the Tall fell to the ground.

The French nobleman had the gates opened, the wounded prince carried inside the chateau, and placed on a bed. There, the lady of the manor, Twyla, bathed the prince's wounds. As she mopped the blood above George the Tall's left eye, his right eye noted his nurse was a very attractive woman.

The lady bandaged the wounds; then she left, seemingly in a hurry. A maid brought in a tray with dinner for George. He feigned sleep and did not partake of the soup and bread. Periodically, through the evening, the door to George's room would open, and then it would close softly. At one point, someone entered and removed the tray. By midnight, George thought the chateau was asleep, but he waited another hour. Then he rose, and in stockinged feet, slipped out of his room. Lamps in sconces cast dim light into a long hallway leading to the grand foyer. In the foyer, a stairway led from the ground floor to the first. All was still, up and down.

George peered out a window next to the front door searching for the sentry.

Seven

LOUIS STUDIED HENRIETTA'S FACE AS she slid a mug of beer in front of him and a mug of lemonade in front of her son, Rene. Sometimes her face foretold how *dejeuner* would go. Pleasant or not so pleasant. That day, no hints resided on, for the moment, her passively stern visage.

Henrietta bowed her head, and Louis noted light gray lining the part in the middle of her dark gray hair. Rene bowed also as she said grace, hiding for the moment his neck that swallowed his chin. Rene. Hair as white as Louis', and almost as tall as his uncle, thick through the trunk and arms and legs, but he was still a simple boy. Simple. At "Amen," she looked up and accused her brother with her brown eyes. Every day at every meal she gored him with the look that could have been copied from St. Peter when he condemned a man to hell. Louis had stopped believing in God at the end of the Second War, but his Catholic- educated brain still spun thoughts like that because they were so perfectly descriptive. Plus, he was never sure if her disapproval came from what he was thinking about her son. Most likely it was about God, though.

At the end of the war, Louis had stopped believing in God, but that's when Henrietta had begun truly believing. Believing in her heart, and not just because nuns and priests and parents had pounded the lessons into her. There was no way she could handle what had happened to her if there were no God to help bear her moral burdens. That's what she'd said when they still spoke of those things.

She rose from the table to dish up dinner.

Henrietta was a sturdy woman. When he was thirteen, just before the Second War, and Louis joined the clump of fifteen- and sixteen-year-olds after Mass on Sunday, they spoke of their ideal wife. She should be sturdy, they'd said. She would serve the men of the farm breakfast, deliver her baby, serve the midday meal, and be in the field plowing in the afternoon with the baby strapped to her chest.

Louis thought his sister was sturdy all right, and not just physically. Her ideas of right and wrong were set in stone, like the nuns who taught them in grade school.

Puh! A nun with a son!

Henrietta opened the door to the oven and glorious aromas filled the kitchen. His sister could cook. Well, at least with the oven. Louis looked up and found Rene's expectant eyes on him. Time for their Sunday dinner ritual. A part of Louis was irritated. The two of them had been playing the same game, Sunday after Sunday after Sunday, without variation, for decades. On the other hand, the boy derived great pleasure from it. And how many times did he have a thing to be happy about?

Louis sighed and said, "Your mama is the best cook in all of Hainaut Province."

Rene's face glowed more intensely, like one of those lightbulbs with multiple filaments when you switch it from dim to bright. "Mama is the best cook in all of Belgium."

"I think she is the best cook in all of Europe." Despite his earlier aggravation, Louis felt himself getting caught up in the spirit of the game.

"No." Rene beamed brightest. "Mama is the best cook in the whole world."

Louis raised his mug. The boy raised his. "To the best cook in the whole world," Louis said, drank, and clunked his mug on the table. *Clunk.*

Louis frowned. Always these little pleasant interludes ended in irritation. The boy, sitting across the table from him, mimicked his moves. He clunked his mug. The boy clunked, too. Irritating. The boy miming him always made Louis think he was seeing his reflection in a mirror, that he was seeing himself born that way.

Henrietta slid plates in front of the males and filled one for herself. The aroma from the mutton set Louis' juices flowing. Henrietta could cook all right. He wondered if she'd gotten some new spices from the gypsy, Anastasia, who lived with her husband Ivan in the forest behind the chateau. He didn't ask though. She was so touchy. Asking about the spices, she might interpret it as an implication she was not a good cook, that only Anastasia's spices saved her mediocre productions.

"Smells wonderful," he said as she sat.

Usually, Henrietta was hungry at Sunday dinner. The butcher in *Toussaint* told Louis once, "At the after-Mass lunch, your sister never eats. She talks. She is hungrier for female conversation than for meat and potatoes."

Which was fine. At least he could eat his dinner in peace, not have to watch his words so carefully lest he set her off into the nasty unpleasantness so close to the surface these days. When had she gotten to be such a crabby old woman?

"Alonzo bought his wife a gas stove," she said.

Louis stopped his fork centimeters from his mouth. The look on her face. She wanted a gas stove. She expected a fight. Or did she *want* a fight? Not this time.

He put on a smile. "Of course. I will take you to Mons tomorrow. You can buy a new stove."

That surprised her. It had been a long time since he felt like he'd come out on top in one of their encounters.

The dinner passed pleasantly, more so than for a very long time. They finished their plates and dessert. Henrietta served coffee to

Louis and refilled Rene's mug with lemonade. Then she loaded plates and silverware into the dishwasher.

Lemonade, Louis thought, *proof the boy isn't Belgian.*

Belgian boys drank beer.

"Tell the story, Uncle," Rene said.

"Please," Henrietta said, and her boy "Please"-d.

"Which one?"

"The first Louis captured the French nobleman. Then George the Tall gave him this farm. Then your grandfather named you after him."

"You know the story, Rene."

"You tell." Rene looked at his mother. "Please."

"Ach," Louis said, but only to sound aggravated.

"It was 1790," Louis said.

Rene: "George the Tall came to Belgium."

"Yes. He asked the first Louis to help him capture a castle from a French nobleman so he could give the castle to Belgium. George the Tall and First Louis won the fight."

Rene: "But the Frenchman tried to escape. First Louis captured him."

"As a reward for his help, George the Tall gave First Louis the land for the Defonce farm."

"It was my great, great," Rene used his fingers to track and total up the six he needed, "grand-*pere*." Rene beamed.

Louis couldn't help it and smiled at Rene. The boy's effusive enthusiasm, despite having heard the story thousands of times, still lifted Louis.

"When you were born," Rene continued, "Grand- mama, with no greats, wanted to call you George. But Grandpapa was stubborn."

Set in his round innocent face, the boys blue eyes sparkled and startled Louis. He'd looked into those eyes countless times, but each time it was as if he was seeing them for the first time. There was an unmeasurable depth, an un-understandable depth to those eyes.

"Grandpapa pointed to the ceiling and said, 'He is Louis.'"

Rene dropped his finger after demonstrating his grand-papa's gesture. "The end," he said and rose to use the bathroom.

The end. It was the end. Louis knew why his mother had not wanted him to carry the name. He knew why his father had burdened him with it. Papa expected him to ensure the family perpetuated. But he'd failed Papa. The only Louis since that first one was Louis the Last. The Jourdan family would not perpetuate. Its history would end, fade, and disappear. Instead of finding a wife and building his own addition to the Defonce family history, he'd had to care for his sister, and her … and Rene.

Henrietta placed her hand on his arm. He had to suffer before she would show him affection. Louis looked up at her. They exchanged a smile reminiscent of October of 1944. Together they'd overcome the disaster of August.

August. When the Germans killed Mama and Papa and Uncle Marcel and destroyed the farm house and raped Henrietta. Together they'd overcome that tragedy, and in October, with the detestable Germans all returned to their detestable homeland, they could see a glimmer of hope for themselves. Louis had begun rebuilding the house. Dreams of the giant Gestapo sergeant hurting her, stopped waking Henrietta from sleep breathing hard and biting a finger to keep from screaming. October.

October was when Henrietta realized she'd missed her monthly, and had missed the one before.

A balloon of cynicism inflated itself and bubbled up and out of his belly. A part of his mind thought it would have been better if the German's had killed Henrietta, but Louis convinced himself that what he really thought was *It would have been better if the Germans had killed the two of us.*

The war had destroyed so many family histories. But the Defonce history survived. It survived because Louis kept it alive. But now—

"No," Louis said.

He would not allow his mind to sink further into that line of thought to ruin his Sunday. "No." He would push himself back to the story, to complete it. The story of 1790 Louis formed the cornerstone of the 1990 Louis.

Louis went back to 1790, with George the Tall climbing out of bed in the chateau. George surprised the sentry in front of the chateau and slit his throat. Then he opened the gate and fifteen Belgium for Belgians snuck into the chateau and began slaughtering the sleeping French warriors. No one had known the nobleman had built his mansion with a secret escape tunnel.

1790 Louis and two other men had been tasked with approaching the chateau from the rear. They were to wait for a signal that that sentry had been dispatched. As they waited, suddenly, in front of the three, the forest floor lifted and light spilled out. The French nobleman climbed out his escape tunnel and, in the light from his lamp, he found three men armed with pitchforks and flails confronting him. The nobleman pulled a pistol from his belt and shot one of the men. Louis and the other survivor stared open-mouthed. The Frenchman drew his sword and stabbed Louis's companion. That stirred him to action and he jabbed the nobleman in the throat with his pitchfork. A woman screamed from down inside the tunnel.

1790 Louis grabbed the woman and her daughter. He took them to George the Tall, but he did not tell him about the tunnel, or the bag of money he'd found with the Frenchman.

George was pleased to see the beautiful Twyla again, but much more pleased with the delectable daughter. The daughter was the reason the Swabian prince awarded 1790 Louis land for the farm adjacent to his new chateau.

Louis sighed. The men of the Defonce family knew the deeper history. His grandfather and father insisted he know and remember and tell the story to the males of the family. Which, now, was Rene. The men of the Defonce family knew of the secret escape tunnel and what was hidden in there: one small sack of coins from 1790, a box of gold and silver the Germans had pillaged at the end of the war, and weapons Louis and his resistance friends had taken from the Germans as well.

"Bah," Louis muttered.

He recalled his fortieth birthday. That was when it dawned on him that he would never marry, that the Defonce line, the Defonce history would be buried with him. It had seemed such a tragedy at the time. One akin to the human race disappearing from the earth like the dinosaurs. A tragedy of monumental importance.

The sound of canned laughter came from the TV in the parlor.

Canned laughter! Leave it to the Americans to put laughter in a can.

That's what the human race has come to. Maybe the end of humanity could be contemplated as something other than a tragedy.

"Bah," he muttered again.

Maybe he'd done enough contemplating for this Sunday. He rose from the table, walked to hutch against the east wall. He opened the top doors.

"Zut!"

The bottle was not on the shelf. Henrietta had used his Calvados in her cooking. He didn't ask much of her, just to leave his apple brandy alone. If she wanted brandy to cook with, he would buy her some. But she used the Calvados. Maybe he should tell her where and how he got the Calvados. She would never touch it again.

But now, there was nothing for it. He had to go the escape tunnel entrance in the forest behind the chateau and get another bottle from the cases in the tunnel. A part of his Sunday ritual was to drink some of the apple brandy from Normandy the Gestapo sergeant had pillaged as the Germans fled ahead of the invading Americans and British. He drank the sergeant's brandy to the memory of his fallen comrades of the resistance.

Eight

K ate Marshall, dutiful navy wife, stood slump shouldered in the crowd around the dead luggage carousel in the Brussels airport. Fatigue buzzed in her head. Everything hurt. Muscles. Bones. Her hair hurt.

Seat 34C. For seven hours and forty-five minutes, 34C tortured her butt and back. Even now, free of it, everything still hurt.

Everything hurt. Just before her mother died, when Kate asked her what was wrong, that's what she said. Her husband Bill had said, "Crabby old women exaggerate their aches." Wrong! She hadn't been exaggerating.

Her mother, Louella Mary O'Reilly, at sixty-nine had been a pistol. She wasn't crabby. Neither age nor arthritis slowed her down. Her ready laugh infected all in earshot with joy and a desire to be included in her adventures. Then two months ago, she stopped going out. She stopped smiling. But she had not been crabby.

Dear God, Kate thought. She had spent the last two months trying to get over being mad at Bill for saying what he did about her mother right before she died, and for betraying Kate. Claire, her boss, her partner, had talked with her endlessly to get Kate to see that the most important thing, when she got to Belgium, was to look forward, to mend the strains put on their marriage, to put the difficulties behind them, forever. Kate had agreed and before the trip started, she was determined to do just that.

But that was before her blind date with 34C. She had no idea how long she'd been awake. There'd been an early morning flight to Dallas. A terminal change dragging bags and children. In New York, the trek to the International Terminal in the middle of a flock of migrating passengers, none of whom seemed to care if they ever got to where they were going.

Someday, she told herself, you'll laugh as you tell people at a cocktail party about the "trip from hell."

"Hey!" William, junior, JR, shouted next to her to her left.

Heather, eleven, poked and antagonized her eight- year-old brother. JR fought back, but did so smiling.

"Knock it off," Kate snapped.

The two smirked at each other. They'd be right back at it in a minute, as they'd been since the flight attendants served breakfast on the plane. Through yet another marathon trek through the corridors of the huge Brussels terminal, the two had delighted in their game of picking on each other, rather than being attentive to things like not getting separated in the press of people, not bumping into other tired, cranky passengers. Her body was drained of energy, but her oldest and her youngest, they made her soul tired. The crowd of people around her stared when she'd barked at her children and stilled the babble of gentle voices. That didn't matter. She was too tired to care.

Her other daughter, nine-year-old Sally, stood quietly to her right, holding her hand passively. Kate thought, as she often did, that God had endowed Heather and JR with a combination of Louella Mary O'Reilly's bright, bubbly personality, and in equal measures, Bill's spirit. But God had withheld from Sally any manifestation of her grandmother's or her father's personality.

Is there a sort of genetics of the spirit world as there is in the physical?

Sometimes a family physical feature appeared in one child,

skipped over the next, and showed up again in the third. Like the deformation of cartilage—the slight deformation of cartilage—at the top of Kate's left ear. Her mother had had it. Heather had it. Sally's ears were perfect. JR's not.

When he saw JR the first time, Bill had said, "My son is marked with the O'Reilly disfigurement."

Sometimes Bill's black, navy-fighter-pilot, gallows humor was just black. And hurtful. Deeper meaning lived below the surface of his words: Your *womb is defective. You're a defective, disfigured, disappointing woman.*

Thinking made Kate's brain buzz like a tired old fluorescent bulb about to blow.

Come on, you stupid carousel. Move!

It didn't. It didn't care about her agony in 34C. On other trips of this kind it had been boisterous Heather and JR that had been so very aggravatingly memorable. This trip, it was that … that seat.

She needed a bath. She needed to wash her hair. She needed a bed. To sleep in. For a week.

A sudden honk jarred her. Sally had been jolted, too. Kate and her middle child both had exaggerated startle responses. "Skittish as a mare in heat with a stallion in the next corral over," Bill had teased, once. She'd bitten his head off for saying such a crude thing in front of the children. Bill. A Wyoming cowboy in his youth and then a US Navy fighter pilot. Kate could not imagine two worse things to build a man around.

The carousel jerked into motion.

Finally, their luggage came. Finally, the line of passengers pushing luggage carts and dragging wheeled suitcases snail-ed through customs and oozed them through sliding doors. She saw Bill behind a waist-high barrier. He waved and a luminous smile lit his face. Heather and JR screeched, ran, and swarmed him. Kate nudged Sally to go to her father too. Then she pushed the luggage cart to the side so she wouldn't block the stream of passengers behind her.

Bill untangled himself from the children and came to her. "I missed you, gorgeous." He kissed her firmly; then hugged her hard. "How was the flight?"

"Fine," JR butted in. "I was going to watch a movie last night but I fell asleep."

Bill took the cart from Kate and headed for the door with JR prattling on one side and Heather on the other. Sally took her mother's hand. They tailed the happy engine towing them.

At the sidewalk in front of the terminal, Bill suggested they wait there with the luggage while he retrieved the car. They'd never manage all the bags on the bus.

"How long will *that* take?"

Foggy headed as she was, she knew her words had dripped ugly venom. Bill reacted as if she'd slapped him. Guilt toasted her soul and released a wisp of remorse. She thought about apologizing. But regret was no match for the resentment boiling in her stomach.

"I should be back in twenty minutes," Bill said. "Or so."

Kate hissed. "Can't we just walk?"

"Too long," Bill said, as if it was obvious.

"We'll walk!" she snapped.

"The sidewalk doesn't go far. We'd have to walk in the street with that." Bill nodded at the two lanes of bumper-to-bumper cars, taxis, and buses inching along. "Be reasonable. Stay with the cart."

Kate was sick and tired of hearing *Be reasonable*. When Bill said it, it was the same as saying: *Don't be stupid. I know what's best for us to do.*

Kate breathed out a sigh as deep as a final deathbed exhale and moved the cart against the front of the terminal.

Bill set off at a rapid pace. Heather and JR refused to wait, but Sally stayed beside Kate. They watched JR lurch in a jerky half run to keep up. Bill said something. Heather and JR laughed.

Probably laughing at me, Kate thought.

Waiting stewed up the betrayal. And the resentment.

Until the betrayal, life for Kate had been pleasant enough. She had the children. After twenty-three years of marriage to the US Navy and Bill—and it felt proper to put them in that order—the moves every two years no longer bothered her. At the next duty station, she'd always made new friends. But through all of it, Kate and the children lived, not their own lives, rather they each lived a small piece of Bill's grand life. And as much as Claire talked against the notion, at that moment, Kate did still feel betrayed.

———∿∽⌒∘⌒⊙⊙⌒∘⌒∽∿———

Standing beside her mother outside the terminal, Sally watched it happen. Her mother became angrier and angrier. The grayness inside her grew darker and darker and colder and colder.

The black and chill frightened Sally. It was as if her mother were leaving her. She squeezed her mother's hand, but she didn't squeeze back. She used to always squeeze back. Before Nana O'Reilly died.

Before Nana O'Reilly died, Sally never thought about her ability to *see* inside her mother. But it was impossible to *not* see her mother's inside brightness and warmth get pushed out of her by a cloud, dark gray and cold. It wasn't really a cloud, only sort of like one. And Sally did see it. Not with her eyes. But it wasn't smelling, tasting, touching, or hearing. It couldn't be those. So it was seeing.

After her father had been gone a few minutes, Sally noticed the gray inside her mother wasn't quite so dark anymore. It wasn't much of a change, but she saw it. A bit of warm softened the hard cold. She saw that too and pressed against her mother's leg.

Sally watched the stream of people flow past, not noticing her, as if she were invisible. She wondered if her mother thought she was invisible too. Then her mother squeezed her shoulder. Sally smiled, but her face didn't.

She let go of her mother's hand and finger caressed the turquoise bead in the pouch on the cord around her neck and under her top.

Please make it okay again.

When someone died, people were sad. Nana O'Reilly was Mother's mother. But after Nana died, Mother wasn't just sad. Something else happened then too. Sally didn't know what it was. But it was bad, bad, bad.

Please make it okay again.

Then her father parked the car at the curb and hopped out.

Some of the luggage went onto the rack on top of the car. Heather and JR wrestled some of the smaller bags into the trunk.

Sally's place in the car was behind her father. From there she could see more of her mother.

As the car eased into traffic, Father said, "Kate, listen. I know you can't sleep on airplanes. I know you're exhausted, but don't take a nap today. Stay awake until normal bedtime tonight, and your body clock will be adjusted in the morning. If you take a nap, it'll screw you up for a week."

Mother replied, "When we get to the hotel, I'm going to take a bath. Then I'm going to sleep. I don't care what happens to my body clock."

"The guys I work with warned me about it when I flew over. It worked for me."

Mother didn't say anything, and Father kept talking. Which was unusual for him. While he was driving, he didn't say much. Normally.

But things were not normal. Normal was when Sally saw warmth and brightness inside her mother. But then Nana O'Reilly died. After that, what she saw inside Mother changed.

Sally shifted her attention to the back of her father's head. She had always thought of him as big. Uncle Norman Marshall was taller than Father. His arms were thicker. His hands and feet were larger. But Father was *bigger.* Riding behind him in the car, she saw that Father wasn't as big as she remembered. Something made him smaller. And the brightness she saw in him reminded her of the porch light at Uncle Norman Marshall's ranch in Wyoming when they visited at Christmas. It was always so cold there. And that porch light, she always thought if she touched it, it wouldn't feel warm like light bulbs did every place else. It would feel like touching a glowing ice cube. Inside the house it was too warm. Before she could pull her coat off, Uncle Norman's loud laugh would hurt her ears, and Aunt Beth would gather and lift Sally and JR in a crushing hug. It had been last Christmas, after Auntie set her and JR back on the floor and grabbed a reluctant Heather that Sally noticed Father standing next to Uncle, and that Father was bigger. Uncle was taller. His shoulders were wider, but there was something about father that was bigger.

But that part of Father wouldn't be bigger any more.

Sally smiled inside, for a moment, as she thought about Aunt Beth. First, she recalled her welcome hug, but then she remembered the pain in Auntie's heart. Auntie loved children. She wanted her own but couldn't have them. As they drove away after the visit last Christmas, Mother and Father talked about Aunt Beth. Listening to her parents speak, Sally understood what she had seen in Auntie to be pain. And she knew what the pain came from, and seeing it in her memory, she cried. But didn't cry outside.

During that Christmas visit, Sally attached herself to Aunt Beth and stayed beside her almost continuously from breakfast to bedtime. When Aunt Beth was cooking, Sally was beside her, helping. Gathering eggs from the henhouse, Sally carried the basket. Sally was drawn to her by something she sensed, but didn't understand as pain, until the ride home, and she heard Mother and Father talk about Aunt Beth.

For her part, Aunt Beth treated Sally like a daughter. After a week, they left to return home to San Diego. That's when Mother and Father had talked. Heather and JR always fell asleep as soon as the car started moving. Sally had her eyes closed too, but she was awake.

"Poor Beth," Mother had said. "Sometimes I think bringing the children to visit just adds to her pain."

Father replied, "If ever a woman was meant to be a mother, it's Beth. And you could see in her face how much she loved being with Sally this past week. And you could see how much it hurt her to say goodbye to her. But, you know, however much pain the goodbye caused, I bet Beth wouldn't trade this past week with Sally beside her constantly for all the comfort in the world."

"Bill!" Mother had said.

"What? The world's greatest fighter pilot can't have a sensitive side?"

Sally had opened her eyes and seen brightness and warmth glowing, filling the front of the car.

"Did you know," Father said," Beth is part Arapaho?"

"Really?"

"Yes. Beth's grandmother, and I can never remember how many greats go in front, was a little girl when her parents were killed somewhere along the Bozeman Trail. The girl wound up as the squaw of a medicine man and she had a daughter. The army raided the village. The medicine man was killed, and Beth's great, great and the daughter were rescued. When we were in grade school, one of the kids found out Beth was part Indian, and the teasing and hounding began. Norman stepped in and beat up anybody, boy or girl, who said a word against Beth."

Near the end of the Christmas visit. Auntie Beth gave Sally a turquoise bead in a pouch hung from the string to wear around her neck. "Turquoise wards off evil spirits," Auntie said. "Keep it with you always."

Mother wanted Sally to take the pouch off at bedtime, to put it on the nightstand when she slept. Sally always obeyed Mother. Except about the bead. Aunt Beth said, " … always with you."

Often during a day, she would touch the bead under her clothing and pray. *Please help it not hurt so much inside Auntie Beth.*

Sally felt the car accelerate, which ended her Christmas reverie. They were driving onto a highway.

"Highway's are called auto-routes over here," her father said.

Mother stared straight ahead. She wasn't asleep. The most important thing was, inside Mother hadn't gotten darker again.

Next to her, Heather and JR slept. Heather leaned against the side of the car. JR used her lap for a pillow.

The motor hummed. Her father's voice droned. She put her hand over the bead pouch. Her mind grew heavy. Her hand slid down onto her lap.

Bill kept an eye on Kate. The guys at SHAPE had gone on and on about how hard the trip from the east coast to Europe was on the body clock. So, he talked. About his job, the people he worked with, the countless interesting historical sites within a two-hour drive from Mons.

Kate's head nodded forward.

"The Germans are interesting," Bill said, and she looked at him. "No matter what we start talking about at lunch, at a dinner, at the bar, sooner or later, World War II comes up. Sometimes, a Belgian brings it up, or a Dane, or an Italian—and of course Italy was on Germany's side back then—but it's like, in all of Europe, when the war is discussed, everybody is a good guy but the Germans."

"How do the German's react?" Kate asked.

"At lunch, at a dinner, at the bar, we are all talking, laughing, telling jokes. Then the war comes up, and the Germans shrivel. Their bodies seem to become less solid, and, I don't know, they make their souls smaller. I think they know they will never be forgiven for what happened.

When someone wants to talk about the war, there's nothing they can do to stop it, so they sort of fade into the background. Once the group moves on to a new topic of conversation, the Germans come out and play again."

"I thought the German economy was strong, that Europe's prosperity depended on it."

Bill was pleased to get her engaged. "Yes. That's pretty much the case."

A sign indicating an exit for Waterloo approached the car.

"See that?" Bill said. "Waterloo. The exact place where Napoléon ran out of luck. General Sampson himself gave me a tour of the place one Saturday."

Bill smiled recalling how the general described the arrangement of forces across farmers' fields, and the general's driver taking them to farmhouses demarking the east and west ends of the battlefield, then the one to the south where Napoleon had established his headquarters.

Stupid!

He'd had her engaged in a conversation, which he then cleverly dead ended. And Kate's head lolled.

He put his hand on her thigh. Her head popped up, she grabbed his hand and moved it off her, and she glared at him.

"Sorry. I was just trying to help you stay awake. I … I didn't mean—"

Kate didn't say anything, just stared straight ahead.

"Can we talk about things?"

"Not in front of the children."

"They're asleep."

"Not in front of the children," she insisted and glowered at him.

A couple of kilometers purred by. They passed an exit from the autoroute. Bill pointed it out.

"On Sundays, they have a *brocante*, a f lea market there. I've found some interesting things there. Like a German bayonette from World War I."

He glanced at her. She sighed.

"I resigned from *Daley and Marshall*. I moved over here because nothing is more important than keeping our family together. And not just together physically. But right now, physically, I'm at the end of my rope. Give me some time. I'm trying to work this out. Just … don't push me."

"Okay, Kate. I will be Mr. Self-restraint and Moderation himself."

She rolled her eyes.

He thought that might be a good sign, but just then he felt like a German. He had an unforgiveable sin on his soul, but Europe needed his economic engine to pull it to prosperity. An unforgiveable sin balanced on a teeter totter by a strong Deutsche mark.

Nine

K ATE'S EYES SNAPPED OPEN. THE car was slowing. The turn signal tick, tick, ticked.

"Are we there?" JR wanted to know.

"Not yet. But we're close, about five, six kilometers," Bill said.

"That's five clicks, right Dad?"

"A click is the same thing as a kilometer," Heather piped in. "Even a goober third grader ought to know that."

"I'm in fourth grade."

"They'll probably set you back a year over here."

Heather and JR slept so soundly, but they woke and went right back at it.

Bill turned off the autoroute and onto a two-lane blacktop. Ahead of them, she saw a small cluster of buildings, not big enough to constitute a real town.

"The *ville* of Toussaint," Bill said.

"I thought we were living in Mons," Kate said.

"Mons is where I work. It's ten kilometers south."

"What's a *ville*?" JR asked.

"It's like a village. Over here, they call it a *ville*."

Toussaint wasn't much. A tiny church and a long row house occupied Kate's side of the street, a couple of shops sat opposite. The windows of the businesses looked expectantly at the row house. Forlornly, Kate thought.

"You can't see it, but there's another street behind the main drag. It's all single-family houses except for a bakery. And you will love the bread here, Katie girl. But the important thing about Toussaint is the speed limit. It's forty kilometers per hour. And they have photo speed traps at both ends of town. When we get you your Belgian driver's license, you'll need to be mindful of that."

In Kate's head, conflicting ideas vied for predominance. Kate wanted to stop Bill's blah-blah-blah-ing and go after him about living in the boonies. In the boonies, people were isolated and lived far apart. Kate needed people around her. She wanted to resurrect her commitment that the relationship with her husband was on a healing path. But it was slipping away. She didn't want to worry Sally. Sally seemed to sense her moods. Kate closed her eyes.

The white light of a migraine hurt her eyes, though they were shut tight. The headache triggered queasiness in her stomach and spritzed vinegary bile onto her tongue.

She reached into her sweater pocket for the rosary. It had been her mother's. With the beads in hand, the ephemeral promise of blessed peace began to solidify and surrounded her anguish and corralled her issues. Her fingers clamped onto a Hail Mary bead, and she began the prayer.

"Dad," JR piped. "There was a picture of a horse on that building back there. Do they have cowboys in Belgium?"

"Just a moment son. Kate. Kate, look."

She opened her eyes, expecting the light to hurt, but it didn't. *One blessing today.*

"See that black pole on the side of the road? There's a Doppler radar on that pole. And the next one has a camera. If you speed, it takes a picture of your license plate. Then you get notice in the mail to pay a thousand BF fine."

"What's a BF, Dad?" JR asked.

"Belgian Franc. Thirty-two equal a US dollar."

"What about the horse on the sign, Dad?"

The edge of the ville slipped behind. The car accelerated.

"Okay, son. Before I answer your question, I'll just remind you we are in Belgium. This is not the US of A. That sign is on a butcher shop, and it means they sell horsemeat."

Heather: "*Eeeuw!*"

"Belgian people eat horses?" JR asked.

Dear God in heaven! Kate was a city girl, but she was from Wyoming. Indians ate horses and dogs. Wyoming white people did not. She started another Hail Mary.

Through the windshield, fields, pastures, and clustered farmhouses, barns, and outbuildings appeared and flashed by in the side window.

"What kind of hotel would be out here in the boonies?" Kate asked.

A big grin split Bill's face. "We are not going to a hotel. I've got a surprise for you."

"A surprise?" from JR. "What is it?"

"If I tell you, it won't be a surprise, will it?"

Even with the rosary in her hand, the relationship between JR and Heather and their father annoyed Kate. It was as if no else on the planet existed but the three of them. Only what they wanted to say to each other mattered. They tuned everyone else out.

Others complained how unfair it was for a woman to do all the work of bearing and raising a child, and then have the youngster look not at all like the mother, but entirely like the father. Unfair. Heather and JR were blonds, like their father, and JR's facial features resembled Bill's. Heather, however, looked somewhat like her Aunt Beth, only a slim version. But the two were definitely chips off Bill's spiritual block.

Bill lifted his foot off the accelerator and the car slowed. "Almost there. Everyone close your eyes."

"Bill! I do *not* feel like playing games. I just want to get out of this car and into a bathtub."

Bill started braking. "Hands over your eyes, Kate."

"Mom!" JR insisted.

"The quickest way to a bath is for you to cover your eyes."

"Has anyone ever told you how aggravating you can be, Bill Marshall?"

"Only you and most of the admirals in the US Navy."

"Mom!" JR again.

Kate turned and encountered Sally's big, black, innocent eyes, and her face, which somehow managed to convey beatific beauty through a shadow of sadness. That young angel face, those eyes, they were not fit places to house worry and concern. But worry and concern were there as if troweled on by a palette knife.

"It's okay, Sally. Really." And Kate made herself be that way for her daughter.

Then Kate shook her head at Bill, still grinning, and she sighed and covered her eyes with her hands.

The car sped up.

"Won't be long," Bill said. "Just a click."

JR: "Tell us when it's a half click, Dad."

Heather: "Just shut up, JR."

The car slowed. The turn signal ticked. The car turned left. Tires crunched on gravel. They stopped.

"Okay," Bill said. "Open your eyes."

Bill had stopped halfway through a gateway in a tall stone fence facing a huge two-story—what? Hotel, or palace maybe? Kate wasn't sure.

"Is this our hotel? It doesn't look like there are any guests."

"Katie girl." No clown ever wore a bigger grin painted on his face. "This is our house. We live here."

"It's a castle!" JR blurted.

"This is our home? We're living here? By ourselves?"

"It's ours, Katie girl. For this tour of duty. Cool, huh?"

"It's sure big enough to be a castle," Heather said.

"Big? It's huge. There are ... seven windows, fourteen, twenty-eight just on this side. I am not living in a house with more than fifty windows. I. Am. Not. Cleaning fifty windows."

"But, Mom, It's a castle, and we can live in it."

"There has to be more than fifty rooms! Bill, have you lost your mind?"

"It's not like that. We'll just live in a one-house-size piece of it. There won't be any extra work."

Kate frowned. "How old is this place?"

Again the huge grin. "Here's the really cool part. This place—"

"This castle," JR insisted.

"This castle was built in the 1790 by Prince George le Grand, George the Tall. The road we took from the auto- route is named for him. He was part of the family that eventually became the royal family of Belgium. George's palace ... actually the Belgiques would say George's chateau."

"*Shah toe*, that means castle, right Dad?"

"Close enough, son."

Kate shook her head.

Bill said, "We are twenty minutes from the French border, two hours from the Netherlands. We can take a day to travel to London via ferry from Calais to Dover and see *Cats* that night. We can drive a day heading east and see where the *Sound of Music* was filmed. And the history! Every time you turn around, you bump into something hundreds or thousands of years old."

"But the coolest thing is we get to live in a castle!"

Bill turned and smiled at the boy.

Kate started another Hail Mary on her mother's rosary.

Bill's voice, as he talked about the chateau, diminished to where it was like a mosquito in a dark bedroom. The sound was annoying, but as long as she heard the whispered buzz, the little beast wouldn't be sucking her blood.

Blessed art Thou among women.

At least one of us is.

For sure, that was a sin, one she'd have to confess.

Overhead the October sky was a sullen, lead gray. Not that sunshine would make a difference.

Exhaustion reclaimed her. She was too tired to pray any more.

"Anyway," Bill said, "the royals used this place as a hunting lodge. It's called *Chateau du Chasse*. See the long buildings with all the doors to either side? Those are stables. See up there to the front door in the center of our new house? Well, when the noblemen were here to hunt, they'd descend those steps, and a groom would hand them the reins to a horse."

"I'm guessing there are no horses in the stables now," Heather said. "We couldn't be that lucky."

"Sorry. The last time the royal family used the place for hunting was just before World War I. The stables are garages now. After the Second World War, it was used as a hotel, but the guy who leased the place died ten years ago, and it's been mostly vacant since."

Kate was having trouble getting a thought in edgewise. As happened more and more, it was Bill, Heather, and JR ganged together in excluding her and Sally.

Sally. It was easy to forget her. She was so quiet, while the others just filled time and space with themselves. Kate turned and saw worry on her daughter's face. Kate had been so consumed with her own troubles. She reached between the seats and touched Sally's hand.

"It's okay," Kate said to her.

"Great, Katie girl. I knew you'd come around."

Come around? How could Bill not *see what was happening with Sally?*

Bill started the car forward. Below the steps rising to the main door of the chateau, and in the center of the circular driveway, stood a statue of a royal huntsman on a horse. The horse had been planted in the center of a bed of densely packed red geraniums. The red flowers made a dramatic splash of vibrant new life in front of the ancient … chateau.

Bill glanced at Kate. A goofy little smile tried to find a comfortable home on his face, but it failed. She knew he was searching for something on her face. *Bill had planted the flowers. For me. He's trying to see if I know.*

He was also trying to fix things between them.

"I know," she whispered.

He halted the car behind the stone huntsman and faced her. She could see on his face that he was glad she knew he had planted those flowers for her. She could also see that Bill considered what he'd done in planting them was just a small thing. She could see how much he loved her.

For a moment, she wished that she could just be mad at him, even hate him. But it didn't work like that. Life had to be complicated, filled with contradictions. In many ways, it had been easier with Bill in Belgium for the last two months.

There were many things to love about her husband. One of those was his sense of morality. He'd told her once, "It was Adam and Eve who picked the apple, but it was you and me, Katie girl, who bit off bites, chewed, and swallowed."

Bill. But now, she had the trip from hell, and the reunion, both these had drained her of strength and energy. She wasn't sure she had the strength to get out of the car.

He did, though, and stepped out and pulled the seat forward. JR and Heather boiled past Sally. Sally stayed in her place.

Bill ascended the stone steps and unlocked the door as Heather and JR elbowed and shoved to enter in first. As usual, Heather won with JR on her heels.

Kate shook her head, marveling that the two rowdies didn't trip over each other's feet. Bill waved to her.

"Come on, Katie girl. You *have* to see this."

"Let's go," Kate said.

Sally nodded, and Kate opened the door and stood on the cobblestones. Standing wasn't so bad. She walked to the steps. Walking was okay. She climbed the steps and her calf and thigh muscles complained. Her ankles, knees, and hips might have squeaked. Stepping into the foyer, her mouth fell open.

The foyer was a huge square space. And the ceiling was way, way up there. It was like being in a cathedral or the Capitol in Washington D.C. To her right, the wall held a flight of stairs climbing to a level walkway, which traversed the front of the building above the door they'd entered, to another flight of stairs, affixed to the other wall, connecting to the second level of the chateau. The walls and stairs were of dark wood. Oak? The ceiling was decorated with square, carved panels painted white. At some earlier time, the carvings in those panels might have been gilded with gold.

The ceiling was so high. It was nothing like a house she could live in. More like something the kids would visit on a school field trip. Maybe if she wasn't so tired, it wouldn't be so … so foreign.

"Right here in the center of the foyer," Bill said, with JR holding his hand and Heather on the other side. "We'll have our Christmas tree. It'll be as big as the national tree back home."

JR's face was alight. Heather's face said "Ho hum." But Kate thought her daughter felt obligated, in whatever convoluted way almost-teenaged girls reckoned obligation, to show disdain for such a childish thing as Christmas. But Heather's eyes sparkled.

"Can we see the rest of *our* castle, Dad?"

"Upstairs first or down?"

"No," Kate said.

Bill and the two children looked at her as if she'd burped loudly during a quiet part of Mass.

"I am dirty and tired and—"

"Where's Sally?" Bill asked.

Nine-year-old Sally stayed beside the car. A petite figure. Her shoulder-length, black, straight hair framed a face as smooth and white as Mary's in Michelangelo's *Pieta*, the one in St. Peter's Basilica. As her mother ascended the steps and entered the house, she heard JR babble. Then her father spoke about a Christmas tree.

Sally's eyes were drawn to the right, all the way to the end of the big house. Her gaze settled on the last two windows on the bottom floor. Those windows were like eyes. She frowned. The window-eyes were watching her. A cold shiver shook her petite frame. She touched the bead pouch.

"Sally," her mother called from in the house.

Sally ran up the steps and through the door to her mother's side. It felt safe there.

Sally peeked around her mother, through open double-doors, and down a long dark corridor. Those windows were down there.

She slipped her small hand into her mother's.

"Heather," her father said. "You're in charge of the luggage working party. Get the small stuff out of the car and bring it up to the second level." Heather bolted out the door. Her father grabbed JR and leaned down close to his face. "Don't try to handle the big suitcases, Mister. I'll get those after I get your mother's bubble-bath going."

As soon as her father released his arm, JR charged after his sister.

"Go on, Sally," her mother said. "Go with them."

Sally squeezed her mother's hand.

"Sally, help Heather and JR with the bags. Are you afraid? This house is just different from what we're used to. There's nothing to be afraid of. It's okay."

It's not okay. Why don't you know that, Mama?

"Help with the bags," Mama said, and pushed her away.

Ten

L ouis Defonce parked his truck in his machine shed and walked to where he could see the chateau. The talk in Mons and in Toussaint concerned the royal residence, and that an American military person would be occupying it. Opinion gelled around the notion that it would be a general, an important one with a large staff.

"Garibaldis has had a truck at the chateau for the last two weeks," Louis said. Garibaldis was a cleaning and building restoration business based in Mons.

"The Americans already have two top generals," someone said.

"The Americans have lots of everything, including generals," from another.

"The two top dogs, one is army and the other is air force. Maybe this new one is navy," another speculated.

"Then it would be an admiral," another informed. "Navies have admirals."

"Admiral, general, what difference does it make. Whoever this man is, he must be important. *Chateau du Chasse* is bigger and grander than the chateaus any of the big generals at SHAPE live in."

Besides the two Americans, the UK and Germany both had four star generals assigned to the headquarters in Mons. Nobody said it, but Louis knew they were all thinking the same thing: With all the other four stars, it was only fair that Belgium, the host country, have one, too. But then, what does fair have to do with anything? Nobody said that either, but they all contributed to the puddle of thought the circle of conversationalists stood ankle-deep in.

Louis, now, standing in his drive, frowned. The chateau didn't look any different. Maybe the important American hadn't arrived yet.

He climbed the steps at the rear of the house into the mudroom, changed from work boots to house slippers, and entered the kitchen.

The aromas from the new gas stove were, as usual, mouthwatering. Henrietta was pleased with her new appliance. She hummed as she cooked, which she had stopped doing with the electric dinner destroyer in residence.

He greeted his sister. She continued stirring at the contents of a pot on the stove and smiled over her shoulder. Louis also saw her judge him, and his mood.

Rene sat at the table, his eyes on his uncle.

"Ah, Rene. Does this kitchen not smell like it belongs to the best cook in the whole world?"

"Best cook in the whole world." Rene's face glowed with pleasure at the variation on their game.

It promised to be a pleasant dinner. These days, those were hard to come by it seemed. Louis washed up in the downstairs bathroom. When he returned, he mentioned the conversation he'd heard about an American general moving into the chateau.

"He's here," Henrietta said.

"We watched them from the upstairs bedroom window," Rene said. "Mama let me use the telescope. It was one man, one woman, one boy, and two girls."

"That's all? No servants?"

"One man, one woman, one—"

"Yes, yes. Perhaps they were servants, sent early to get the house ready for the important officer."

"I do not think so," Henrietta said. "They did not look like servants."

"Bah," Louis said. "What do you know of how servants look?"

"Yesterday a moving van unloaded furniture there," Henrietta said. "It was enough for one family, not a houseful of servants."

"This happened yesterday? Why didn't you tell me?"

"You were in one of your moods."

Bah! You're the touchy one. And even if I am moody, don't I have good reason to be?

After giving up everything to help Henrietta raise her Gestapo's bastard, Louis expected an occasional sign of gratitude from her.

He kept his mouth shut. If he said something, it would provoke her. A provoked Henrietta spewed such venom into the kitchen that not only dinner, but sleep would be ruined as well.

Louis sighed and sat at the table.

Henrietta and Rene bowed and prayed.

Louis felt it happen. It was as if his soul ripped silently into two parts. He did not believe in God or souls, but there was some other than physical entity, other than his mind, to his makeup. Soul was just a word, and it was useful in describing or thinking about things of the spirit. So, it was his spirit, or soul. And it was pulled apart as he sat at the table and Henrietta prayed.

Half of this spirit Louis spoke with Rene and with his sister and enjoyed the excellent meal.

The other half stewed over the injustice of her ingratitude. The other half dredged up the fall of 1944. Thirteen-year-old Henrietta became aware she had missed her period two months in a row. Bad enough the Gestapo sergeant had raped her, but, so much worse, he'd planted his bastard in her womb. The sergeant was tall, and his face bore pig-like features. Louis could not help but recall the stories of George the Tall.

Louis wanted her to get rid the German devil's spawn. But would she see the wisdom of doing that? She would not. Stubborn, even then. He took her to live with the Ormands, a family living in Louvain, east of Brussels. Louis met them through his activities with the resistance. When the baby was six months old, he brought Henrietta and Rene back to the farm to live.

Their neighbors would ask about the boy. Louis urged Henrietta to tell them she'd been in love with a resistance fighter, but the Germans killed him.

"I will not tell such a lie," fifteen-year-old Henrietta said.

"Then," eighteen-year-old Louis commanded. "You will not say anything. You will not shame the Defonce name."

Henrietta had hung her head. For a moment. "I tried to stop the German, The Pig, but he was too big, too strong. I have done nothing to be ashamed of." Henrietta paused as she glared at her brother and he stared back. "But you are ashamed of me, Louis. You think I should not have run away from The Pig. I should have stayed and let him kill me like he killed Isabella."

Louis remembered vividly when and how his sister had spoken those words to him. It was like a slap, but not to his face. It was a slap to his heart. Also, during that … conversation, he discovered he had two souls. A part of him wanted to hold his sister and take upon himself some of her hurt, but the other part … the other part wished she had been killed by The Pig. That other part, too, had been sure when Henrietta delivered her baby, it would have the face of the giant Gestapo sergeant. The boy, however, looked nothing like his father. But there had been no relief in that fact as Rene's face bore the signs of his condition from the first.

The sin of how Rene had been conceived lingered in the body of Henrietta and disfigured the infant in her womb. That's how Louis saw it.

Sitting at his kitchen table, with Henrietta and Rene in the parlor with the TV, Louis recalled the struggle he'd had to put his two souls back together as he'd spoken with his sister, with infant Rene in her arms.

In the end, the conflict inside Louis resolved itself by a slim margin. He had been specifically named for the man who had established the Defonce farm and family name, and he, Second Louis was obligated to preserve them both. To do so, he'd have to throw Henrietta and her bastard out. But his sister was sprung from Mama and Papa as surely and purely as he was. She was a Defonce, and he could not throw her out. Throwing his own sister out, with an infant, would so devalue the family name, it would be worthless.

Back then, at the end of 1945, his souls had come together again with the decision that Louis Defonce was obligated to care for his sister and her son, even if that meant he could not find a wife to fulfill his other obligation.

Thus, Louis spent his young-man years guarding and caring for his sister and her child. And keeping them clear of the shame which would have smeared the Defonce name if anyone learned of Rene's origin.

Sitting at his kitchen table with his coffee, as Henrietta and Rene sat in the parlor with the television manufacturing happiness for them with the sound of manufactured laughter, Louis reminded himself that happiness was overrated.

Then, Louis felt his souls begin to come back together again.

Then he remembered his American neighbor.

Les Americains. Les 'Ricans! They saved Europe with their Marshall Plan, some believed. But they were the ones who drove the Germans out of Normandy. As the Germans retreated, some of them pillaged and raped their way back to their *vaterland.* That's why the Gestapo sergeant, The Pig, had entered his and Henrietta's lives. The Americans drove him to them. And The Pig killed Papa and Mama and raped Henrietta.

Normally, Louis only drank Calvados on Sunday evenings to remember his fallen resistance fighter comrades. It was not Sunday, but Louis needed a brandy.

He swallowed a big mouthful and gasped. It had been like swallowing cool fire. The liquor took his breath away. He sipped at the next glassful.

Les Ricans!

They did not save Europe. They destroyed it with Disneyland and McDonalds.

A burst of canned laughter erupted from the parlor.

... and television, he appended to the thought.

Eleven

KATE KICKED HER PANTIES ACROSS the tile floor toward the trashcan. She'd thought about burning the undergarment. If they— Panties were plural, but the pile of ivory fabric was a very singular item.

Ever since her mother died, she, at times, found strange thoughts volleying back and forth in her mind. She was so very tired, and in a way, she hadn't gotten a good night's sleep since that horrible day back in San Diego. Why was she thinking about if panties were plural or was singular? It *was not* important. But she could not push the stupid thought out of her head.

If the panties were so dirty the laundry could not restore them, then a bath could not clean the filth from her body.

Forget the bath. Take a nap.

Bill told her to stay awake. He was probably right about that.

A nap. A picture of her head on a pillow, her eyes closed, a blissful smile curling up … Sally's lips. Where did that come from?

Something other than herself directed her thoughts. *Am I possessed*?

In the Bible. Jesus and the apostles drove evil spirits out of possessed people. In one story, an evil spirit was driven out of man's body and cast into a herd of passing swine.

There's never a herd of swine passing when you need one.

Kate shivered. Her arms wore sleeves of goose bumps.

What do you expect? The ceilings in this place are so high, and all the heat is up there, and you, Katie girl, are down here, standing on a tile floor. Of course you're cold.

Kate stuck a finger through the layer of bubbles in the tub, expecting to find the water had gone cold. But it hadn't.

She was too tired to talk to herself any more. Another shiver shook her.

Holding onto the side of the claw-foot tub, she stepped in carefully. Tired and fuzzy headed, slipping and hurting herself were real dangers. Slowly, she lowered herself until the bubbles tickled her chin.

"Aaahh!" she whispered as she closed her eyes, for a moment, and feather-floated down into comfort.

Her eyes opened … to the red rose in the bud vase on the dressing table. Bill was trying. He'd made sure she had bubble bath.

And it was a luxurious, large bathroom. Besides the mirrored dressing table with a cushioned seat against one wall, a double sink above cabinets with drawers occupied the other wall. One of the sinks even had a sprayer attachment on a hose for washing her hair. The toilet. And a bidet. Carved panels decorated the ceiling, as they did in the foyer. The pattern in the wallpaper above the wainscoting, Bill told her, was the coat of arms of the Belgian royal family. The bathroom was fancy, luxurious even.

Their bedroom, on the other hand, was plain. Walls and ceilings plain and painted white. At another time, she probably would have cracked, "If any room needed interesting things on the ceiling, it's our bedroom." But that was then, and not when there was healing to accomplish, and that by baby steps.

If she didn't like anything else in her monstrous house, she was going to love the bathroom. The tub was deep. The toasty radiator was next to it.

Aaahhh!

A fist pounded on the door. Kate splashed water onto the floor. The fist stopped as suddenly as it started. Her heart pounded harder and like it would go on until it exploded.

"Kate. You awake?"

She put her hand over her chest. Awareness dawned. She saw the puddle she'd made on the white tile floor. It had missed the bathmat. Her startle response, Bill liked to tease, was like a kernel of popcorn.

"Kate?"

The doorknob turned.

"I'm awake. I'm awake."

The water was still warm. She thought about staying in longer but feared she'd fall asleep again.

"I'm getting out of the tub."

The doorknob unturned itself.

"I'll have lunch on by the time you get dressed."

Bill was trying. It should have helped. Instead, she found it annoying. A little. Sitting in the tub of warm water, she wondered, *Maybe I don't want things to get better with Bill.* But no. She'd been over it. And over it. And she always came to the same answer.

"Phooey!" she muttered.

Then she stood up, and allowed the cold to have its way with her.

Their dining room table, without the leaves, accommodated six. The room itself, however, had room for one three times as long. From the doorway, Kate headed for her place, the seat nearest the kitchen.

"No, no. Today I'm the serving wench," Bill said. "And you, Kate O'Reilly Marshall, sit at the other end. Today you are the master of the 'ouse."

Kate had descended to the lower level restored. After the warm bath, and clean hair and clean clothes, she was ready, she thought, to begin the process of getting her head around her castle-house, around Belgium and kilometers and people who ate horses. She was not, however, ready for giddy exuberance.

Master of the House!

After Bill had arrived in Belgium, he called Kate, and the children, every two weeks. During the calls, she forced herself to be civil, even though she seethed with anger and hurt. The calls were expensive, and venting in front of the children would never do.

A month ago, General Sampson had taken Bill along on a visit to a NATO headquarters in the United Kingdom. There they also stopped in London and took in *Les Mis*. Bill fell in love with the character Thenardier. He even sang "Master of the House," for Kate and the children during a phone call and promised they would all see the musical together. As Bill had enthused about the play, Kate's anger began to boil. He had betrayed and abandoned her in California, and he was in Europe having the time of his life! But then he sang the song and he so obviously got into the character, she couldn't help herself. She'd laughed.

That was then. Now she was trying to control the rate at which strange things came at her. It overwhelmed her, or tried to. If she allowed herself to be swept up, the flood would rip essential bits out of her soul. So far, she'd been able to hang onto the essential bits.

Bill seated her.

"Umm. Your hair smells … Well, it does smell good. And it feels good that we are all together again."

Bill took his—her— place, said grace and attached a few extra thank You-Gods, and began to ladle from the tureen into bowls.

"Mom," JR said. "Our castle is so cool. Wait until you see it."

Bill smiled, obviously pleased that the boy liked the house so much.

"Even Heather likes it," JR gushed.

Kate raised an eyebrow.

"She liked the attic. I like the cave, which the Belgians call the basement, right Dad?"

Heather shrugged as she passed a bowl to Sally next to her. "When the chateau was built, lots of the rooms had fireplaces, and the brick chimneys ran through the rooms without fireplaces to heat them too. Up in the attic, all the chimneys come together so there are only two smokestacks going out through the roof. One on each end of the house. How they did things, in the old days, it's interesting."

"I think Heather got civil engineer genes from someone," Bill, proud owner of a BSCE, said.

"But the cave is the coolest," JR said. "The Belgians call a cellar a cave."

Heather stood to bring Kate her soup.

"The cave has a real dungeon, with cells and everything."

"Yes," Bill said. "They did indeed build two cells into the basement, or cave."

"And the cells have leg irons and everything!"

Kate frowned. A dungeon with leg irons. That was the stuff of children's nightmares.

"And we're going to have the coolest Halloween party down there."

"What?" Kate glared at Bill. "A Halloween party! We're not even unpacked."

"Now, Kate." Bill held his hands up, stop-sign like. "We have a couple of months. The kids and I will do the work. They can invite their classmates."

"They haven't started school yet," Kate said. She felt her heart throb in her head.

"But we will soon," JR said.

Heather took a spoonful of soup, and said, "Sally and JR and me, we'll make up the invitations. We won't take them the first day."

"We'll take the invitations the second day of school," JR said.

"It's all planned out, Kate," Bill said. "There's four guys I work with, all colonels, two US and one German Air Force and one from the Norwegian Army. All four of them have kids in school on base. The guys will help me with decorations. Their wives will bake cookies. Katie girl, you won't have to lift a finger."

"Right!"

"Mom." JR was worried. "This will be the coolest Halloween ever."

Bill told the children to eat before the soup got cold. Then he cast a sheepish glance at Kate before, he too dug into his lunch.

Sally. Kate had forgotten her middle child. Sally stared at her bowl and absently stirred her spoon around in the soup.

"Eat," Heather told Sally.

Sally took a spoonful.

Heather turned to her brother across the table from her. "Stop slurping. Slow down."

There were moments when eleven-year-old Heather acted so mature, so sure of herself. And the younger children listened to her and accepted her authority. Of course, there were the other times when her oldest and youngest nipped at each other like rowdy puppies. Heather wore her dirty-blonde hair short as a boy's. She refused to let it grow long enough to hide the O'Reilly deformation at the top of her ear.

"Sally," Heather said. "Tell Mom what you like about our house."

Sally looked up. A tiny smile played with the corners of her lips. "I get to have my own room."

Kate had no trouble interpreting Heather's expression. It said, "Everybody's happy here but you, Mom."

"I'm finished," JR said. "I'm going back down to the dungeon."

"You can't go down there alone," Bill said.

"Hurry up, Heather."

"No," Kate said, louder than she'd intended. "Your father or I have to be with you."

Heather rolled her eyes.

"Kids," Bill said. "Finish eating, then clear the table and load the dishwasher. I'm going to show your mother the house."

There were two doorways out of the dining room. The one behind where Bill sat opened to the kitchen.

Bill led her through the other door into a large room with their living room and family room furniture arranged into a conversation group and a TV viewing group.

"I could have set this up in separate rooms, but we don't have enough furniture to fill them. I think we should call it the front room. The window looks out onto the drive, past the stables and through the gate to the road. Front room okay with you?"

"How high are these ceilings?"

"Four meters."

"In feet."

"Um, thirteen I think."

"Thirteen? That would be bad luck."

"No. It's four meters, not thirteen feet."

Bill left the front room through a doorway into the expansive foyer. He had pushed Christmas at her when she walked into it the first time. At lunch, he forced Halloween down her throat. She tasted that more than his soup. Why couldn't it be just what it was, what it was supposed to be? Early September. And the days, she should be able to cross them off one day at a time. Instead, it was as if Bill was ripping weeks and months off all at once. She couldn't keep up.

"Kate. Kate," Bill called from across the foyer.

He stood beside double doors open to a long corridor.

"This is the west wing. Nothing but bedrooms and bathrooms on this, the ground floor. That's what they call it. The ground floor, not the first floor. To them, first floor is what we'd call the second."

"For the … Can't anything be simple here?"

"Now, Kate, it's not that bad. You'll get used to it."

Anger tried to make her say something hard and nasty at Bill, but she clamped down on it.

Bill opened a door to the first bedroom to the left.

"Almost all the rooms are like this. A bed, dresser, wardrobe. This room, of course, faces the rear. Nothing but forest back there. Stretches for a kilometer. It was where they hunted deer and boar in the eighteen- hundreds. And back there, see that tombstone? That's George the Tall's grave."

A narrow strip of lawn held tall towering trees away from the rear of the chateau. A slab of white marble rose perhaps six inches above the grass. Upright behind the flat slab rose a white marble tombstone. It looked rather plain.

"That marble slab is less than two meters long. Supposedly, when George the Tall died, they cut his legs off at the knees so he'd fit in the coffin they had."

Kate almost said, "What do you expect from people who eat horses."

Almost.

Bill crossed the hallway to the opposite bedroom. Furnished the same, except it faced the front of the house.

"Both these rooms have radiators," Kate said. "They all must. It's going to cost us a fortune to heat this place."

"No. The only thing it costs us is our housing allowance. We don't pay utilities. We are so lucky. Apparently, this is the best deal for housing in NATO. I don't know what the US Army pays the Belgian royal family for this place, but I was told the royals aren't interested in making money on it. They just want someone to live here. They think the chateau is happier with people living in it."

"I do not feel lucky. I do not think this house is happy."

Tears burst out of whatever was containing them.

Bill's arms were around her. There was such comfort, and ease, as her burdens fell off and outside the circle of his arms. She pressed herself further into the embrace. After a moment, she took in a deep breath and exhaled a teacupful of turmoil. It helped. A little. She placed her hand on his chest, and pushed, gently. Bill's arms sprang open, and she stepped back. She gave him a smile. A little one. Her eyes touched his blue ones and bounced off.

"Um, so like I said, bedrooms and bathrooms down here. The last couple of rooms to the rear are small, servants' quarters. And there's a staircase down into the basement. Above us is all bedrooms and baths too."

Bill closed the two bedroom doors and led her back into the foyer.

"We'll keep the west wing closed off," he said as he latched the knob-less half of the double door in place, and then he closed the other part.

"So, Kate, we can walk through the rest if you want. Our wing is pretty much the same thing, except of course the ground floor. It's kitchen, front room, dining room. From the kitchen, by the way, there's a doorway to a corridor with four small servant rooms. That's royal family storage, and they are all locked. There's the attic and the cave, the cellar."

"The attic and the cellar, not today."

"We can unpack our kitchen stuff. I only opened a couple of boxes to get a few things out. I figured you'd want to organize your things."

"I'm thinking about a nap."

"Kate—"

"I know. You told me a hundred times. Let's work on the kitchen."

Bill started to turn away.

Part of her didn't want to. Another part did. She grabbed his arm.

"Bill, I know you're trying."

There was more to say, but she stopped there.

As they unpacked dishes and stacked them in cabinets, they talked as if nothing was wrong. The air of phoniness suffusing their act of normalcy bothered Kate, but it was better than the anger that ate holes in her stomach.

Twelve

Louis Defonce drank beer, as did most Belgian males. *Instead of mother's milk; instead of water,* according to their European neighbors. Prior to that day, the Calvados was for Sunday only. Henrietta and Rene attended Mass to remember God and His Son. Louis, though he didn't care for it, drank a single glass of the apple brandy in memory of his resistance cell comrades.

On Sundays, he dutifully swallowed his glassful. The liquid sluiced like cold fire down his throat, puddled warm in his belly, and a minute later, he would feel the liquor in his head. The liquor seemed to burn away time's fuzziness, to sharpen his memory, and he saw their faces clearly.

Jacques, Eric, and Claude. Jacques, the oldest, but not yet twenty, had been the leader. Louis drove a truck for his uncle between Mons and Louvain. He transported meat and resistance activity reports north and Brussels-brewed beer and weapons, explosives, and target information south. He constantly begged to go along on an ambush, but Jacques would not hear of it. He was too valuable in his current role. *And at sixteen, too young to go along on a mission.* Jacques never said that, but Louis knew he thought it.

"We do our missions at night," Jacques said. "We ride horses forty, fifty kilometers to set up an ambush. Then we ride back to our coal mine before sunrise. The old mineshaft we live in, it's like we are back in Neanderthal times. As it is, you get to sleep in your own bed. Besides, if you go with us, you will have to sleep during the day, and you won't be able to make the runs to Louvain. Worse, your papa and mama will find out you are part of the resistance. That would be dangerous for them and us." Jacques put a hand on Louis's shoulder. "What you do is worth more than what we do."

He knew that for a platitude. He wanted to go on a mission to shoot Germans. The accursed Huns had confiscated the Defonce's neighbor's farm and built an airfield there. The neighbor, Albert Jourdan, had raised goats. The Nazis called their new military airfield Goat Air Base. Albert, his wife, his two oldest sons and a daughter were loaded into boxcars, men and women in separate cars, and taken to Germany to work in factories.

The Devil-spawn Huns also loaded Uncle Guillaume and Aunt Marie onto the same train.

That night, Papa wanted no supper. "Eat!" he'd shouted at Mama. "Who can eat with these Germans destroying everything a man has to live for? Goat Airfield they call it. To remind us they are almighty Germans and we are just goats."

Then he shouted at God. "And where are You? You haven't used Your fire and brimstone since Sodom and Gomorrah! You should burn the despicable race and their detestable nation from the heart of Europe."

Mama had slapped Papa for blaspheming in front of Louis and Henrietta. "Shame on you," she said. "You spew such hatred here, in this house, in this kitchen, at this table, where we knew such love."

"Bah! You are like Lot's wife." Papa's voice had been so loud, Henrietta covered her ears. "Looking back when you should be looking forward."

The door to the mudroom jerked open. Louis thought for a

moment it was Gestapo, come to shoot them for blaspheming the Third Reich. But it was Uncle Marcel.

"Stop this yelling. I could hear you clear out to *Rue* George the Tall. You will get us all killed. Stop it now!"

Uncle Marcel stood in the doorway of the dark mudroom. Louis wondered why he didn't come in to the kitchen.

"If the Defonce family is to survive," Uncle Marcel said. "we have to be smart. We have to keep our wits about us. The Nazis have taken many able-bodied men and women for their factories and work camps. I have registered my sons and Louis as drivers for Defonce Brothers Trucking. Henrietta is registered as a farm worker on the Defonce farm. I have you," Marcel looked at Papa, "registered to provide vegetables and produce for the Gestapo headquarters in *Chateau du Chasse.*"

"I will not feed them," Papa raged. "I will get my shotgun and shoot one of them."

"And they will shoot you and all of us," Mama screamed.

Marcel stepped in to the room. He had a young raven- haired snip of a girl by the arm. She was younger than Henrietta. Her black eyes were big in her alabaster face. She was afraid. Of the shouting. Afraid of something else, Louis thought. But she was the most beautiful girl he had ever seen.

"You must stop the shouting. Now!" Marcel growled.

"A Jewess?" from a stunned Papa.

Mama went to the child, knelt, and embraced her. The girl wrapped her arms around Mama's neck. Mama asked her her name.

"Isabella."

"And how old are you?"

"Nine."

Louis's eyes drank her in, all of her.

"You say my yelling will get us killed," Papa said, with a normal speaking voice. He shook his head. "And you bring a Jewess here?"

Louis, sitting at his kitchen table, felt the memory dissolve and awareness of where he was and when it was form. He raised the glass to his lips. *Bah*! Empty. He scowled. The bottle too was empty. It had been more than half full.

He thought he should get up and go to bed, but then he remembered what the Americans had done.

The day before The Pig killed Mama and Papa, Uncle Marcel and his sons had been pressed into service with their trucks to help the Germans escape from Normandy. American planes had blown the trucks up and killed uncle Marcel and Louis' cousins. The Americans had killed as many of his family as the Germans had.

A wave of dizziness swept through him.

Out of the fog filling his head, an image of Isabella formed clear and sharp. It took his breath away, just as it had in 1943 when he saw her for the first time. It stirred him, just as it had in '43, and every time since, when she appeared to him.

The subtle taste of apple from the brandy on his tongue soured, became vinegary. Louis rushed out into the backyard and vomited.

Sally Marshall lay in her bed staring up into darkness. Something scary was out there in the house. Or it might even be inside her room, too. She rubbed the pouch with the turquoise bead. It seemed to push the scary thing back, so there was some space between It and her.

Her bedroom door opened and a huge dark figure stood there, looking at her. She gasped.

"I'm sorry, Punkin." *Father.* "I didn't mean to frighten you. Maybe we should turn on the night light. Should I do that?"

Now she could see that it was her father. With her other eyes. It was as if she'd been so frightened she hadn't been able to hear what her eyes—her other eyes—were trying to tell her.

"Yes, Daddy, please."

There was a click. The lamp turned the ceiling gray and made the bed seem like a boat floating on a pond of light.

"Better?"

It wasn't better, but she knew what her father wanted to hear. "Yes, Daddy. Thank you."

"Think you'll be able to sleep now?"

"Yes, Daddy." He wanted to hear that, too.

Her father kissed her on the forehead. "I love you, Punkin."

"I love you, too, Daddy." He did not know how very much she loved him, and how happy she was to see things begin to grow lighter and warmer again with Mother.

He closed the door softly.

The light did nothing. The scary thing she sensed in the house, if it came for her, she would not see it with her regular eyes. She would only see it with the other ones.

Mother prayed with Nana's rosary. Sally fingered her turquoise bead. That wasn't praying. Exactly. But it wasn't not praying, either.

Bill closed the door to Sally's room. She'd always slept with Heather. Heather wanted it dark in her bedroom. Bill had thought Sally would want it that way, too. JR could sleep with the sun shining on his face.

He entered the master bedroom. He'd installed a nightlight there, too. If he or Kate had to get up in the night, neither of them would want to be fumbling in darkness in an unfamiliar place.

As he undressed, he studied Kate's face, framed by her dark hair splayed over her pillow. Her lips were pursed, slightly, as her slow even breaths passed out through them and back in again. Those lips. The kisses they'd given him. Maybe he'd taste one soon.

That morning, when he'd been showing her the house, and everything she'd been through since her mother died overwhelmed her, she'd come to him, wanted him to hold her, his spirit soared. They were husband and wife, and they faced the vicissitudes of life as one. And a split second, after that thought, he became a Neanderthal. He wanted to club her and drag her to their bedroom and take her.

Bill shook his head. The need for her was an ache, a visceral hole in his soul.

Their bed. It was where love and lust intersected. One a sacrament. The other a deadly sin.

Sometimes, God, thinking about the mysteries You've planted in our lives, I worry I'm going to give myself a mental hernia. But, thank you for bringing us together again, husband and wife, father and mother. Amen.

Bill slipped under the covers and turned onto his side facing his wife. He expelled a big breath and the lingering burdens from the concerns of the day. The day had sucked a lot of energy out of him. Sleep would grab him and pull him out of the world. That's what he expected to happen. He closed his eyes.

His hand moved over and rested on Kate's thigh. After months apart, he wanted physical reassurance that she was really there beside him.

She was there all right, and so was his need for her filling and spilling out of his head and flooding down and settling in his loins.

Bill sighed, removed his hand, and rolled onto his back.

How is it, God, that she is right next to me, but just as unattainable as when there was an ocean between us? And why is it, when a man most needs sleep, sleep is the hardest thing to come by?

Kate's eyes popped open.

The high ceiling reflected a weak gray glow from Bill's nightlight. It reminded her of rare low ceilings over San Diego. Bill—armed with the smattering of meteorology training pilots received—described the phenomenon. "An onshore breeze pushes low hanging cloud in to form a ceiling over the city with light-absorbing, moisture- saturated air." When Bill said things like that, she never knew whether to believe him. Was he speaking truth or was he doing what he'd done in Speech class back in college? Supporting, with great conviction, a position he didn't believe in.

Snake oil salesman. That's what her classmates had called him. She'd fallen in love with the salesman. She propped herself up on an elbow to look at him. It was nice, she thought, to be in love with him again. Not that she'd stopped loving him. Not really.

Kate lay back. She was wide awake. Alert. Her mind was clear. She'd forgotten what it was like to feel refreshed, restored by sleep. Every morning since the betrayal, she woke to find her mind filled with a buzzing, fuzzy roil of anger, resentment, and hurt. And every night since the betrayal, sleep would not claim her because those same ugly thoughts boiled ceaselessly in her head. Sleep would not have her. Only exhaustion eventually agreed to take her body for a moment's surcease. Always she woke wondering if it would have been better to have stayed up all night.

It felt … delicious to lie there, feeling as she did. Free of stomach churning anger. Free of the necessity to get on her knees and pray for divine aid in lifting the weight of enough sin off her soul so she could make it to the bathroom to put her face on, the face with the makeup that hid the raccoon eyes, that would not betray to the children what ugliness fouled their mother's soul.

She stretched, luxuriating, and turned to the clock. Red numbers proclaimed two a.m. 0200.

"Don't take a nap," Bill had told her and told her. At midafternoon, she hadn't been able to stand it anymore. She'd slept for an hour and a half. When Bill woke her, she felt as bad as she had during the ride south from the Brussels airport. Groggy, stomach churning out vinegary tastes to pump up to her mouth and sit on her tongue. The late afternoon and evening had been an endurance contest. Dinner hadn't interested her. She'd picked at it, then left the cleanup to her husband and the children, and she returned to bed and, instantly, to sleep.

It was good to have him there. In the bed beside her.

When he'd been away on deployments, Kate always slept with one eye open. At least that's how she thought of it. She was responsible for the safety of the children, and the burden doubled when Bill was not there to carry his share. When he returned from an extended absence, she felt many things, but always, one of them was, *Now I feel safe.* She'd didn't know how it had happened, that she'd relinquished concern for her safety to Bill. But it surely had. After the children perhaps. Safety meant something entirely different once babies had to be considered.

It was so good to have him there. Even asleep. With him in his place in their bed, it felt safe. Last night she hadn't wanted to deal with all parts of what being together again meant, but she definitely wanted the feeling safe part.

Her rosary was on the nightstand. She reached for it and said the prayers that went with the beads down to the beginning of the loop. She thought she might need to come up with her own list of five mysteries, in addition to the set of church-sanctioned mysteries which ranged from Glorious to Sorrowful. Her new mysteries would be "Thank You, God" mysteries.

Thank You, God, for bringing us back together.

Last night, after dinner, Bill had come up with her. After she climbed into bed, he said, "We always tried to never let there be anger between us before we went to bed. There has been anger between us for two months now. It's all my fault.

"Despite what I did, I love you more than my life. I always have. Ever since college. I always will. And how does that fit with what I did? I don't have an answer for that. I don't know how to explain it. What I did to you was pure and simple a sin. A sin against you and God."

He kissed her firmly, briefly, then he pulled back, and, she thought, he had just opened his soul to her. She saw so much on his face, in his eyes, she couldn't begin to take it all in. There was shame, vulnerability, love … so many things.

After a moment, he told her to sleep loose. Sleeping tight meant tension and an uneasy night in bed. Loose sleep was relaxed, peaceful. Restful. "Sleep loose," he'd said and went back downstairs.

She had slept loose and felt … more than restored. Glorious. Resurrected.

Bill slept on his side, his back to her. *Phoo. Phoo.* Obviously, he was sleeping loose.

Return to sleep, she knew, was out of the question, and she slid out from under the covers and found her bunny slippers. A birthday gift from JR.

There were ten bedrooms on the top floor of the east wing and four bathrooms. The family occupied four of the bedrooms. There was a master bedroom with two baths adjoining it on the ground floor, but Bill had thought Kate would want to be where the children were. He did get some things right.

She checked on the girls and smiled. Sally slept next to Heather. The nine-year old had wanted her own bedroom, but apparently, she wanted the comfort of her older sister more. William junior, JR, how could the boy sleep like that? He had his knees under him. He slept in Child's Pose. Slept soundly, as did all three children. And they'd slept on the plane. And in the car. Watching her son sleep so deep in peace, his little bottom pointed up to heaven, an urgent need to scoop him into her arms and then gather the girls too surged up through her chest and lumped in her throat. She blinked as moisture puddled in her eyes.

Great God in heaven, thank You for the gift of my ... our children.

Closing the door to JR's room, she turned. The nape of her neck tingled.

Down the hallway, past their bedroom on one side and Heather's and Sally's rooms on the other, across the open space of the foyer, which was illuminated by dim ground-floor lighting, she saw a rectangle of blackness. The doorway to the long dark corridor of the west wing stood open.

They had closed those double doors that afternoon.

The back of her neck felt as if bugs were pushing through her hair. Something was there, in that west corridor. Something fearful. Eyes, invisible ones, eyes she could feel slithering over her flesh. She shivered, though it was warm. The lights in the sconces on either side of the hall behind her exposed her, made her want to hide.

Go back to bed. It' ll be safe by Bill.

Another voice in her head told her it was just a big old empty—*except for us*—building.

She wanted to listen to the rational voice, but the sense of evil threatening her pushed her close to panic.

Close the west wing doors, the irrational voice suggested.

She hurried across the walkway above the entryway, and with every step her breathing rate increased. She pulled the floor-to-ceiling door to the left closed and bent to push down the latch at the bottom, but stood bolt upright. She was sure the invisible beast was coming for her. Without worrying about the bottom latch, she pulled the right-side door shut.

Safe, she thought. *Silly,* she thought. *Get a grip, Katie girl,* she thought. Deep breath. Let it out. *There,* she thought. *Not a thing to worry about.*

What just happened? She'd given in to an irrational fear, as if she were a child. Her heart rate was still coasting down, but her mind belonged to her again.

My mind belongs to me again! What did that mean? She didn't know, but it promised unpleasantness if she followed the line of thought.

"Get a grip, Katie girl," she muttered to herself. The way her father said it when she really was a child, and, according to her father, prone to furious outbursts when she didn't get her way. But then, again according to Da, "A bloody miracle it was. She took First Communion and the devil let go a her."

And her mother would respond, "If only the *divil* would let go a you, Sean O'Reilly." And she'd hold up one of his full ashtrays. "This is what hell smells like, and I'd like a miracle to get the smell of it out of my house."

Ma didn't categorize lung cancer as a miracle. Neither did what she said zing Ma's conscience with guilt. "Smoked his fool self to death is what he did," is how she put it. But after saying it, Ma always turned away so no one could see her tears.

"Get a grip, Katie girl," she murmured.

She stood for a moment with her back to the closed doors and considered going back to bed, but, no, she was wide awake. There were boxes of kitchen items to unpack.

As she descended the *grand* staircase to the lower level of the *grand* entryway, she marveled at the place Bill had found for them. She'd been so angry when they'd arrived, but then, she'd been exhausted and saw only the work the place would entail. But now, rested, clear minded, free of anger—and fear—she appreciated the opportunity they had to live in such a place, such a castle JR would insist.

She stepped onto the floor of the foyer. The double doors to the west wing on this level were open. Those had been closed too.

The fear began again on the nape of her neck, and she hurried to the open doors, and closed them, and immediately, the fright evaporated.

Standing in front of the west wing doors, she shivered. It was cooler on the ground floor. On the other side of the hallway was a coat closet. From there she took Bill's flight jacket and put it on. After passing from the foyer to the front room and through the dining room, she flicked on the lights in the kitchen.

The kitchen was, as was everything, huge. Six-burner gas stove with an oven. Double oven besides. Large side- by-side fridge. Separate freezer. Oak cabinets galore. Endless counter space, including a center island. Two dishwashers.

"We can't afford all this," she'd told him last night.

"We can. It cost us our housing allowance. Same as we pay for government housing back in the States. I don't know what the U.S. Army pays the Royal Family for this place, but that's their worry."

"It doesn't seem right, that we don't have to pay for everything."

"Katie girl, things are just different here in Europe. The US Army runs things here."

Kate shook her head. The army running things explained it for Bill.

She pulled open the top of a tall box packed with dishes. She unwrapped plates and stacked them on the island in the center of the room. After unloading the box, she placed her good china in cabinets. As she scooted the empty box aside, she looked out the window. Pitch black out there. *Someone's watching me.* The thought didn't frighten her, not like the open doors to the west wing had driven her near to panic.

She stood at the window, staring at the blackness and wondering if it was an animal, a deer maybe. A friendly deer, like Bambi.

From upstairs, from the west wing, a door *creeeeeked.*

She spun around. The creaking ceased and gave over to palpable silence charged with all powerful menace, to which Kate felt vulnerable, helpless. But she couldn't just stand there in the kitchen. Holding her breath, she tiptoed through the dining room, through the front room, listening intently for a whisper, a claw scrape, back into the foyer to where she could see up to the west end doors on the second level.

The double doors stood agape again. Someone, or something, reopened those doors! She needed to breathe but was afraid it would make noise. Then she had to and inhaled air … and rational thought. She hadn't latched the one double door in place. So the doors swung open. Old house. Hinges need oiling. Nothing to worry about.

With that decided, she climbed the stairs. Despite her self-counselling, the hair on her neck tingled again. She gritted her teeth and forced herself to proceed at a normal pace. She forced herself to resist panic as she bent down to latch the un-knobbed door and to close the other one.

Annoyed with herself for acting like a frightened girl, she returned to the kitchen. She had dishes to unpack. As she slit the tape atop a dish-pack, she heard a mournful moan from just behind the door to the basement. From upstairs, creaking and squeaking as if someone were walking on in-need-of-repair flooring.

Kate Marshall. You are a mature rational woman. It's an old house. It makes spooky noises. Spooky noises are just noises.

As she stacked dishes in cabinets, she repeated the sermon to herself.

Sensing something behind her, she spun around. Her reflection looked back at her from one of the huge windows. A haggard face topped by rat's nest hair, big eyes with raccoon circles, the flannel nightgown, and Bill's flight jacket. The way she looked, ghosts would be afraid of her. Old houses made noises, she told herself again. This one was really old. And she had jet lag. Jet lag of epic proportions, she thought, and laughed at herself. "Epic proportions," a phrase from a Bruce Lee movie Bill loved. *Enter the Dragon*, maybe. Bill used the phrase all the time.

Bill.

It was 0330. Enough unpacking she decided. She went upstairs, brushed her teeth, climbed into bed, pressed up against Bill, and said his name.

He looked up over his shoulder at her.

"Bill," she whispered.

He threw the covers back and hustled to the bathroom. From there, came the sound of water running and his electric razor. She knew what he was doing. He shaved with one hand and brushed his teeth with the other. She also knew he'd be back in bed in less than two minutes.

Thirteen

B EHIND *CHATEAU DU CHASSE*, THE forested remnant of royal hunting grounds stretched away to the south for a kilometer to where the trees were bounded by a road, which then gave way to farmland. Ten meters from the blacktop, screened by dense low brush and tall oaks, a small house trailer rested on concrete blocks. When the sun was up, the light filtering through the leafy canopy cast the color of nicotine stained ancient ivory over the dwelling. Rust dribbled dried-blood streaks down the sides from screws.

It was still hours prior to sunrise. Inside, a small round table with two chairs, a small cupboard for dishes, and two beds filled most of the floor. Atop her bed, Anastasia Kukov's eyes opened. To Darkness. Pitch black darkness. For so many years, darkness hid her, had been her refuge. Darkness still felt like a friend.

Across the narrow gap separating the beds, her brother Ivan breathed in, breathed out.

Thank You, God of All People. The Clan still lives.

As long as she and Ivan breathed, the Clan lived. Infused into Anastasia with her mother's milk was the notion that nothing on earth was as important as the survival of the Clan. For almost fifty years, since that day in 1943, the Clan had consisted only of her brother and herself. Some would say two hardly constituted a clan. That argument of numbers had no power to diminish the force behind *survival of the Clan supersedes all else.*

Such a blessing, to lie in the darkness, waking slowly, the only sound Ivan's inhales, exhales. Her brother slept most soundly at that time of morning. If anyone deserved a peaceful morning, it was him.

Thank You, God of All People, for this morning.

She closed her eyes, and behind the lids saw a glow. It was dawn for the part of her spirit that slept along with her body. Another part of her spirit never slept, never rested, always sniffed for the homicidal hate and anger implanted in men's hearts by the Evil One.

For twenty years, Anastasia and Ivan had lived in their trailer at the edge of the pure and undefiled forest. Through those decades, the mornings had been like the one today. But she never ceased to be thankful for each one. Memories of the First and Second Wars, and the years between, were so vivid with images of how many of those mornings began. The Clan, always ready to flee at a moment's notice, did so, so very often in those years. Then, after 1943, Ivan, not Mama shook her and hissed, "Wake up! Wake up! Hurry! Hurry!" He would grab her hand and drag her as he ran.

All those mornings so very different from the ones now in the blessed forest.

Back at the start of the First War, the Clan numbered twenty-eight and had been in Vilnius for a time. Then, the Byelorussians suspected them of spying for the Russians. The elder led them to Poland. The Poles suspected them of spying for the Byelorussians. And so it went. The Clan found no safety in Latvia or Lithuania. "The Evil One," Papa had growled, "has infected the entire continent of Europe with his hate." The elder moved them constantly. Still hate, suspicion, and at times, capricious whims found them and slew members, including Anastasia's and Ivan's parents near Kiev. But there was no time to mourn the loss of anyone. There was only time for flight. "The Evil One," the elder said, "runs over Europe like a beast too big to cage. But we must hide from it until the war ends. It will be better then."

But war's end brought no surcease. The Evil One's influence was even stronger. Near Prague, the elder was killed. Leadership fell to Ivan. His determination to preserve the Clan drove them ruthlessly, the men, the women, the children, the horses hitched to the wagons. Some died from the inhuman demands placed upon their bodies, and their spirits. The Clan became night creatures, foraging and moving in the dark and hiding in the light. Night after night, Ivan pushed them. Week upon week. Month upon month. Year upon year. North and south and east and west, they fled all through Eastern Europe. Ivan was the will, the way, the strength of the Clan. Short, slender Ivan was a giant of determination, but wherever he led them, the evil found them and killed Clansmen.

In early 1943, he led the ten surviving members from Greece to Italy to Sicily. The Clan lost two in southern Italy and three in Sicily. They arrived in Barcelona and lost three more. Sometimes the executioners were German. Sometimes they were people who were fighting the Germans. Sometimes the people just said, "Gypsies!" and shot them.

Ivan got the two of them to the Pyrenees where they lived like mountain goats. Even after the war, they could not find a place to settle without feeling threatened. Until Ivan discovered the blessed forest.

Anastasia sighed atop her bed. All those horrible, fear-filled awakenings. But now, *thank You, God of All People*, twenty blessed years of peaceful dawns.

Get up sleepy head. That's what Mama always said.

Ivan chided her, "Bah. You live more in the past than the present."

Ivan was right. The past formed her. In the past, beyond the First War, twenty-eight men, women, and children comprised the Clan. Back beyond the First War, Innocence stood out prominently while Evil cowered in the shadows.

Anastasia! When Mama said her name, that meant every drop of parental patience had been poured out.

She threw back the covers, stood on the cold floor, and pulled her sleep dress off.

As a child, her feet had known cold floors. "Fetch wood. Start the fire. Fetch water." When Mama said those things in her memory, Anastasia smiled. She wondered, though, if she had grumbled, as she knew other children of the Clan had grumbled.

Anastasia shivered violently. Outside, she knew, there'd be frost because Frost reached a big hand inside the trailer and laid his feather touch, so subtle at first, on her bare back and arms, but then so stunning as her skin awakened to the thief stealing warmth. And it wasn't just trying to sap the warmth from her flesh, the chill aimed at sucking the life from her. She pulled the shirt over her head and stuffed arms into sleeves and legs into tights.

There, she thought, as if addressing Frost. She imagined the frigid entity replying, "Until tomorrow then," and departing.

Her spirit, the life force inside her, was a gift from God of All People. A temporary gift. Some day He would take it back. In the morning especially, Anastasia understood her spirit was anxious to return to Him. So many things could kill a body and release the life force. But too, the body developed defenses against outside killers, and learned to hold tightly to the spirit.

Anastasia slipped on and buttoned her plain dress and thanked God again for a peaceful morning. It gave her body time to transit gradually from sleep to wakefulness, and her spirit to resign itself to another day confined to earth.

She reached under the bed for her shoes, which were next to the flat boxes with her clothes. Then she made her way to the door, being careful to not bump Ivan's bed, grabbed her coat from the hook on the wall, opened the door, stepped out, and quickly closed it.

Outside, she stood still and opened her senses, her gift. The eyes of her spirit could see farther outside. She paused facing each direction of the compass as she probed for signs of threat, signs of any Other People filled with the Evil One's homicidal hate.

When she'd been thirteen, just before the First War, Grandmamma had explained, "We are just like the Other People. Except we do not see nations' boundaries as fences. Boundary fences keep some people out, and they keep others in. Worse though, fences would define for us who are our enemies and who are friends. We don't look at anyone as an enemy. But the Other People need their enemies as we need our freedom from their anger and hate. They don't understand us, and so, many fear and hate us. Many would harm us."

But that morning, inside their blessed forest, once again she sensed no danger to the Clan from the Other People.

Carrying her shoes and coat, she walked across the beaten path to the cook shed. The hinges squeaked when she opened the door. She'd asked Ivan to fix the squeak. He told her the squeak made his last hour of sleep sweeter. "It means you make hot water and coffee and breakfast."

Anastasia lit the kerosene lantern and lifted the tiny statuette of a busty pregnant woman from the shelf. "Good morning, Earth Mother," she whispered. After a moment, she replaced the miniature stone sculpture and then poked at the ashes and uncovered live coals. With tinder and twigs and breath, she coaxed the embers to give birth to flames under the black kettle filled with water. After adding logs, she pulled on her coat for the trip to the outhouse. She left the shoes. The lantern and fire had ruined her night vision, and it was still pitch black under the trees. Even with good night vision, she would have needed her bare feet to see the way to her destination.

When she returned to the cook shed, she filled the coffee pot with water and grounds and set it on the stone intended for the pot.

Then she reached up and took the tiny statuette from the shelf. First Woman, Grandmamma called the figurine. The tiny woman was a symbol of the gift of life from God of All People. "The life force," Grandmamma had said, "passed through First Woman to all men and women."

"Who was first man?" Anastasia had asked.

"Child," she'd replied. "The Other People have a story about First Man. Our story is about First Woman. It is from ancient times and concerns the spirit world. Many things about the spirit world are unknowable. Or maybe have been forgotten."

Grandmamma had put her hand on Anastasia's head. "Do not be troubled by what I've told you. There is more you need to know. You need to know about the gift."

"The gift of life?" Anastasia had asked.

"No. Another gift."

It was the time before the First War when the Clan had been in Vilnius. Grandmamma and Anastasia were in their booth to the side of the cobblestoned market plaza among other sellers of cloth. The Kukovs sold embroidered tablecloths, napkins, and blouses. Arrayed around the plaza, other booths displayed foodstuff, leather products, clocks and watches, dolls, and vodka.

"See that man standing in the center of the plaza, Anastasia?" Grandmamma had asked. "Tell me what you see in him."

The man was a policeman. He was taller than Grandpapa and Papa. The front of his uniform coat bulged. The ends of his black moustache were curled into loops.

She described him and said, "He reminds me of ravens that look at you as if they are deciding if you'd be good to eat or not."

Anastasia had been proud of her answer. She'd thought it sounded grown up.

Grandmamma, however, had not been pleased. "Bah, child. Did you not hear me? I asked you to tell me what you saw *in* the man. You described the outside of him. Look again."

With Grandmamma coaching, Anastasia had discerned what was inside. Areas, entities of dark and brightness, warmth and chill.

"The ability to see inside a person, to see anger and hate, love and affection, fear, that ability is a gift from God of All People to some women. The gift has been given to women since ancient times."

"Can't men have the gift, Grandmamma?"

"I have never seen it in a man."

"Can women from the others have the gift?"

"Yes. I have seen the gift in a few. But all of us who have the gift, need a guide to help us understand what our spirit eyes behold. The gift resides inside some, but if it is never developed, the woman never realizes she carries it."

And Grandmamma had explained how a body, a mind, and a spirit comprised a human. The body is controlled by the mind. The mind is controlled by the spirit. A spirit will be good or evil by degree. People, by an act of will, open themselves to be influenced by God of All People or the Evil One.

"People want to let the Evil One inside them?"

Anastasia had been surprised at the look on Grandmamma's face. It wore a tiny smile, but, clearly, she was sad.

Over the next weeks, Anastasia enjoyed feeling the eyes of her spirit develop and to discuss with Mama and Grandmamma what those eyes could observe.

A few weeks later, "Child," Grandmamma had admonished. "Your gift is from God of All People. But it is not for you. Certainly not to amuse you. It is for the Clan. You must use the gift to protect us. When you see evil and hate directed at the Clan, warn the elder. He will then move us away from the danger."

The coffee pot gurgled. Anastasia was annoyed to have to return to the present just then.

She added logs to the fire.

The coffee pot had grown silent, and she pulled it back from the flames.

Ivan expected hot water, coffee, and breakfast. Well, he would get the first two, but she had another thing to do. She wanted to study the people who had moved into the chateau at the other edge of the forest.

Fourteen

Louis Defonce picked up scissors to trim his beard, as he did every morning. Tremors shook his hand. He grabbed his right with his left to steady it. Then he looked up and encountered the red-eyed demon glowering at him. *Who the hell are you, and what the hell are you doing in my mirror?*

Then he remembered the Calvados. He remembered the puking. Then he knew why he felt ill in every cell of his body when he got out of bed and staggered to the bathroom. Both his hands shook. He put the scissors away.

His eyes returned to his visage, and he rubbed a finger from the tip of his jawbone to under his left ear, tracing the welt of the knife scar under his short beard. It reminded him how close he'd come to dying in 1944. If the blade had sliced two centimeters lower, it would have severed his jugular.

That would have been merciful.

"*Merde!*" Louis muttered, as he stared at his reflection.

Louis couldn't remember if he'd had that thought before. If he had, it had never been this vivid.

His head felt as if barbwire was wrapped around his brain, but in the center of the anguish, the thought was crystal clear. It would have been so clean, so merciful if Louis the Last had died in 1944 in the cellar of the chateau by the Pig's knife. The Pig already shot, already dying, lashed at Louis with his blade and cut him. Made him bleed. Like a hog with his throat cut to make blood sausage. But didn't kill him.

Louis shook his head to clear it of thoughts of death. He hadn't been mad at God for a while.

"By the sweat of your brow shall you eat bread," Louis mumbled.

How could God think that was so bad? What else was a man to do? Run around in the Garden naked all day and every day the same? Who could take satisfaction from that? But a man who sweats, who tills and sows and cultivates and reaps, a man who tends flocks, and earns his daily bread with his aching muscles and the smell of exertion on him, how good his bread and meat taste when he earns it that way. How could He think that was bad?

What God should have held up to Adam was the anguish He would visit on his soul. That would have had First Man quaking in his boots.

Then he remembered the Kukovs were coming to help with butchering the horse.

"And here I am," he mumbled to the ghoul in the mirror, "I can't even trim my beard."

It was 0430. Henrietta did not awake until 0530. He could not wait that long to get some food in his belly. He needed potatoes fried in bacon grease. He would catch hell from his sister when she found a mess in her kitchen, but then, he caught hell from her every day anyway.

He went to the kitchen and fried potatoes.

Anastasia stood inside the edge of the forest in thick brush. She knew she'd be invisible to those inside the chateau. Through the window, a woman served breakfast to a man and three children.

She used her gift. The woman was filled with warmth and brightness, as was the man. But inside the man's warmth was a core of something hard and cold. In a way, the man was like Louis Defonce. When she and Ivan met him, she had seen that core of coldness and hardness in him. Around the core of Louis was warmth and brightness, but it swirled and changed from a thick sheath to thin. As if Louis's spirit could not decide if it wanted to be good or evil.

Louis Defonce, she knew, had fought with the resistance during the Second War. He'd found his parents murdered by Nazis. Ivan said Louis had killed Nazis. According to what Grandmama had told her, when a person killed another, it drilled a hole in the middle of the killer's spirit and filled it with cold and hardness.

Anastasia wondered if this man had ever killed anyone. The cold core of him was encased in a thick and steady sheath of warmth and brightness.

She smiled as she studied the young boy and one of the girls. These were, as were most children, filled with an absence of evil, which the world, as they aged, would contaminate.

They were not like Rene Defonce. An Innocent, carrying with them to their graves the innocence they were born with. The Other People considered Rene, and those like him, afflicted with a disability. But with the gift, one was able to see the blessing of their elemental goodness, which evil was powerless to corrupt. Not all Down's syndrome persons were pure Innocents, as was Rene, but most of them were endowed with more than average warmth and brightness in their spirits.

Then her gaze shifted to the other girl, and Anastasia's mouth dropped open.

This girl was not filled with the temporary innocence of youth, she was not filled with anything.

For a moment, Anastasia wondered if she was seeing in this child what she saw with her gift in drunks.

"When a man drinks too much alcohol," Grandmamma had explained, "it is as if the alcohol deadens the brain and the connection between the body and the spirit is temporarily broken. I do not know what happens to the spirit, but, even with the gift, we cannot see his spirit until his body rids itself of the poison. Then the brain awakes from its coma and finds its spirit again."

This child could not possibly be a drunk. Anastasia employed her gift again. The girl was at some distance and inside a building, which diminished the observational power of her gift. She concentrated on the girl, who was about ten years old, she judged. And then she saw it. This girl was not like a drunk. She was like a new born infant. The girl's body and mind, as far as she could tell, had developed normally, but her spirit had not developed.

If only Grandmamma could be there. Grandmamma would help her understand what she was seeing. She did say once that the spirit world was a place of mystery. Even those of us with the gift can see only a small part of it.

Anastasia closed her mouth. Ivan had been talking about moving. "Twenty years in one place!" he said. "I have grown complacent. I am not sure I would recognize danger if it bit my buttocks." She could not let him move. Not now.

She felt a strong compunction to study this girl, to understand her. God of All People had brought her to this spot in the woods to observe this girl for a reason. Grandmamma had cautioned against jumping to the conclusion that it was God behind every compulsion to do something. Anastasia was always mindful of the things Grandmamma had told her, and as she hid in the brush behind the chateau, she prayed, *God of All People, as it is in my power to discern Your will, I believe it is my duty to try to understand this girl.*

To find this phenomenon next door to the Defonce farm, next to where Rene, an Innocent lived, concerned Anastasia.

She recalled the Innocent Grandmamma had shown her in Vilnius. "An Innocent is very rare," Grandmamma said. "God of All People creates a few of these spirits who are all good and invulnerable to the Evil One. In the darkest of times, when it seems as if the Evil One will prevail, an Innocent will appear as a message that, in the end, God of All People will not abandon those who love Him."

During the First War, the period between, and during and after the Second War, Anastasia had not encountered another until she met Rene. Now this girl with her strange spirit, a mere kilometer from the Defonce farm. No. They could not leave now. There was a purpose behind why God of All People brought her to this spot to see this girl. She could not allow Ivan to take them away before she better understood the girl. And whether the girl threatened the Innocent.

Kate walked to the dining room window and peered out into the darkness.

"What is it?" Bill asked.

"I think someone's out there watching us."

"What? Like a peeping Tom?"

"No," Kate said. "Not like that. That would be scary. This isn't."

"Are you sure?" Bill asked. "I'll go look."

"It's just a feeling. Maybe it's getting used to a strange place."

"Maybe the house is haunted," JR said. "That would be so cool."

Sally *saw* the woman at the edge of the forest with her other eyes. It was … strange. She had never seen so much warmth and softness in a person. After sensing the scary thing in the house last night, *seeing* this woman there, watching them, was comforting.

Her mother walked to the window and blocked Sally's view.

Then her father stood beside Mother.

Immediately, Sally noticed how warm and soft the two of them appeared to her other eyes.

"I don't see anything, Kate," Father said.

"I don't see anything either."

"But you think someone is there?"

Mother nodded.

"So, this is like when you get a sense someone is looking at you, and you turn around to discover that yeah verily, someone is looking at you?"

<center>~~~~~~~~~~~~~~~~~~~~~~~~~~~~~~~~~~</center>

Bill didn't know what to make of what Kate said. If there was a man out there watching them, he was a threat. No two ways to cut that apple.

But Kate had come to him that morning, surprised him with her affection. He would not disbelieve her. Not openly.

"Straight out from the window? Is that where he is?"

"I'm not sure it's a man."

"A woman! What would a woman—"

Bill cut the words off. He shook his head, exasperated at himself. Exasperated at how quickly a man could bridge the gap between a good and charitable intention and aggravation.

"I'm going out to check," Bill said.

JR hopped down from his chair.

"You are not going out there, young man."

"Mom!"

"Sit."

"Come on, JR. We can watch from the window."

Bill saw irritation manifest itself on Kate's face. Heather hadn't asked, just took over and issued an order. That personality trait, in their oldest, not only rubbed Kate the wrong way, it frightened her. Back in San Diego, Kate told him, "Heather is so headstrong. A situation develops, and she just charges in. She doesn't consider the consequences. She scares me. And JR is right behind her. They both scare me."

Bill couldn't remember how he'd responded. Probably with a, "Now, Kate, ..." Truth be told, Bill admired that part of Heather's make up. She was a bright kid. And contrary to how Kate found cause to worry, he thought Heather took in a situation, understood it in a flash, knew what to do, and did it. She, he thought, had the makings of a great fighter pilot. She was the oldest. Oldest siblings made the best fighter pilots. Stats proved it. JR was the only, and oldest boy, and therefore, he would be a great fighter pilot, too.

Bill, it's time to check out the backyard, he told himself.

Yes, dear, himself told him.

He grabbed a flashlight from the counter in the kitchen, exited through the door in the east end of the chateau, and walked to the grave of George the Tall. Playing the light over the brush at the edge of the forest, he stopped, cocked his head, and not sure if he heard something or not, decided it might have been a small animal. Bill turned and flashed a thumbs up to his family in the window. Heather and JR were there and Kate was behind them.

Fifteen

At times, Anastasia considered Henrietta Defonce and Louis to be like she and Ivan, the last of a Clan, physically human, but apart from all the Others spiritually and mentally. Just under the surface of the initial thought, though, was the certainty that Henrietta could have been a member of the Clan, but not Louis.

The Clan believed that evil, when it manifested itself in one or more of the Others, was a thing to flee, that fighting it, and even vanquishing it, left a man or a woman tainted, corrupted, with a residual lust for fighting and killing. Anastasia saw, with her gift, Louis could not and would not accept that philosophy. The disposition toward fighting and killing were strong in him. Ivan did not see it, even though Anastasia had told him a number of times what she saw in him.

"Puh. Louis is a good man," Ivan believed. "He dedicated his life to caring for his sister and her son."

What her brother said about Louis was true, but it was a shallow truth.

Still, Louis was fond of she and Ivan. Once, years ago, not long after they'd met, Louis said, "Ivan, you are a runt of a man, but you do the work of two giants. Anastasia, after Henrietta spends time with you, she becomes almost pleasant."

She was certain that the source of any unpleasantness between the Defonces dwelt in Louis, not his sister.

Anastasia relished the occasions when her friend invited her to help with harvesting vegetables or fruit for canning. Or the butchering.

That day, the two women placed the large, rimmed aluminum trays on the table in the backyard. The trays prevented the blood from soaking into the wood. They laid out knives and a saw. Rene was inside baking tarts. The radio was on. It disturbed him to hear the gunshot that slaughtered an animal, and today it was a horse.

After all the evil Anastasia had witnessed in the earlier decades of her life, it was pure joy and a blessing to be with Rene. He always manifested some sign of his undefiled goodness, like with the gunshot inflicting more pain on him than the animal would feel. It was as if Rene said, "Don't worry, Horsie, it won't hurt. I will take your pain." Every time she was with Rene, she thanked God of All People for allowing her to live long enough to meet another of His Innocents.

Henrietta befriending her also constituted an extraordinary blessing. Anastasia knew their relationship was mutually beneficial. It had taken ten years for their friendship to develop before Henrietta told her about how Rene had been conceived.

Today, as they worked, Henrietta rambled on about how the children of her friends at church were drawn to Rene and he to them. The ramble was of low substantive, but high in comforting emotional, content and Anastasia's thoughts meandered to that day Henrietta confessed the rape.

As Henrietta unfolded the story, Anastasia saw pain sculpted on her face and an anguished spirit staring out through dark eyes. Henrietta had tried to tell herself that the German rapist was the sinner, that she had done nothing wrong. The day *it* happened, Louis's resistance friend had taken her to live with a family near Louvain. They told her the same thing.

"But I feel such shame," Henrietta told Anastasia. "I have never talked about it to anyone."

Anastasia, too, had felt a compunction to offer the same condolence, but she kept quiet, lest she disturb Henrietta's story.

During the summer of 1944, the Defonce family hid a nine-year-old Jewish girl, Isabella, in their cellar. Isabella was permitted into the fenced backyard from 1200 to 1230 to eat lunch. The Germans in the chateau religiously ate at noon. That day in late August, Henrietta sat across the table from Isabella. Isabella closed her eyes and raised her face to the sun. Henrietta smiled to see the nine-year old derive such pleasure from such a simple thing as a half hour outside in daylight.

Suddenly, from the side of the Defonce farmhouse, Henrietta heard the motor of a truck roar, a shotgun boom, and a crash. The side and rear walls of the house collapsed amid a cloud of dust. Stones and lumber fell to the ground a meter from their table. Henrietta jumped to her feet. Isabella ran to her and grasped her around the waist. It was very quiet for a moment. Then a gruff voice spoke. German. The shoulders and head of a soldier appeared over the top of the fence. His face was pig- like. The man was huge and frightening. He stared at Henrietta. Isabella clasped her more tightly.

Pig-face ripped open the gate, licked his lips, and charged in to the yard. Henrietta wanted to f lee but she was frozen to the spot. All she could do was to hug Isabella more tightly.

The huge soldier grabbed Henrietta and Isabella by an arm, pulled them apart, and took them to a truck. The truck conveyed them to the chateau. There, Pig-face dragged the sobbing girls to the basement. He bound Isabella's hands and feet, then he turned his attention to Henrietta. He ripped her clothes and fell on her more like a wolf than the animal he looked like.

The day Henrietta told her story, they were sitting across from each other in the Defonce kitchen. Anastasia felt the acute pain of the violation her friend had experienced. She started to rise from her chair, to go to her friend with the tears streaming down her cheeks, seeking to be comforted as much as to comfort, but Henrietta raised a hand.

"After ... after—" Henrietta's breath of audible short bites of air huffed in and out. "After he finished with me, he left me lying on the dirt floor. And he clumped up the stairs.

"He'd hurt me. I was bleeding. I knew I should untie Isabella and flee. I knew, but I just lay there and cried. Until I heard the boots on the stairs, coming back down. Then I just jumped up and ran down the center passageway, away from the sound of the soldiers. I found another set of stairs and ran up and out the door and hid in the woods behind the chateau.

"I didn't even look at Isabella. I just ran and left her to Pig-face. To do to her what he'd done to me. She was just a little girl. And I left her."

Whenever she recalled that day of revelation, Anastasia remembered how the thought struck her that thirteen-year-old Henrietta had been brutalized but was more traumatized by her own sin of abandoning the nine- year old. She was a good woman and a most appropriate mother for an Innocent.

Henrietta had stopped speaking. The two women's eyes met.

Anastasia could see Henrietta knew what she was thinking.

Louis' rifle popped.

Anastasia followed Henrietta's eyes to the kitchen window. Rene stood there, looking out, but not at anything of the world.

Then she remembered the girl in the chateau. Anastasia did not understand what she saw in her. Not understanding was of concern, especially so close to Rene. Evil, Grandmamma had told her, feared and felt threatened by Innocents and sought to find and exterminate them. It had been a very long time, since the end of the Second War, since she'd seen Evil, as pure in its form as Rene was in his. As she recalled Henrietta's story, or confession, Anastasia knew she would have recognized the pig-faced man as pure evil. Chateau-girl was certainly not evil, but could she become so? The spirit world was full of mysteries. Like how could such a reprehensible act, the rape of Henrietta by a pure evil man lead to the creation of Rene, a pure Innocent? There was no answer to the latter question. The former one, however, Anastasia determined to watch to see if there was an answer to it.

Louis and her brother Ivan worked quickly and efficiently. It seemed like not nearly enough time since the rifle shot before the men had the entrails buried and one quarter of the horse delivered to the table in the backyard.

Anastasia and Henrietta began carving and wrapping roasts. Rene came out of the kitchen and handed the men a bag with sandwiches, a jug of water, and a coffee thermos. The men departed in the truck to deliver the rest of the meat to butcher shops in Toussaint and Louvain and the hide to a tannery in Mons.

The women finished with the meat. Rene stowed it in the freezer, segregating the packages marked with a "K" for Kukov on one end. Anastasia cleaned the butchering table as Henrietta and Rene laid out lunch in the kitchen.

After they ate, Henrietta announced that they would take one of the apricot tarts Rene had baked to the Americans living in the chateau.

As Henrietta drove on Rue George the Tall, Anastasia could feel the anxiety mount in her friend.

"This is the first time you have come to the chateau since 1944, yes?" Anastasia asked.

"Yes. It is one thing to look at the chateau across a kilometer of fields. It is quite another to come right up to it." She sighed. "It is so much like what is in my memory. What happened to me … and Isabella, is there but far away." She slowed and turned onto the lane leading to her neighbor's house. "Now I am getting close to what happened, just as we are getting close to—" She nodded at the mansion.

Henrietta parked the car. "Rene, you carry the tart."

Anastasia remained in the passenger seat in front.

Henrietta pressed the doorbell button.

Anastasia wondered if she'd get to see Chateau-girl. Through the open car window, she heard the sound of running feet clomping on wooden flooring. The door ripped open. The older girl and the boy jostled to see which would go through the door first. The woman appeared behind the two.

"*Bon jour, Madame.* I am called Henrietta Defonce. Sorry. English not good. I am neighbor." Henrietta pointed to the east, across a field. "In auto is *amie,* friend, Anastasia Kukov. And here is son. Rene bake for you a *tarte. Abricot.* To say *Bien venue.*"

The woman's face bloomed a smile, like a lamp being turned on.

"How very nice of you," the woman said. "I am Kate Marshall. And this is Heather and William junior."

"We call him JR," Heather said.

"Hush," Kate said to her daughter. Then the lamp- like smile re-illuminated. "Come in please. I will make coffee."

"No, no," Henrietta replied. "Cannot." She turned to Rene, and, in French, told him to give the tart to the woman and say welcome.

"*Bien venue, Madame.*"

The woman, Kate Marshall, took the tart and thanked Rene.

"*Abricot,*" Heather said. "That must mean apricot."

Then the other girl appeared beside her mother.

"My other daughter, Sally," the American woman said.

Anastasia could see only the side of Henrietta's face, but she sensed a sudden burst of fear in her friend. Henrietta took a small step backward drawing near to the edge of the small porch, three steps above the ground. Anastasia opened the door, and was about to go to Henrietta to keep her from falling, when the scene playing out in front of the chateau stopped her.

Henrietta stared at the youngest girl and raised her hand to her mouth. Anastasia watched a radiant smile bloom across Rene's face. Then he knelt, and the girl came to him. Rene embraced the girl, then they separated and smiled at each other, like the very best of friends, separated a very long time, and now, suddenly, reunited.

Anastasia sat, transfixed. Such a pure communion of spiritual interchange flowed between Rene and the girl. *God of All People, are You here?*

The moment passed. Anastasia felt as if she had to find her way back to earth.

"Je'm appell Rene."

The girl extended her hand to still kneeling Rene. "I'm Sally."

One spoke French, one English, but they understood each other. Perfectly, Anastasia was sure.

Awareness of the others returned. Heather and JR poked at each other, silently and oblivious to the adults and to Sally and Rene. Kate Marshall, Anastasia saw, understood something extraordinary was transpiring. She turned from Rene and her daughter to Henrietta.

"Are you all right, Mrs. Defonce?" Madame Marshall asked.

Henrietta shook her head side to side as if saying, no, but said, "Yes. Yes. Okay. I … I see *fantome. Votre fille est Isabella.*"

She frowned at the French.

"Your daughter, Madame," Anastasia said, "looks very much like a person from Henrietta's past, during the Second War. It was a shock, like seeing a ghost. You understand?"

"Oh. Yes. I understand." She turned to Henrietta. "Please, won't you come in and have coffee?"

"No, no. We go now." Henrietta walked down the steps and around the car. "Rene, come."

Rene entered the rear of the car and rolled down the window. *"A bientot, Sally,"* Rene said to the girl.

"See you soon, Rene," she replied.

The American woman, Anastasia saw was confused. The visit and the gift of the tart were warm and welcoming acts. The leave taking, however, was abrupt. Rude. Anastasia wished she could stay and explain what had happened.

As they drove away, Anastasia watched Henrietta concentrate on driving. She'd thought she understood Henrietta's motivation. Taking the tart to the Americans was an excuse so Henrietta could go the chateau and face the demon possessing a corner of her soul, and, hopefully, in facing it, expel it.

The American woman, Madame Marshall, invited them in for coffee. Henrietta refused. Anastasia understood that would have been too much all at once. Her friend had approached the chateau, gone right up to the door and rang the bell. *Perhaps on a second visit, Henrietta would go inside.*

She said she'd seen a ghost, that the Marshall's daughter *was* Isabella, not looked like Isabella, but actually *was* her.

Seeing the girl, Sally, deeply disturbed Henrietta. Instead of beginning to heal the wounds of being raped and her abandonment of the little girl, seeing Madame Marshall's daughter ripped open the scab, and it bled fresh and red anew.

"You won't cry, will you, Momma?" Rene asked from the backseat.

Henrietta shook her head. At the end of the lane, she turned onto Rue George the Tall and accelerated toward her home. "No, Rene. I will not cry."

Anastasia was not going to cry either, although she was upset with herself. She'd been so taken with how Rene and Sally had reacted to each other, after having the opportunity, she'd failed to study the girl at close range with her gift. Rene was obviously very strongly attracted to the beautiful black-haired child. Was that how Evil managed to get close to an Innocent, to destroy him?

God of All People, help me find the way to some of Grandmamma's wisdom.

Sixteen

Louis Defonce felt like an old man. All strength and energy had drained from his muscles. He wanted his dinner. Then he wanted to sleep. Without dinner, he did not think he'd be able to climb the stairs to his bedroom. He drank off half his beer and replaced the mug on the table.

Across the table, Rene, for once, wasn't imitating him. Usually, the boy mimicked his actions, which irritated Louis. But tonight, he didn't. Louis found that irritating. The boy just stared at him.

Henrietta slid filled plates in front of Rene and Louis. Rabbit. It would have upset Rene to eat horse meat on the day one was butchered. *Everything revolves around the boy. The forty-six year-old boy!*

Louis leaned over his plate and started eating.

"You do not wait until I sit and we say the prayer? You stick your snout in your plate like swine at a trough and snuffle up your food!"

It was inevitable. After a day like today, he would have to catch grief from his sister before it could be complete.

"It would have been nice to eat dinner with the Kukovs, but you and your rotten mood drove them away."

Her voice was like a bone saw working on his skull.

"It was the brandy, wasn't it?"

If she knew the pig-faced Gestapo brought the brandy—

"You drank too much."

"Mama, don't fight, please."

"You should listen to the boy."

"You should be like him instead of a bitter old man driving your family and friends away with your nasty manners."

"We went to see the Americans," Rene said.

"What?" Louis glared at Henrietta.

"I wanted to meet the Americans. I do not hate them as you do."

"I have a new friend," Rene said. "Her name is Sally."

Color drained from Henrietta's face.

"What is it?" Louis demanded. "What happened?"

"Sally is Isabella, Mama said."

"Hush now, Rene." Henrietta sat. "The American woman, her name is Kate Marshall. She has three children. Two daughters. The younger … she, she looked just like Isabella. I thought I was seeing a ghost."

Louis pushed his plate away.

"Mama said she is Isabella."

Louis stood and left the kitchen and stepped into the back yard. He had to get away from his sister and the boy. The Calvados. He'd drunk it all last night. He considered going to the chateau escape tunnel to get another bottle.

The air was cool and crisp. Above, stars crowded together in front of the deep black, almost as if the stars were trying to get away from that utter darkness, almost as if the darkness were trying to devour the little dots of light.

Outside the kitchen, it was easier to think.

His only thought, however, was of Isabella.

She disturbed the rhythm of his heart beat. Heat suffused his face. Isabella was, had been, such a still creature, almost like a baby bird fallen out of the nest and huddled in the grass beneath the tree hoping nothing will find her.

Birdlike, too, her raven hair, aglint with a spot of purple fire in the sunlight. But her face was alabaster and smooth like it belonged on the statue of an angel.

Isabella, so utterly delectable.

Anastasia didn't say anything until Ivan turned the *camion*, the panel van, onto Rue George the Tall. "Why did you refuse Henrietta's invitation to dinner?"

"Henrietta wanted us there. Louis did not."

"Louis has had his moods before, but after we sit down and begin to eat, he gets over it."

"This time was different. Always before, when we worked together, we had things to talk about. Not today. In the morning, his hands shook holding the rifle. I offered to shoot the animal. I didn't want it to suffer if he only wounded it. But he would not let me. And all day, the smell of alcohol was in his sweat, and, all day, he was sullen. He wanted us gone, and I did not want to be with him anymore."

In the glow of the instrument panel lights, she saw Ivan gripping the steering wheel with both hands. He glanced at her briefly. "Did you not see Louis' spirit?"

"I was concerned with Henrietta."

Ivan turned to look at the chateau as they drove past. Two windows on the ground floor spilled light as did two in the upper floor.

The chateau dropped behind them.

"Henrietta? Is something wrong with her?" Ivan asked.

"I told you what happened to her in the Second War, and that it happened in the chateau." She related the visit to the American woman and how the sight of the daughter affected Henrietta.

Ivan humphed and turned the van left to skirt the western edge of the royal forest.

"You think us women are all befuddled by our emotions."

Anastasia knew, as did Ivan, that her statement had taken them to the edge of a precipice. They'd had the argument many times before about emotional females and logical males. "If men are so logical, can they not see the futility of war? Who leads one group of the Others to war against another? Men." The decades of the struggle to survive formed and turned Ivan's arguments into cured concrete. Her own experiences set her arguments hard as stone. Only anger and hurt would result from arguing, Anastasia knew, as did Ivan.

The van motor purred. Anastasia stared out the windshield. Riding in a vehicle at night, was for her, a curious mixture. She had a feeling of security, of being invisible and flying above the earth and far from the threat of evil. At the same time, she sensed imminent danger. The headlights illuminated only a few meters, and Evil was out there just beyond what her eyes could see.

Ivan turned the van left again to skirt the southern edge of the royal forest.

"We will leave in the morning," he proclaimed.

"I do not want to leave. Henrietta needs my help."

"Something has happened with Louis. He is a threat to us. We leave."

"I do not want to."

Ivan exhaled air and impatience.

"There is something else. What is it?"

She could not tell him of her concern over the American girl, how attracted Rene was to her. Ivan knew what Grandmamma had said about Innocents attracting evil.

"Yes, there is also Rene. If something is happening with Louis, I must help Rene as well. They are like Clan to me."

"Bah. There is no *like Clan*. A person either is, or is not Clan. You feel a responsibility, because of your gift, to take care of the Innocent. But the safety of the Clan is the preeminent concern. I decide for the Clan. We leave in the morning."

"The safety of the Clan is not the most important thing. The Clan will die when we do. In the old days, our people frequently lived more than one hundred years on earth. Back then, there were young people to care for the old. You and I, Brother, God of All

People will take back the life force He gave us to use for a while. Then, the Clan will die, and soon."

"I cannot think that. I will not think that. In the morning, we depart. And there will be no more talk about it."

No more talk about it. That part of Ivan's dictum she would observe.

Ivan parked the van next to the trailer, and they went inside and prepared for bed. Frosty silence filled their small dwelling.

They climbed onto their beds and pulled up the covers.

"Good night, Sister."

She did not reply. In the blackness, she heard him hiss. That made her smile for a moment. *There will be no more talk about it,* he'd said. He was bound by the order as much as she was. The smile lasted but an instant before the gravity of what she intended doing in the morning assailed her with guilt and worry.

Ivan had worked hard during the day. He slid quickly into sleep, his irritation with her powerless to prevent it. Anastasia listened to him breathe for a time. Then she allowed herself to drop into a state of what she thought of as half-sleep. That night she had to keep her senses alert, just as she had each night of all those years of running from ubiquitous evil. She had to be gone before he awoke. That was more important than the more restorative sleep.

She came fully awake at what she estimated to be two hours before Ivan would awaken. She dressed and left the trailer. In the cook shed, she took Earth Mother statuette, and carrying it in her hand, entered the forest, as at home as the small creatures naturally in residence there.

Louis called, "Uncle. Uncle." His voice, he thought, sounded strange. *Where am I? Why is it so dark?* Fear gripped his stomach. *Am I lost?*

"Uncle, uncle."

Louis saw the shadow figure next to his bed and sat up, his heart pounding.

Rene stepped back.

Louis rested his face against the palms of his hands and took a deep breath; then he huffed it out.

"What are you doing here, Rene?"

"Mama said, 'wake Uncle.'"

Louis checked the bedside clock. *Merde!* 0700, he'd not slept that late since … he'd never slept that late. Papa had gotten him up to help with the morning chores since before he'd started primary school.

Louis was about to throw the covers back when it dawned on him. It was cold and wet. Down there. *Jesus, Mary, and Joseph.* At age sixty-four, he was going through puberty again. He had been dreaming about her.

"Go back to the kitchen."

"Alonzo is here to work on the combine. Mama said—"

"Back to the kitchen. Now."

Rene went back to the kitchen.

Seventeen

KATE SAW HER CHILDREN, AT least Heather and JR, as adaptable. Back in the States, when they moved, the two of them settled into new schools and made friends so easily, it was as if every place in the US was their home and they fit right in with no effort at all. Of course, they hadn't tested that theory in all the states, but they had moved up and down the west coast and twice crossed the country. Now as she and Bill left the children at the school on the base, Kate thought she would have to amend the theory. The world is their home.

"Schools over here are managed by the Department of Defense," Bill said. "They try to make the kids all feel equal. There is no appreciation for the father's rank, or what service he is in, or even what country the child comes from. Some of these kids have fathers who are army and air force generals. Others have enlisted men. It's a good system. I think the kids will benefit from this experience."

Heather and JR embraced the new school eagerly. In fact, the two of them didn't seem to have to make any adjustment at all. But Sally?

When they'd moved to San Diego, Kate asked Heather to watch

after her sister when they enrolled the children for their respective classes.

"Sally would do better if you didn't baby her so much, Mom," Heather had scolded.

"I'll look after her, Mom," JR, a kindergartner at the time, had enthused.

That morning, at the DOD school on the military base in Mons, Belgium, JR had said the same thing. "I'll take care of Sally, Mom."

Kate had wondered a number of times if Heather was right about her babying Sally. Sally did cope … with the assistance of an older sister laden with all the sympathy of a US Marine Corps drill sergeant, and a smaller, younger *big brother*. Still, it pained Kate to turn Sally over to her teacher as her daughter looked up at her with her big eyes, almost as if she were pleading, *Don't leave me, Mama!* It tore a piece off Kate's heart.

"I'll take care of Sally, Mom," from JR stuffed a lump in her throat and moistened her eyes. Bill had put his hand on her elbow. Which helped. He didn't say anything. That helped even more.

After depositing JR in his classroom, Bill took Kate to the gendarme post on base to get her a Belgian driver's license. There were forms to fill out. Gendarmes, Bill had explained, were a combination of policeman, state trooper, sheriff's deputy, and FBI agent. One of them took her picture. Fifteen minutes later, the officer, in his natty blue uniform with red trim, which reminded Kate of the US Marines more than any of the things Bill had used to describe the man's role, handed Kate her license.

Kate frowned. "I want a new picture."

"Let it go, Kate," Bill had hissed.

"This is the ugliest driver's license picture in the world."

"Take the license. Let's get out of here."

He took the license from the gendarme, grabbed Kate's arm, and propelled her out of the office. Outside, they stood beside their BMW.

"I told you," Bill said, "they delight in snapping ugly pictures of Americans. Other nationalities too. It's best to just go along with them. It doesn't matter, really. You use your US ID for most things."

"You told me, but I never expected it to turn out so very ugly."

"Come on, Kate. It's not that bad."

"It's terrible. And why didn't you argue with that, that—"

"It wouldn't do any good. All the guys say it's a mistake to fight with the gendarmerie."

"You always fight bureaucratic stupidity."

"Yes. I have. And I do."

They locked eyes. She, and he, had the same thought: *Look where it got you/me!* Bill had laid the foundation of a promising navy career, progressing through the ranks rapidly. He'd established a reputation as a strategist, a tactician, a leader, and a good fighter pilot. He'd made captain and been detailed into an airwing commander slot, a plum assignment, and springboard to admiral. He had a good relationship with the commanding officer of the aircraft carrier, but he butted heads regularly with his boss, the admiral commanding the battlegroup. Battle group commanders, Bill had told her, as a rule, were invariably top-notch leaders. But as luck would have it, her husband had worked for the one exception that proved the rule.

All during that tour, Kate had listened to Bill grumble about Admiral Ditzhead. "He has no sense of what a powerful weapon an aircraft carrier with eighty planes aboard can be. And has no sense of what limitations a single carrier has. Eighty planes seem like a lot, but not if you have to cover operations twenty-four hours a day, days at a time. Then you have to manage the planes and the crews. I've tried to tell him how it should be done, but the blockhead won't listen."

Kate knew many of Bill's arguments with the man had been in front of his staff. Bill had known he was killing his chances of promotion by arguing the way he did. "But it matters," Bill told her. "There are five thousand men aboard the carrier and all of them deserve at least a mediocre leader."

Bill had fought with his boss, but he wouldn't take on the Belgian gendarmes.

"Kate, if we make a stink, we get on their list as troublemakers. The guys in the office told me that is not a good idea. General Sampson's executive assistant said us guys on his staff have to keep our noses clean with the host country. If we get on their list, they will take it out on you, and I won't be able to help you.

"Come on, Kate. Get in the car, please?"

"Ditzhead gendarme," Kate grumbled as she pulled open the door on the passenger side.

"Why don't you drive?" Bill asked, and handed her the laminated card. "You have a driver's license."

Kate didn't want to smile. She tried to contain it, and a most unladylike snort had her worried about her nose and lip.

Bill offered her his handkerchief with an absolutely straight face. She laughed, then took the hanky, wiped her nose, and gave it back.

With Bill providing direction, she drove to the commissary and exchange compound, and then they returned to the chateau. Bill got his car and followed her, ensuring she had mastered the navigation to where she would do her shopping. He then went to work.

A US military commissary in Belgium, thankfully, was a US military commissary. Familiar arrangements of familiar items on shelves, familiar process at the checkout counters, all that grounded her, propped up her self-confidence. Belgium, she admitted to herself, intimidated her.

With the trunk and rear seat of her car filled with bags of groceries, she negotiated the route back to the chateau without difficulty. She unloaded the perishable items. The groceries in the trunk could wait for the children to carry in after she picked them up from school.

Bill had pointed out a bakery in Toussaint. Croissants for breakfast tomorrow sounded good. Maybe someone in the shop would speak English. Croissants. The word probably meant the same thing in French and English. And she could always point at them through a display case. How hard could it be? She returned to the car and drove to Toussaint.

After Louis discussed the required machinery repairs with Alonzo, he walked across his field to the forest behind the chateau and entered the trees. There he stopped and watched behind him, to ensure no one followed, the way he'd been taught by Papa. Then he tore branches from a holly bush and stepped to the dense scrub brush covering the hatch over the escape tunnel and lifted it. The edge rose silently fifty centimeters. He spread the small piece of tarpaulin on the ground, dropped onto his belly, slipped into the tunnel, and closed the hatch.

The Defonce family, according to Papa, never told George the Tall about the tunnel. Original Louis had figured out how to open the hidden doors built into two rooms in the chateau by studying the unlatching mechanism from inside the tunnel. This knowledge was passed on to male members of the family.

On top of crates stacked against the wall, Louis felt for and found the flashlight and clicked it on. Strong beam, but he always carried spare batteries and a spare flashlight in his pockets. Besides the half-dozen cases of Calvados, other wooden boxes contained American and German rifles, pistols, grenades, and explosives. There were also bags of gold and silver coins.

Atop another stack of crates, he found the long dagger, which had belonged to the Frenchman who'd built the chateau. The dagger served as the trigger to open hidden doors from the chateau into the escape tunnel.

Louis had visited the forest entrance to the tunnel when he needed money or Calvados but had not transited the tunnel to the chateau since the war. After Jacques accepted him into his resistance cell, Louis led him through the tunnel and into the structure to spy on the Gestapo headquartered there.

Beyond the cases, spiders had woven tattered gossamer curtains across the tunnel. He used the holly branches to sweep away the cobwebs. The going was slow, but he'd expected that. The tunnel led into the east end of the chateau in the basement. Once inside, the webs thinned to mere annoyances.

From the entry chamber, Louis could take two paths. Through the hidden door into a servant's room in the basement and on into the chateau or climb steps to the lower spy passageway that ran the length of the building. He climbed.

The French nobleman, according to Papa, obviously thought listening to the private conversations of his guests was necessary to his success at court, and maybe to his survival in his own home. He'd constructed his mansion, and the spy-way, to afford good acoustics into rooms adjoining the passageway. If voices or noises were heard, a small plug could be extracted to peer into the space. Louis began walking carefully down the man-wide corridor. He heard nothing but pulled the eyehole plug from the dining room. He saw no one.

At the west end of the chateau he climbed more stairs to the upper spy passageway. Traversing the length of the building again, and listening for sounds indicating one or more of the Americans were home, he heard nothing. At the east end of the passageway, he pushed open the hidden door built into the brick fireplace. He stood still and listened. Silence. He closed the hidden door. To open it he would have to stand up in the fireplace and insert the dagger into a slot more than two meters above the grate. The same opening mechanism operated in the servant's room in the cellar.

He exited the room into the upper floor hallway and checked bedrooms on both sides. None showed signs of occupancy until he reached the last two on each side before the grand entryway. The first of these was a boy's room. A bookcase held toy trucks, farm machinery, and horses. And a toy pistol.

Americans and their cowboys!

The room opposite and fronting Rue George the Tall was a young girl's room. *Hers?* The quilt on the bed was pink and white. Tacked to the wall above the bed was a large poster of a skinny young man with wild blond hair, wearing black clothing, and holding an electric guitar. The eyes of Poster Man seemed to glow with a demonic energy. The eyes drew and held his attention. Louis could see the passion involved in creating the young peoples' primitive, drug-fueled, bestial imitation of music. *Another gift from* les Ricans. It pained his ears to look at it.

The last room on the other side of the hall before the grand foyer was obviously the master bedroom. Opposite it, another girl's room. Pink and white quilt. No posters. Books in a bookcase and one primitive doll. Disappointment chilled the core of him. New Isabella's. Where the surety came from he didn't know, but he knew. And the room was on the side fronting Rue George the Tall. No spy passageway on that side of the chateau.

Merde! He had wanted to watch the American girl, to see if she was as much like Isabella as Henrietta thought. He could watch her in the dining room. It wouldn't be the same as peeping into her bedroom. Muttering another curse, he closed the door and crossed through the foyer and opened the door into the hallway of the west wing. He wanted to see if the Americans used any of those bedrooms. He had checked five rooms, all of them lacking signs of occupancy, when he heard a vehicle turn onto the driveway. He pulled open the bedroom door the *rue* side. Sheer curtains covered the window.

A car with a woman driving passed between the stables converted into garages. Louis tore out of the room, considered running to the east end to enter the spy corridor there, but he did not want to pass through the foyer with the large windows. He ran to the east end of the chateau, descended the stairs into the cellar, ran the length of the building to the entrance to the escape tunnel.

"Why does even the simplest thing I try to do wind up humiliating me?" Kate muttered at the windshield as she drove out of Toussaint and back to, no. She almost thought *home.* But that monstrous building Bill got for them to live in, this infuriating nation populated with women looking with disdain and amusement at her stupidity, no, there was nothing *home* about any of it.

She had gone into the first "bakery" on the main street of Toussaint and asked for croissants. The proprietress behind a display case and two customers in front of it, looked at her as if she had burped loudly in church just after the priest asked for a moment of silent prayer. The astonishment on the Belgian women's faces morphed into amusement. After much fumbling with language, spoken and pointing at items in the case, she understood she had entered a "pah tiss er ee," *patisserie,* a business that sold cakes and pies only. For croissants she had to go the "boo lan jer ree." At the *boulangerie,* it happened again. More humiliation heaped upon her embarrassed soul. Fortunately, the proprietress of this shop had a teenaged daughter who spoke English. Croissants, it turned out, were sold out by ten each morning.

"So, you see, we have no more the croissants. Perhaps, Madame, you would like a baguette? Yes?"

She bought a baguette, and on the way back to the car, wished she'd had the presence of mind to say, "No, thank you. The only thing I like about French speaking people is croissants." But she never thought of saying those kinds of things until it was too late.

As she was leaving Toussaint, she admitted to herself that it was probably her guardian angel saving her from spouting a rude and cruel attempt to injure. Even having the thought required confessing the sin. *Get a grip, Katie girl,* the voice of her father remonstrated.

A sudden flash from the side of the road startled her. *Oh, foot!* The photo speed trap at the edge of town. Bill had warned about it again that morning.

The driver's license photo, the croissants, the speed trap. And it was only midafternoon. Plenty of time for a lot more things to go wrong.

Ahead of her, a man stood next to the passenger side of a car parked on the shoulder. It was obvious what he was doing. Urinating. Bill had told her to not be surprised to see Belgian men do that. Public restrooms cost a few Belgian francs to use. Belgians drink a lot of beer, he'd said and shrugged.

The people eat horse meat. The men urinate in public, *and I let them humiliate me!*

Kate turned into her driveway and began passing between the garages to either side. Suddenly, she jammed on the brakes. Someone was in the house, looking out a window of an west wing, upper floor bedroom. *Could it have been an odd reflection off the glass?* She wasn't sure. With all the things roiling around inside her head, it was hard to be certain about much of anything.

Get a grip, Katie girl!

She would call Claire. Nine-hour time difference to California. She did the math: 5:30 a.m. back there. Claire woke at 5:30. She wouldn't mind.

Kate drove up to the house and entered the foyer and listened for a moment. She heard nothing. Glancing up, the door to west wing hallway on the upper level gaped open.

She bolted back outside and down the steps. Glancing toward the west end of the chateau, expecting to see someone coming for her, and about to jump into her car and race away, she heard her father talk to her again.

That door to the west wing had swung open before. She'd been upset and wasn't sure a man had been in the window. *I am a mature, competent, logical woman*, but then admitted those things were true in her own country, not in this place.

I am not juvenile and hysterical. I will go in my house.

Once in there, though, she would call Claire.

After two rings, "Yes?"

"Sorry to wake you."

"Kate, what's the matter?" The sheets rustled.

"Oh, Claire, I just needed to hear your voice. Belgium is more foreign than a foreign country."

"I'm sure it seems strange, Kate. Give it a little time. You'll get used to it."

"You know how men are from Mars and Women are from Venus? Well, what's the planet farthest from the sun? That's how far Belgium is from the US."

"The farthest planet? Let's see. As I recall, sometimes it is Pluto and sometimes it's Neptune."

"What? Even that question doesn't have a straightforward answer?"

"Actually, Kate, that is a straightforward answer."

There was a momentary pause.

"Except for one thing."

Kate groaned.

"I recall an argument as to whether Pluto is a planet with a moon, or if Pluto's moon might not be a planet, too."

Kate burst out laughing, close to hysterically. After the laughter coasted down, Kate said, "Smoothly shifting the subject, how are things at the office?"

They spoke for thirty minutes. Then Kate left to retrieve her children from school. The next day, they would ride the bus to and from.

Eighteen

After Ivan awoke, he called for her. A few minutes later, he tromped off through the forest with a f lashlight. Anastasia had no trouble following him without betraying her presence. His skills in the forest had atrophied. Hers had not.

Ivan led her to the rear of the chateau. The ground floor windows were all dark. Dim light showed through two in the upper floor. He studied the building for a moment, then continued on to the east, toward the Defonce farm.

Henrietta was Anastasia's only friend. Ivan would ask Louis and Henrietta if they had seen her. When Ivan crossed Louis' field, Anastasia stayed at the edge of the woods.

Dawn was a glop of gray. Not much light oozed through the clouds. Anastasia could not see Ivan for long. She pictured what he'd do. He'd knock on the door. Henrietta would answer. "Have you seen Anastasia?" Her reply: "No. But, come in. Have breakfast." After refusing, he'd return to their trailer, get in the van, and drive back to the Defonce farm. Ivan would know she'd followed him and expect her to call on Henrietta as soon as he left.

What a blessing it would be to visit her friend at this time, but she couldn't. Ivan expected to catch her there. And, too, she did not want to involve Henrietta in the sin against Ivan and against the Clan.

Anastasia returned to the chateau and watched Madame Marshall serve breakfast to her family. Sometime later, all the Americans left together, and Anastasia spent the day wandering through the woods, her favorite pastime.

Kate called Bill.

"There was a man in the house. I thought maybe it was just a funny trick with light off the window; that I imagined it, but I didn't. There are footprints."

"Slow down. He's in the house now?"

"No, no … actually, I don't know. This afternoon, coming back from shopping, I thought I saw a man in an upper floor window in the west wing. But I wasn't sure. I came inside and didn't hear or see anything. I convinced myself there had been no man. But he *was* in the house. He left footprints."

"Get the kids and drive to Toussaint. Park on the main street. I'll meet you there."

He hung up.

Kate had been worried about the man being in the house that afternoon. She wanted Bill to do something to make sure he couldn't come back.

Bill was worried the man was still in the house! He was right. The intruder could be anywhere in the huge chateau.

Kate stood in her bedroom holding the phone, frozen to the spot for the moment as panic welled up out of her chest.

The children!

Get a grip.

She looked at the phone in her hand, then hung up. Out in the hall, she saw Sally at the east end looking into the open bedroom door. Heather and JR were arguing about whether the house was haunted or not.

Kate started walking toward the east end, then broke into a run.

"Heather, JR, get your jackets. Now"

"What's the matter, Mom?" Heather asked.

"Get. Your. Jacket. Now."

Heather stared, making up her mind as to what to do. Kate was about to rush forward and grab her arm and drag her out of the house, when her daughter decided to do what she'd been told.

Kate herded the children in front of her while they collected jackets. "Just the jacket. No books. Nothing else. Move."

Bill disconnected the call to Kate and called Warrant Officer Herb Lang to tell him he was leaving the office and why.

"Hang on," Herb said.

Bill could hear mumbled conversation.

"Captain," Herb said. "Hustle down to the office. Hondo will go with you."

Hondo was the head of General Sampson's security detail. Another US Army warrant officer. Six-foot-four with a hard belly, broad shoulders, gorilla arms and hands, stubble for hair, and a welded-on scowl. Hondo drove fast. He turned on the warning blinkers of the heavy Mercedes. He had one hand on the wheel. The other held a microphone. Into it, he spoke French to the gendarmerie, then he hung up the mic.

Bill said, "I just remembered. This morning, at breakfast, Kate thought someone was watching us from the woods behind the chateau."

"She saw someone?"

"No. She said she *thought* someone was watching us."

Hondo's head twitched. Bill decided not to tell him Kate thought it was a woman, and there was nothing to fear from her.

Hondo took the exit for Toussaint at a speed that pushed Bill first toward the driver, then back the other way. Other people flying a plane or driving a car he rode in scared Bill.

There wasn't anything to grab onto. He braced one hand on the dash and pushed himself against the door.

Hondo applied the brakes. The car slowed as they approached the ville.

"The blue Mercedes. That's Kate's car," Bill said.

"Tell her, follow us."

Hondo screeched the car to a halt. Bill lowered the window. Kate lowered hers.

"Follow us, Kate—"

Hondo tromped on the accelerator. It wasn't quite plugging in the afterburners on an F-14, but it was close. The flash from the roadside camera winked as they sped past the edge of the ville.

Bill looked out the rear window. "Kate hasn't even pulled away from the curb yet."

"Good."

Hondo used everything the engine had to give until it was time to put the brakes to use. Then he abused them, took the turn hard, pressing Bill against the door. He raced between the garages, stopped the car pointing at the chateau, bailed out, and pulled his army Colt from a shoulder holster.

They bounded up the steps.

"Bill, unlock the door. Then step aside."

Hondo poked his head and pistol around the doorjamb clearing to his left, then jerked back out again. He shifted the gun to his left hand and cleared to his right and again pulled back out. Then, holding the Colt in a two-handed grip, he stepped into the foyer, stood there as he swept right and left a couple of times.

Hondo growled, "That damned Herb Lang. I'm going to kick his ass. He didn't tell me how big this place is. Christ! I was expecting a house, you know, like normal people might live in. I should have ten guys to clear this friggin' hotel.

"What's layout, Bill?"

He told him.

"And you don't know where your wife saw the man?"

"Sorry."

Hondo ordered Bill to stand in the foyer and watch the closed west wing doors while he cleared the kitchen and dining room. "If anyone opens a hallway door to that wing, holler my name, then you get in the car and drive away. Fast. You hear shooting, get in the car and drive away fast. Got it?"

Bill had it.

"One more thing. If I die in here, you kick Herb Lang's ass for me." Hondo had *fierced* up his glower. He was holding a .45. Bill nodded.

Hondo entered the front room and flicked on the lights. Dusk was settling.

Kate pulled up behind General Sampson's vehicle.

Bill held his hand up to keep her in her car.

"Pull around the circle," he shouted, "and get it pointed back to the road. Keep the motor running."

Good girl! She did what she was told.

Hondo returned to the foyer. "I called from the kitchen. Herb is sending me two more of my security detail and the gendarmerie is sending another two men."

The gendarme car arrived first and parked with its flasher continuing to flicker blue light against the façade of the chateau. Five minutes later, Hondo's men arrived. Hondo and a gendarme, probably a sergeant, Bill thought, conferred and began, clearing the basement first and working their way up to the attic. At each level, they left every door to every room open and lights in each room illuminated. A gendarme or security man was left watching each floor.

Their efficiency impressed Bill.

With the house cleared, the gendarmes checked each external door for signs of forced entry. The security men checked the windows on the ground floor. Bill established the children in the front room with a movie as Hondo and the gendarme sergeant had Kate show them where she thought she saw the man in the upper floor west wing.

Bill joined them as they all stood in the hallway outside the last bedroom on the upper floor east end to the rear of the chateau.

"Madame, where, precisely, did you observe the footprints?" the gendarme asked.

Kate pointed. "Just in front of the fireplace, to the side, there."

"I see no footprints."

"They were there. We all saw them. My children and I."

Bill saw the look pass across the Belgian policeman's face. Apparently he didn't think much of women and children as witnesses. And Kate was American to boot. He also, probably, resented foreigners inhabiting a royal Belgian chateau.

But Bill didn't see footprints either.

"When you thought you saw the man, Madame. Describe that for me again please."

Kate sighed. "I was returning from shopping. I turned off Rue George the Tall. When I was between the garages, I saw something in an upper floor window. I thought it was a man. I stopped the car. But I wasn't sure. I thought it might have been a reflection of sunlight off the windshield of my car onto that window. I wasn't sure. I came in the house and listened and looked for signs of an intruder. I found nothing. So I thought it could have been reflection I saw. But then after I picked the children up from school, my son, JR, likes to explore. He found the footprints right over there."

She pointed again. "That's when I called my husband."

"But, Madame, there are no footprints."

Hondo dropped to his hands and knees and shone a flashlight across the floor. "Sergeant," he said. "There are footprints. Look. *Comme ca.* Like this."

Although irritated, the man dropped to his knees and shone his own light. "*Zut!* The light. It must be just so."

Bill knelt also to see for himself.

Fifteen minutes later, the gendarmes and Hondo's men departed.

Bill, Kate, and Hondo sat at the dining room table.

"Mrs. Marshall—"

"Kate, please."

Hondo's head twitched. "Mrs. Marshall, you did the right thing, calling your husband."

"Those gendarmes thought I was a foolish woman. A foolish foreign woman."

Bill put his hand over Kate's atop the table.

"The Belgians can think what they want. Don't second guess yourself on this. You thought you saw something, weren't sure, checked it out, found no substantiating evidence, and dismissed your first impression. Then you got a second piece of evidence. For the safety of your children and yourself, you did absolutely the right thing."

Hondo, Bill thought, tried to put a smile on his face, but didn't quite know how to hold it on. Did the ends of it loop over his ears like eyeglasses?

"Mrs. Marshall, eyes are wondrous instruments. They see things in all manner of color and detail. What they see goes into the brain. Sometimes the brain doesn't know what to make of what the eyes send them. Fear, anger, too brief a glimpse of something, all those things can muddy up what a witness *thinks* he sees."

Bill was sure Hondo had used the male pronoun on purpose. Kate, he thought, wanted to believe him.

"Listen," Hondo said, "the very best thing that can happen to a security guy on any given day is to be notified of a threat, and when he checks it out, he finds out there was no real threat. Understand?"

"Are you the Incredible Hulk?"

Hondo spun around on his chair. JR stood in the doorway behind him. Bill saw that smile thing try to happen again.

"Don't make me mad," Hondo said. "I've ripped up three uniform shirts already this month."

"No, Sir. I won't make *you* mad."

"Come here."

JR's eyes grew big, but he walked up to Hondo, and he lifted the boy onto his knee.

"You're JR, right? And you found the footprints, right? That was good detective work."

After Hondo departed, Bill and Kate worked on getting dinner together.

"You think I was a foolish hysterical woman, too, just like those Gestapo gendarmes."

"No, I don't, Kate. I do know Hondo is right about eye witnesses and sometimes what they think they see or hear is not what actually happens. We see the same thing investigating airplane accidents. You take every witness statement, but you keep compiling evidence until you amass enough to draw a reasonably sure conclusion.

"Those gendarmes were right about one thing. Those footprints could have been left there by workmen a long time ago. Whenever there was maintenance done the last time. The prints are hard to see. Nobody goes into that room. Except for our little explorer.

"I do not think you are a foolish, hysterical woman. You are intelligent, grounded, brave—"

"So I could be a Boy Scout except for one thing?"

"Mrs. Marshall, are you trying to seduce me?"

"No."

"Well, you have."

"If I had spinach stuck in my teeth, it would seduce you."

Bill had her in his arms with a lascivious grin on his face.

"Oh great," JR said from the dining room. "Mushy stuff. We'll never get dinner."

The red numbers proclaimed 2230.

Bill lay on his back, staring at the ceiling. Kate slept on her side, her back to him. She would think this was funny. They'd made love, and she fell asleep and he didn't. At least he thought she'd find it funny. He still thought of what he'd done to her as a betrayal.

The betrayal altered Kate. Sometimes he felt like he didn't know her, know what to trust from her. He'd never worried about that before.

Hell, the betrayal altered all of us. Well, maybe not the children, *but it sure as shootin' messed with me.*

Then out of the rear of his mind, what he had to do the next day crowded forward. He had to figure out how to use American military aid, and European nations industrial capability, to put into several of the NATO nations the kinds of equipment they needed to be able to participate, meaningfully, in the new NATO strategy of mobility in lieu of static defense. He sighed.

Kate was a puzzle these days. At times, she was the old Kate, loving, warm, giving. At others, she pulled herself inside a hard, cold protective shell, as if she were some artic species of turtle. Belgium, he knew, was harder on her than on the children or him. Maybe with a little more time, the old Kate would come out of the shell and stay out. In many ways though, things had gone better with Kate than he'd anticipated. *Thank You, God.*

So maybe, God, You can help me get the strategy together tomorrow. What do You say?

The house was quiet. Barefoot, Sally stepped into the hallway, and, staying near the rue-side wall, hurried to the east end, and opened the door to the last room on the rear side. Standing in the center of the corridor, she stared for a moment into the dark space. A frown wrinkled her forehead. She glanced down the length of the long passageway to the door closed on the west wing. After frowning again at the dark room, she closed the door carefully and returned to her room.

She opened that door and stepped back.

"Don't be afraid," the soft voice advised.

Nineteen

Louis Defonce flung the covers back and sat on the side of the bed. One in the morning. Sleep would not come. His plan to enter the chateau to see the new Isabella at dinnertime the previous day had been thwarted by the gendarmes showing up. What did that mean? Their appearance had to be related to his visit.

Could the American woman have seen him when he looked out the window? Yesterday, he hadn't given the matter any thought. He'd spent maybe two seconds at the window. He'd stood to the side. Then, as soon as he was sure a car was approaching, he ran. He remembered to close the bedroom door. *Or did I?*

If *la Americaine* saw him, why did it take the gendarmes two and half hours to show up? That didn't make sense. *Unless I left some sign, and they didn't find it for a while.*

That bedroom door, if I did forget to close it, even an American wouldn't find cause to call the police over that. Zut! The east wing hallway door. Did I close that?

It couldn't be doors. Jesus, Mary, and Joseph. The door to the escape tunnel in the upper bedroom. Did I leave that open?

Louis pulled on his pants and descended the stairs to the lower level and kitchen. His bedroom had gotten filled with unsettling thoughts and worries with no solutions. He'd placed a new bottle of Calvados on the upper shelf of the hutch. He poured a glass and stood leaning against the sink. Sitting at the table was not something he wanted to do just then.

The first slug of liquor sliced down his throat like a double-edged sword, razor sharp and cold on one edge, and razor sharp and scalding on the other. Then the warm puddle formed in his belly. Some of the fog in his head burned away. The second sip tasted of apple above a layer of cool alcohol.

It became crystal clear. He had to find out if he'd left the door to the escape tunnel open.

Back in his room, he dressed, descended again, and hurried to the entrance to the tunnel in the forest. With his light, he scanned the ground for signs someone had exited the tunnel and disturbed the soil or brush. Nothing.

Then he remembered clearly and distinctly. He had closed the escape door in the upper bedroom. For dead certain, he'd closed it.

He returned to his kitchen. He poured another Calvados.

Dead certain I closed it. In the kitchen, it didn't feel certain. *Perhaps I shouldn't risk the spy passageways for a bit. So how can I set eyes on New Isabella without using the tunnel?*

Louis took a sip.

Then he smiled. A new plan had formed in his head. He swallowed the Calvados down, went up to bed, and slept like a free-from-sin first communicant.

Sally stepped into the doorway to her room.

The girl in a long-sleeved, long silky gown stood at the foot of the bed. She smiled. "Don't be afraid."

Sally fully entered and closed the door.

"I am Sophie. I have been waiting for you for two hundred years."

Sally woke. The nightlight cast the ceiling above her in soft gray. She remembered entering the room. The girl told her to not be afraid. Her name was Sophie. She remembered the story Sophie told her.

My father built this chateau. We moved here from Normandy. One night, an evil man named George the Tall attacked. My father and mother and I fled. George's men captured us. They killed my father and turned Mother and me over to George. To save me from him, Mother killed me.

"And now, at last, you are here."

Sally lay still. She sensed the menace. But that morning, she did not fear it.

Anastasia spent the night in Louis Defonce's hayloft. Rising early, she returned to the woods around their trailer. The van was there. The trailer was dark. She settled herself to wait for Ivan to wake and to see what he would do. After looking all the previous day, would he, this morning, depart without her? As well as she knew him, as well as she could predict what he'd do in many circumstances, she did not know what he'd decide in this one.

"Anastasia!" startled her out of her nap.

"I know you are out there. Stop this foolishness. Come here this instant!"

She smiled. He would not leave without her.

The hinges of the cook-shed door creaked. She was close enough to hear him grumble. He hadn't had a fire yesterday. There were no embers. A new one had to be built. It had been twenty years since he'd had to do that for himself.

Was he really building a fire for coffee and breakfast and warm water for shaving? She thought he was.

Retracing her way back to the Defonce farm, she peeked in the kitchen window. Rene sat at the table. Henrietta stood in front of the stove.

She climbed the steps and rapped softly on the door. Footsteps approached. Henrietta opened the door.

"Anastasia! I was so worried about you. Ivan was here several times yesterday. Oh, goodness. Come in. Come in."

"Thank you, but I cannot. I just wanted to ensure Rene and you were all right."

"We are. Why do you ask?"

"Henrietta, I don't know how to explain it. Something bad is about to happen. Something bad. So, I wanted to make sure it hadn't happened to you or Rene.

"Louis is not here?"

"He is here. Still in bed. *Him* I worry about. The last two mornings, he sleeps late. He has had his moods in the past. This time though, it seems worse or maybe just different.

"But what has happened between you and Ivan? In all the time I have known you, I have never seen you angry with each other. You have always made me wish it could be that way with Louis and me."

"I have never been angry with my brother. He is angry with me now because I do not obey him. He wants us to leave and move away. I do not want to leave you and Rene. You are like clan to me.

"Now I must go. Ivan will be back looking for me."

"Wait. Where did you sleep last night? Have you had anything to eat?"

"I slept in your hayloft. I find things to eat in the forest."

"Wait one minute. I will wrap some food for you. A thermos of coffee. I could not go two days without coffee."

Thank You, God of All People for such a friend.

After serving her children and husband, Kate sat next to Sally, creamed her coffee, sipped, and surveyed the children. They were eating. The bus was due in forty-five minutes. She refrained from mentioning it, as much the words were anxious to be said.

"Bus comes in forty-five minutes," Sally announced.

Across the table, Heather stared at her sister as if she wondered what ungodly thing had happened to her docile sister. Kate wondered the same thing. Sally, she would have said, had not one assertive bone in her body.

Kate looked at Bill. He noticed the change also. His face said, *What's with her?*

Kate shrugged.

Behind the screen of brush, Anastasia ate her sandwich and waited for the American family to come to breakfast. She felt compelled to check on the one called Sally.

She'd had half the coffee earlier. Drinking more now was out of the question. Her breath might steam and betray her presence. All those years of running and hiding from evil she was always thinking of survival, or Ivan was reminding, chiding, hounding her to be mindful of it. Even after twenty years of security and peace in this blessed forest, the self-preservation considerations rose naturally to the surface.

A light blinked on in the chateau dining room. The American woman walked through the room and disappeared. Anastasia smiled. Madame Marshall would be doing what she did, preparing breakfast. A dash of chill regret pumped through her heart. *I am sorry, Brother, to have to defy you.*

Another survival trait: regrets were acknowledged and quickly shoved aside.

The husband entered the dining room and sat at the table. Madame poured him a coffee and sat beside him with one of her own. The man touched the woman's shoulder. The way they looked at each other touched Anastasia's heart. Another regret, and a tinge of envy, flitted through her.

Sally entered and sat. Anastasia opened her senses; then she dropped her sandwich.

Another surprise! Another thing Grandmamma had never spoken. She *saw* two spirits inhabiting the girl's body.

Anastasia tried but was unable to discern if the spirits were good or evil. The spirits she beheld were neither warm nor cold, neither soft nor hard.

God of All People, why have you put me here? I do not understand what I see. How then can I serve your purpose?

The answer to her prayer, she knew, would come in His time.

Kate sat by the front room window watching her children stand at the end of the drive waiting for the bus. Heather held the flashlight. She shined it in JR's face. He tried to take it from her but she held up, higher than he could reach.

Lights shone from down the road to the left. A splash of fear pulsed through her veins. The bus was coming. The children were not paying attention. They were fighting. It was pitch dark.

Sally grabbed Heather's arm, pulled it down, and took the light away from her.

So many times Kate wondered about Sally, if there was something wrong with her, with her mental state. She did well in school, but she had been so withdrawn. Bill once said if life was a train, Sally seemed to think she could only watch it go by. She could not get on board and ride it.

But this new Sally, she was not watching life from the side.

Out by the road, she took JR's hand and when the bus stopped, she held him back as he tried to push past Heather to get on first. Heather mounted the steps; then she allowed JR to enter. Sally turned and waved to her mother; then the bus swallowed her and roared away.

Kate shook her head, unsure as to whether to be pleased or worried over the transformation.

She pulled the rosary from her sweater pocket, and prayed for her daughter, for all her children. And for Bill, that the work he was doing, and had him worried, would turn out well. *And please, Lord, give me a day where no Belgian woman snickers at me. But Thy will be done.*

Twenty

For Kate, dinner with her family at her table, with her dishes, helped make JR's castle like her home. A little. Also, Bill and Hondo had worked hard to convince her she had done the right thing to call about the footprint. She wanted to believe them and did, mostly.

Sally offered to help dish up and deliver plates of chicken enchilada casserole to the table. Heather looked at her mother. Kate shrugged and Heather sat, her waitress job usurped by her younger sister.

The dinner served, the prayer said, the diners sliced a forkful off their tubular main course.

JR chewed once on his mouthful and swallowed. "Our school is so cool, Mom. In my class, I have a Belgique, a Deutscher, a Dutchman, an Italiano, and a Norwegian. I don't know how to speak Norwegian yet."

"I speak Norwegian," Bill said.

Kate rolled her eyes.

"Here it comes," Heather said.

"Mom rolled her eyes, Dad. Show her. Say something in Norwegian."

Bill grinned. "Yumpin' yiminee!"

"Oh brother!" from Heather.

Kate shook her head but a smile snuck onto her face. It had been a long time since her dinner table had been flooded with light-hearted good cheer. They ate, bantered, laughed, poked fun. Laughed. Kate felt her heart expand, as if it wanted to see how close it come to bursting without doing so.

Heather and Sally cleared plates. Kate brought the tart in from the kitchen, and as she served it, JR brought up the Halloween party haunted house they would set up in the basement.

Kate again shook her head. Bill was more the boy than their son. He ticked off the rooms they could create: ghost room, headless-man room, witch room.

"How about a pirate room?" JR asked. "A pirate with a sword stuck in his gizzard."

"Pirate room. Great idea."

Bill was so wrapped up with planning a spooky Halloween, he'd forgotten how he might be distressing Sally.

It was Kate, however, who'd forgotten about her younger daughter's new personality.

Sally looked just like her mother, people said. Same black hair, though Sally's was straight, while Kate kept a curl in hers. And Sally's complexion was milky rather than tanned. Bill said she and Sally had the face of Mary in Michelangelo's Pieta.

"Your eyes are green, hers black. But the eyes," Bill told her, "in yours I see a soul with depth. In Sally's, there's a shallow flatness to them."

Kate, for all her ability to read jurors, found Bill better able to see what was going on with their younger daughter.

Kate was watching her, when she turned and their eyes met. Sally smiled as if to say, *They are such children, aren't they, Mother?*

In Sally's dark eyes, Kate perceived a depth in them now. Before—

Was it just yesterday?—her eyes had been just as Bill described them. *What happened?*

There was a knock at the front door.

"I'll get it."

"JR, you stay right there," Kate said.

Bill went to see who called.

A man's mumbled voice and Bill's indistinct response floated into the dining room. Then Bill said, "Come in. Come in."

The front door closed and boots clumped across the foyer. Bill was with a man of his same height but thicker through the chest and belly. Older, sixty something, Kate thought. The man had a neatly trimmed white beard, wore a tan jacket, dark trousers, and nervously spun a wool short-brimmed cap in his hand. The man stared at Kate a moment too long and too intensely.

"This is our neighbor," Bill said, "*Monsieur* Louis Defonce."

Bill then introduced his wife and children. At "Sally" Kate saw surprise, maybe even shock, f lash over Mr. Defonce's face. For an instant.

"Sorry. I stare. You look like my niece," Mr. Defonce said. "You look very like my niece."

Kate recalled how Mrs. Defonce had reacted to Sally. The gypsy woman said it was like seeing a ghost. But they hadn't said whom Sally looked like.

"Can I meet her?" Sally asked. "I'm nine, and my birthday is April 7th. It's my turn to have a party next year."

Another expression of surprise f litted across the neighbor's face, as if he'd been suddenly slapped.

Kate was sure the man lied.

"*Alor.* My niece lives in Denmark."

"Let's get through Halloween first," Bill said. To Louis: "Sally left all her friends back in the States. She's lonesome.

"Have a seat," Bill said. He didn't seem to think there was anything untoward with Mr. Defonce's behavior. He pointed to the empty chair across from Heather. "Would you care for a piece of the tart your wife made for us?"

"No, no. Is for you. And Henrietta is *ma soeur*, my sister. Sorry. English not so good."

"Well, please thank her," Bill said. "The tart is very good. Sit down, please. How about coffee or a beer?"

"Okay. Beer. If it is not trouble."

Mr. Defonce unzipped his jacket, sat, and dropped his cap on the floor beside him. Bill went to the kitchen to fetch the drink.

"Mr. Defonce—" Bill began.

"Louis. Call me Louis, please."

"If you're Louis, I'm Bill."

In the kitchen, Bill popped the tops off two bottles of beer.

"Bill. Is William, right? I have … had an Uncle *Guilliame*." Louis rubbed his hand across the tabletop. "Good oak table. Not new."

"I love this table," Kate said. "Bill and I grew up in Wyoming. Western US."

"I know Wyoming. Cowboys," Louis said.

Kate nodded. "In the old days."

"Now too, Mom," JR piped up.

Kate held her finger up to her lips to shush the boy.

"Anyway, Louis, I bought this table at an estate sale. I've always wished I'd taken the time to inquire about the history behind it. But I didn't."

Kate saw anger f lash across Louis's face. Gone, though, as suddenly as it had come. Maybe, she thought, I imagined it.

"Here you are, Louis," Bill said, as he placed a glass and an opened bottle next to Louis.

Kate now saw anger cloud Louis's face again. This time, there was no mistaking it. He pushed the Paulaner bottle away from him. "Allemand!" he said and stood up.

"Oh. Sorry," Bill said. "You don't like German beer. I should have asked. I have Stella and American. Don't leave. Sit, please. I didn't mean to offend."

"Please, Mr. Defonce, Louis," Kate said.

"Not beer," Louis said. "*Chermans!* I not like the Germans."

Bill apologized, asked Louis to sit, and took away the offending bottle.

From the kitchen, he said, "So, Louis, you weren't very old during the war—"

Bill didn't want to re-offend, Kate thought, so he just left the thought unfinished.

Bill placed a Stella Artois in front of his guest, returned to his place, and swigged from his bottle. Kate could see the light in Bill's eyes. He was excited at the prospect of talking to someone who had experienced a little-known part of World War II.

Louis picked up his bottle and poured and looked at Kate as a tiny abashed smile played at the corner of his lips. She thought he was probably ashamed over his outburst. He turned his head and faced Bill.

"Not very old when war started," he said. "When finished, I was old man."

Oh, Lord! The look on Bill's face. "Dear, perhaps Louis would rather not talk about it."

Bill had been leaning forward, eager to hear what Louis would say. He sat back and frowned.

"Is okay," Louis said. "I tell one thing. My papa and I learned the English. To listen to radio. The British. During second war."

"Were you with the resistance?"

"Bill, let Mr. Jourdan be." Kate turned to her guest. "I'm sure you didn't come to talk about the war. Did you want something?"

Louis expelled a breath with a *puh*. "I forget. Stupid old man."

Kate did not think Louis was stupid or old and feeble. She sensed an aura of solidity. Down inside him, she'd caught glimpses of a hard, fierce, angry passion. Twice she'd seen it burn through the outward shell of nonchalance he wore like work clothes.

"Yes, Mr. Marshall, Bill, I ask favor?"

"Of course."

"I show, okay?"

Bill followed Louis to the east wall of the mudroom beyond the kitchen. Louis pointed to a panel next to the rear door.

"Alarm. For cow."

"You mean cows might try to break in to the house?"

Louis laughed. "No, no. Belgian cow bred to have large baby. Cow must have Caesarean. By *veteranaire*. Alarm tell when cow have baby. Call *veteranaire*. You see?"

Louis handed Bill a slip of paper. "Two numbers. Top is me. Alarm go on, call me. Henrietta is home. If not, call bottom number. Is *veteranaire*. You can do?"

Kate was standing behind Bill.

"Okay, Kate? You'll be here during the day."

Kate nodded. "But what if I leave the house to go shopping?"

"You call. Henrietta is home."

"Okay," Kate said. "So, you must have lived here for a while."

"Yes. For one year. I have new electricity put in our house, and new, um, plumbing. And don't worry. I will move alarm next month."

"For a year, you lived here, you and Henrietta?" Kate asked.

"Me, yes. Henrietta, no. She not live here. She stay with friends in Louvain."

"Mr. Defonce, can I ask you a question?"

"JR, don't interrupt adults when they are talking."

"Is okay," Louis said. "How you cowboys say, shoot. Not so?"

JR looked at his mother and plunged in. "Is this chateau haunted?"

Louis rubbed his chin whiskers. "Some people think so, including my sister."

JR ran back to the dining room.

"Heather. Heather, the chateau is haunted. Mr. Defonce said so."

Bill said, "We'll pay attention to the alarm, and, if it's not too difficult for you, would you mind talking to me about the resistance?"

"Is okay. We do that one day soon. You and me."

"Madame," Louis said. "Thank you for allowing me into your house. Sorry I interrupt your dinner."

"Not at all, Mr. … Louis. It was a pleasure to meet our neighbor."

Anastasia checked the trailer throughout the day. Each time she found Ivan working on the van.

She returned to the rear of the chateau at dinnertime. As she studied the younger daughter and her two distinct Spirits, Louis Defonce entered the dining room.

Ivan worked on the van. Louis was visiting the Americans.

Anastasia hurried to the Defonce farm, and when Henrietta invited her in, she entered and ate with her and Rene.

Anastasia said, "I saw Louis calling on the Americans."

"When?" Henrietta asked.

"Just now."

"He didn't tell me. He didn't even tell me he would not be home for dinner. He is acting very strange lately."

"Is he unwell?"

"There is nothing wrong with him physically." Henrietta hesitated but then continued. Two nights ago, he drank too much brandy, made himself sick. He hasn't been the same since."

"The day of the butchering, no?"

Henrietta nodded. "He has had these moods before. It stems from some things that happened during the war. On Sundays, he remembers three men. He drinks a glass of brandy. The brandy is from Normandy, and the Germans, The Pig, the one who—" she glanced at Rene.

Anastasia nodded. She understood.

"Anyway, the Germans, as they f led from the Americans and British in Normandy, pillaged and looted. They headed back to their country with truckloads of furniture, paintings, money. And brandy. Before, Louis drank one glass of the brandy. I didn't think he liked it. He drank it to honor his friends who were killed by the Germans shortly after … after what happened."

Rene sat at the table at his usual spot. Across from Anastasia. His hands in his lap. He watched his mother. Seeing pain in others, especially his mother, distressed Rene. He knew Henrietta was talking about something very close to pain. If he sensed it, Anastasia knew, he would want to take it out of her and into him. It was a blessing to be in the presence of an innocent.

"Louis sacrificed everything for Rene and me. But I know it built a kernel of resentment in the heart of his soul. He used to keep it hidden. As he, as we, have gotten older, he doesn't keep it hidden so well anymore."

"Are you afraid of him?"

"No. Of course not. He would never hurt either of us." Henrietta had gotten one glimpse into the extreme depth and breadth of evil that could spring from the heart of a man. Out of that violation of her body and mind and soul had come Rene. A miracle from God of All People. From an evil seed sprouted and flourished an Innocent. But, too, Anastasia knew the Evil One worked miracles of his own.

Anastasia would continue to watch over her friend and her son, and watch, too, over the other one, in the chateau. The one who had been an innocent.

Twenty-One

Mʀ. Mᴀʀsʜᴀʟʟ, Bɪʟʟ, ᴡᴀɪᴛᴇᴅ ᴏɴ the top step in front of the chateau until Louis entered his Pugeot. Then Bill went inside. *Thank God!*

Louis feared the American would stand there until he drove away.

Louis was shaken to the core. He needed a moment to collect himself. The wife, Kate, she bore a stunning resemblance to Isabella. The face. The raven hair. The green eyes were different. *Different?* Kate's eyes glowed with an alien, other-worldly emerald aura.

The new Isabella, though, she was beyond stunning. The black hair, the same face as Kate's, but pale, as first Isabella's face had been. New Isabella was old Isabella brought to life again. And how was this possible? He had watched as the pig-faced Gestapo slit her throat. He'd watched the blood puddle around her head. Yet here she was again. Alive. Flesh and bone. And she didn't just look like Isabella. No. The mother *looked like her.* This— whatever name the Americans stuck to her—was Isabella. Totally. Mind, body, and spirit. Rene and Henrietta were right. This girl *is* Isabella.

The clothes were different. Decades had passed. But wearing today's clothes was yesterday's Isabella.

Merde!

Back in '43, when he'd first met Jacques, and he'd asked Louis to join his resistance cell, Jacques submitted Louis to endless mock interrogations. Louis had to be able to answer German questioning without betraying fear or any emotion.

"You are a truck driver," Jacques said. "The war is not your concern. What does it matter who rules? Belgians, Dutch, English, French, Spanish, Mongols, Celts, Huns, Norsemen, Romans. Germans. We have always been ruled by someone. All you want to do is to deliver your vegetables and meat to Brussels and bring back beer and clothing from there to markets in Mons."

Jacques would have been very disappointed in Louis's performance in front of the Americans. His emotions had shown. He had felt those emotions heat his face. But Americans were shallow people with shallow powers of perception, Louis told himself. Jacques would not have been swayed by the rationalization.

Louis had no idea how long he'd been sitting there outside the chateau, but he knew it was time for him to drive away. He did and turned right on George the Tall.

Isabella.

She came to live with them in 1943.

For a year, she, from the cellar, had tortured Louis in his bedroom two floors above. His nights were filled with forces pulling and pushing at him. One pulled at him to go to her, to take her in his arms, to meld their flesh, to become one flesh.

Become one flesh. There was no good or bad to the desire. She was a child, but that did not matter. The yearning was so clear and pure. The yearning pulled at his soul strong enough to rip it from his body.

What Papa and Mama would say if he gave in to the longing constrained his body atop his bed. "A Jewess!" from Papa. "She is but a child!" from Mama.

And, he knew, all that had shown on his face to the Americans.

Even if the Americans were shallow people, non-perceptive, hubris blinded as had been conquerors since the beginning of time, he should have hidden his feelings as Jacques had drilled him to do.

That day in 1943 materialized. He watched Uncle Marcel bring Isabella into the kitchen. In his vision, Isabella stood illuminated as if by automobile headlights driving down a dark road, and there was only a short narrow tunnel lighted and all around, the whole rest of the world was darkness. He saw only the alabaster face of an angel framed by raven hair.

"Isabella," he said as he drove.

Papa argued having the Jewess in the house endangered the entire family. Marcel had a plan to keep the family safe and together. The argument sounded as if it came from far off, not right there in the kitchen.

Isabella's dark eyes met his, entered his, and he felt something in the center of him melt. If he hadn't been sitting, he might have fallen.

Louis gripped the wheel and leaned forward. Death did not prevent Isabella haunting him and ruining his sleep all these decades. What would this new, this reborn, this living Isabella do to him?

Suddenly, it dawned on him. He was about to enter *Toussaint*. He'd driven four kilometers past his driveway and hadn't even noticed. *Merde!*

Without checking for headlights behind him, he stopped and turned around. His visit to the Americans had not gone as he'd expected. He had been so sure Henrietta had been mistaken about the girl. But he had to see for himself. And he had seen. Seen Isabella. Alive. Not a dream. Not a remembrance. In the flesh, he had seen her.

This time, he found the driveway.

The lights were on in the front room. Henrietta and Rene would be watching the television.

He parked the car in the machine shed, turned off the motor, and sat and stared into blackness. Going into the house, subjecting himself to Henrietta's interrogation, which would come as certainly as sunrise in the morning, no, he would not do that. In his heart and in his head, he felt those pushes, those pulls of so long ago, still working on him with superhuman strength trying to pull essential bits of him, out of him. He had to come to grips with these forces, to fight them into submission, and it would take all his concentration and all his strength. No, he could not go in the house and let Henrietta cut loose at him, poking with her questions into the interior of his heart and head.

Calvados!

On the top shelf of the hutch in the kitchen sat a bottle of the brandy. Maybe he could go in and get it and leave without being seen or heard. *Bah!* Henrietta would hear, would see, would know he was there. *To the escape tunnel, then.*

In the tunnel, with the hatch closed over him, in the light from the flashlight, Louis worked the brittle cork out of the bottle. In his house, in the hutch, he kept a box of new corks, but he had no new corks in the tunnel. *No matter.* There were always bits of cork floating on the liquor. *No matter.* He lifted the bottle and swallowed a mouthful. The slug of brutal liquor made him gasp and it watered his eyes. When he could breathe normally again, he felt the brandy branch out from his belly up through his chest and into his head and out his arms. The Calvados tamped down the raging forces pushing and pulling inside him.

Louis sighed. It was if he'd had a toothache. One that had bothered him for weeks and had gotten worse and worse each day until he could feel the toothache in his toes, and suddenly, it was gone. He raised the bottle and sucked in a smaller slug than the first swallow. This one went down more smoothly.

He left the tunnel, closed the hatch, and returned to the machine shed and looked toward his house.

The light from the kitchen window lit the backyard. And the fence. Mama had Papa build that fence so Isabella could sit in the sun for half an hour when the Germans ate lunch. Henrietta loved to sit with her. Even in the rain. Henrietta would hold an umbrella over the two of them. Louis loved to watch Isabella from the hayloft. From there he could see over the fence. From there he could see her. And she and Henrietta, in sun or rain, twittered like happy birds.

Most days, Louis got those minutes of seeing the real Isabella. Every night, though, images of the take- your-breath-away, hurt-your-heart beauty, flickered in his dreams like a silent movie. A movie on a screen, at once so near he could reach a hand and touch it, but at the same time as far away as the moon.

Some days, he didn't return in time from his morning round trip to and from Louvain in Uncle Marcel's truck to climb to the loft to see Isabella.

Isabella. It hurt his heart when he could not see her. *Puh!* It hurt his heart when he did see her.

Louis shook his head and leaned against the machine shed. Reassuring solidity pressed on his shoulder. For a moment, he'd been in 1944.

He pushed away from the shed and peered across his field to the chateau. Lights were on. Not the kind of lights left on in an empty building. No. These lights proclaimed someone lived there. New Isabella … no. Not *new* Isabella. *Isabella* lived there.

Louis had his thumb over the opening of the bottle. He'd carried it that way from the tunnel to keep the Calvados from sloshing out. Lifting his thumb away, he took a drink, swallowed, and closed his eyes.

He saw what the alcohol was doing. It hadn't killed his anguish, as an antibiotic would have killed invading bacteria. No, the brandy worked only on the pain. And it hadn't killed the pain, only pushed it back. Temporarily.

He drank again. *Isabella.* In his head, he saw a thick black line against white. One end of the line was 1944. The other, 1990. The line collapsed in on itself and became a dot.

There was not time. There was only now.

The barn sat next to the machine shed. Louis walked to, entered it, and climbed to the loft.

When Anastasia had climbed into Louis's hayloft two nights ago, she'd expected to find it filled with a jumble of loose hay.

She had been in haylofts in eastern Europe, Germany, Greece, Italy, Spain, and France. Always before, she'd found loose hay. This time, she found rectangular bales, stacked in an orderly fashion, filling the loft to within a meter of the roof. During the last twenty years in the trailer at the edge of the blessed forest, as she and Ivan had talked, she'd gotten a sense that the Other People had developed marvelous machines to farm the land, to build roads, to manufacture all sorts of items in factories, but she'd never developed the sense that some machine could bundle up hay in such compact bundles. Surely it had been a blessing from God of All People.

She, as she found it necessary to do often, reminded herself of His name: God of *All* People. Not all of His blessings were reserved for the Clan. And as she always did at such moments of self-perception, she bowed her head. For a moment. Then she set to work to create a cubby hole for herself among the bales and wrapped herself in her cloak. She prayed for Ivan, for the Innocent, for Henrietta. And for Louis. He, perhaps, needed prayers more than the others. And she thanked Him for the blessings of the day.

Then she sank down and down, into dark and darker. Where nothing threatened, nothing worried, and no one hated.

She'd had two nights of sleep as glorious as those nights in the trailer next to her brother. This third night, she started to sink, with a vision of Grandmamma's hand on her shoulder saying, "Sleep well, my child. You will need your rest for tomorrow," when a noise from the ground floor of the barn arrested her descent. More noise. Someone was climbing the ladder. Light, from a flashlight, bobbed on the roof over the loft.

Anastasia sat up so she could see out of the crevice between the bales. A man, a tall, broad shouldered, thick chested man stood upright after clambering off the ladder. *Louis?* She wasn't sure. She opened her senses.

Empty! Inside the man, she sensed no spirit.

Anastasia recalled that day when Grandmamma and Mama had just begun to speak to her about her gift, about understanding it, about understanding what her spirit eyes perceived.

The Kukov women were in a booth in a town square selling embroidered blouses and tablecloths. "See that man?" Grandmamma asked as she pointed.

"I see him."

"What do you see?" Grandmamma asked.

"A man. Not tall. Not short. Small belly. He does not do hard work. Every once in a while, he sort of staggers, walks funny."

"Open your senses. What do you see now?"

"The man is empty. He has no spirit!"

"That man," Grandmamma said, "has been drinking alcohol. Be wary of such men, and women. Alcohol can melt a man's, or woman's, spirit from his body. Not permanently, but for some hours. In that time, good or evil can enter in. Both good and evil are all around. Though many times, forgive me, God of All People, there seems to be so much more evil than good."

From her cubby hole, she watched the man flick off his light and make his way to the big loft door. The door was closed but there was a two-centimeter gap to either side. The man, who might be Louis, plopped onto the loft floor with a grunt. He peered out between the loft door and the side of the barn.

What was he looking at?

Anastasia did not know. She hoped he would not stay there long. In her just before sleep dream, Grandmamma said she needed rest for what was coming tomorrow.

He just sat there and stared, as if he might sit there all night. Anastasia could not lean back and sleep. Ivan had complained any number of times how loudly she snored. She could not allow Maybe Louis to find her. That was as sure as any fact she knew. She had to stay awake.

But what was Maybe Louis looking at?

Twenty-Two

Louis sat on a bale and peered out the gap between the loft door and the side of the barn. He drank from the bottle as he looked, and with his eyes open, saw 1944.

August.

He'd returned from his Monday through Saturday run to Brussels and Louvain delivering meat and produce. In Brussels, he loaded cases of Stella Artois beer, and in Louvain, he filled the remainder of the truck with boxes of men's work clothing and women's dresses. His return load was for bars and shops in Mons.

Sometimes in Louvain, he would be given weapons to bring to Uncle Marcel's resistance friends. When he had guns or explosives to transport, he would deliver most of the rifles, pistols, and machineguns, ammunition, and dynamite to a spot ten-kilometers north of Toussaint, where his uncle's friends awaited it, and the verbal intelligence he'd memorized. On such occasions, he held aside one pistol, or one rifle, a handful of ammo, and a stick or two of dynamite for Jacques.

Jacques wanted to join the resistance. At age eighteen, Uncle

Marcel did not consider him too young, but he did consider him rash, impetuous, and untrustworthy. So, Jacques formed his own cell, which included fifteen-year- old Louis and two sixteen year olds. One of the sixteen- year-olds waited at the turnoff from the Brussels to Mons highway to Toussaint to see if Louis had anything for Jacques. When he did, Louis transferred the bundle of contraband and the intelligence information, and, in a matter of minutes, was on his way again to deliver his load in Mons.

Mama and Papa had strenuously objected to Uncle Marcel using Louis for the runs to Brussels and Louvain. But, he'd argued that he could keep Louis safe, much safer than if the Germans sent him to work in their factories, which were being bombed every night. In the end, Mama eventually capitulated, seeing the tip of the logic iceberg poking above the ocean of motherly concern. Uncle Marcel never mentioned his connection to the resistance or that he'd gotten Louis involved in that as well.

"I need to be able to count on you to keep your mouth shut about this," Uncle Marcel said. "You cannot mention the resistance to anyone. Especially not to your mother and father. If they find out, they will shoot me in the stomach with a shotgun."

At first, keeping a secret from Mama and Papa felt like a sin, like his soul was dirty. But then he recalled how the Defonce men had their secrets from the women. *How is this different?* Louis asked himself. It really wasn't different. It was better that Mama and Papa not know. Besides, the Germans had taken Uncle Guillaume and Aunt Marie, and no one knew if they were alive or dead.

When Jacques approached him to join his cell, Louis did not need much convincing. It was a way for Louis to strike back at the Germans. But Louis had wanted to go with Jacques on the ambushes they conducted, but Jacques would not hear of it. "Any fool can pull a trigger or light a fuse. What you do, driving the truck, is worth more than what the rest of us do. Only you can get us weapons and intelligence. There will be no more discussion of this. You drive the truck for your uncle."

Louis took another drink from the bottle.

And now he saw the day. That day. August, 1944.

Some days, when everything went smoothly, he would return to the Defonce farm before noon. Then he could get to the hayloft in time to see Isabella enter the backyard. He could watch her lift her face to the sun, or even sit under the umbrella to eat her lunch outside. How she loved her few minutes of escape from her confinement in the basement.

As much as she enjoyed being out of her dungeon, so much did his eyes enjoy feasting on her. His eyes seemed to take on extra powers, as if the eyes could feel the skin of her alabaster cheeks, could caress her arms. That day, his eyes were doing that, touching Isabella, touching her skin, when he heard the diesel roar.

Out on Rue George the Tall, a half-track German Army truck was accelerating away from the chateau. Heading toward the Defonce farm. *Were they coming here?* Louis wondered. They had never come to the farm before. More likely they were headed for the autoroute and Mons, or maybe they'd go north toward Brussels and pick up the highway leading to Germany. Some of the Gestapo had already abandoned the chateau to go home.

Last night, he and Jacques had listened at spy holes into the dining room as a lieutenant explained to two soldiers the bad news from Normandy, and that they would be leaving for the fatherland the next day.

"In the morning," the lieutenant said, "you will go to Mons and confiscate a truck big enough to hold the paintings. It can be a butcher's or a baker's truck. It doesn't matter as long as the engine and tires are in good shape and it looks like a civilian vehicle. American fighter planes will be less likely to attack us if we look like civilians and travel alone."

"The Defonce farm has a truck," one of the soldiers said.

"Idiot," the lieutenant snapped. "The one they deliver vegetables in is too small. We need one with a bed four meters long, not two."

"If the major hadn't taken all the money with him and left us nothing but paintings—"

"Silence!"

"The army has already confiscated the trucks around here to help with the pullout from Normandy," the other soldier pointed out.

The lieutenant pulled his luger and laid it on the table. "Tomorrow, early, you will find a truck. The truck will be large enough. The engine and the tires will be in good shape. *Verstehen?*"

The soldiers jumped to their feet, at attention, saluted and "*Jawohl*"-ed.

Louis and Jacques replaced the plugs in the spyholes and exited the chateau and escape tunnel.

"I'm going to get the others. We'll enter the chateau, wait until the Gestapo are asleep, and we'll kill them."

"Wait," Louis said. "Perhaps I should make my run to Louvain in the morning and tell them how things stand here. See what they say."

"Bah! You heard them. They are pulling out and taking their plunder with them. There is nothing to be gained by waiting."

Uncle Marcel thought Jacques was impetuous and rash. "Listen. We do not know if other Germans are coming from the south. If they find slaughtered Gestapo in the chateau, there will be retaliation. I should make my run and find out what they think.

"The Gestapo do not know I have a truck on our farm in the machine shed. If they knew, they would have come and taken it. So, can you make sure the two soldiers don't interfere with my run in the morning? Then when I find out what Louvain knows, we can get together in the afternoon and plan what to do. This is the prudent course."

"Your prudence will let these animals get away."

"Perhaps," Louis said. "But if you rush ahead, you might wind up getting a lot of our neighbors shot. The major, when he left, ordered the lieutenant to stay and maintain the headquarters. If the Germans don't find the chateau manned, there will be retaliation."

Jacques eventually agreed to the *prudent* plan. And he promised to make sure the two soldiers did not interfere with the morning run to Louvain.

That morning, Louis found out Uncle Marcel and his sons had

been sent south by the Germans to help with the pullout. He found no interference with completing his loadout for the trip north.

In Louvain, his resistance contact had told him they knew a rogue cell was operating around Mons, they suspected it was Jacques, but they wanted Jacques to cease with all his independent activities. The next morning, Louis had been instructed, he was to bring Jacques with him to Louvain. There the resistance would decide what to do with him.

Louis had returned to the farm.

First, he'd wanted to see Isabella in the backyard. Then, he would deliver the message to Jacques. Jacques would not like the message. That was clear, but that was for after his time watching the object of his dreams in daylight.

He had only begun to watch her when he heard the truck.

The truck was not one of the vehicles the Gestapo operated from the chateau. Most likely, it was German soldiers on the way home. Hopefully, they were doing just that and would pass by the Defonce farm driveway. But hope did not deflect the truck from turning off the rue and spitting up gravel and dust as it sped toward the farmhouse.

Louis did not have a weapon. He cursed himself for not keeping a rifle for himself. All he could do was watch.

Papa leaned out an open window and fired a shotgun at the truck. The windshield over the driver shattered. The truck careened left and into the house just below Papa's window. Half the house collapsed into a pile of jumbled lumber and stone into the kitchen. The truck stopped halfway between the house and the barn. A tall German, a Gestapo sergeant bolted out the passenger door with a luger in his hand. He ran around the front of the truck sweeping his pistol over the ruined house. Then he swung around and faced the backyard. Louis and the German heard Isabella sob. He saw his sister put her arms around the girl.

The huge German went to the gate and peered over it. Louis noticed then the tall, bald German looked like a pig. The Pig stared at the two girls. A grin, a leer formed and made him even uglier.

Louis sat in the hayloft, frozen, afraid to move, afraid to breathe, afraid the Pig would see him.

"Heinrich," the Pig called.

A soldier climbed out of the rear of the vehicle.

"Get in the driver seat."

Henreich looked through the open passenger door and shook his head. Heinreich stared at the body draped over the steering wheel and shook his head. Papa had fired his shotgun from close range. It would have made a mess of the man.

The Pig holstered his pistol, bared his teeth, grabbed the squeamish soldier's jacket and slapped him forehand, back hand, and forehand again. The he dragged the man around the truck, grabbed the former driver, tossed him to the ground, and shoved Heinrich up onto the seat.

For a moment, the only sound was the hissing of coolant steaming. Then Isabella whimpered. The Pig spun about, kicked in backyard gate, and grabbed the girls by their arms. He dragged them to the rear seat of the truck, pushed them in, and entered behind them.

"Back to the chateau. *Schnell!*"

Heinrich gripped the steering wheel, then removed his hands, and looked at his palms.

"*Schell!* Before we lose all the coolant."

The gears ground and truck backed first, and then rumbled out the drive and turned left on the rue.

"Mama. Papa," Louis said.

He climbed down out of the loft and ran to the house.

A leg cut off at the knee lay on the ground next to the soldier with the bloody ground-meat face. His father's leg. From under the rubble, blood trickled down the side of the house and into a sizeable puddle.

At the rear of the house, roofing material covered the steps. Louis grabbed boards and flung them aside. Mama lay there, head down on the back steps. Her mouth was open, as were her dull eyes. Her dress was up, exposing her white underpants. Louis made her decent.

Dead. Both of them.

"Isabella," Louis said.

From her cubbyhole, Anastasia heard Louis say the name. There were so many things in his voice: longing, anger, pain, and other things.

"Isabella," he said again, this time with pure longing.

Louis took a long drink from the bottle. She heard a *glug, glug.*

Then Louis tumbled sideways off the bale and onto the loft floor. After a moment, he snored.

Anastasia stood. The dry hay rustled. She listened but the snoring had not been disturbed. She climbed down from the loft and knocked on Henrietta's back door.

She told Henrietta where Louis was and what shape he was in. Henrietta took a blanket and climbed to the loft to check on and cover her brother.

Back in the kitchen, Henrietta said, "There is no way to get him down from there. He drank himself senseless, so he will have to spend the night there."

"What if he wakes and does not remember where he is?" Anastasia said. "He could fall and hurt himself."

Rene had been sitting at the kitchen table, listening, unobtrusive as a wall flower. "I will stay with uncle."

Henrietta shook her head.

Anastasia said, "Rene should not be alone with him when he wakes up."

Henrietta said. "I will stay with him."

"No need for you to sleep in the hayloft. I will do it. I am used to it."

"He is my brother. I am afraid of what he might do to you when he wakes. God only knows what foul mood he will be in. No, I can make him listen to me."

Anastasia woke in Henrietta's bed and poured extra fervor into her morning "Thank You, God of All People." She'd had a bath and slept in a bed, and it only took a few days without those to make of them true blessings. She dressed, made the bed, and slipped the Earth Mother statuette into the pocket of her dress; then she tiptoed to Rene's room and opened the door a crack.

A nightlight threw enough light to show Rene sleeping on his back, his hands crossed over his chest atop the covers. Some of the Other People, Anastasia knew, posed their dead that way for burial. The Clan looked on that pose as the dead trying to hold onto the life force, and in death to say, "God of All People, why did You take *my* life force from me?" The Clan lay their dead with their hands at their sides, palms up, to say, "Thank You, God of All People, for allowing me to use the gift of the life force for a time. Here it is back again, and I tried to keep it as pure as when You gave it to me."

"Good morning, Auntie Anastasia."

"Oh!"

"Sorry, Auntie. I did not mean to frighten you."

"I thought you were asleep."

"I was. Then I felt you here. You came to say goodbye. I'm happy you did."

Shadow, from the dim light, shrouded Rene's face. But, still Anastasia felt something different in him this morning. The Other People would have said he sounded *normal,* not afflicted with disability both mental and physical. This morning, Rene seemed sound and whole in both those dimensions, but nothing changed the pure and innocent essence of the child-man.

"It is still early, Rene. You can go back to sleep."

"Goodbye, Auntie."

"Goodbye, dear Rene."

Anastasia left the house and entered barn. She stood at the foot of the ladder to the loft and listened. Louis snored with gusto. "Henrietta," she whispered into the silence between snorts. But there was no other sound from above.

Anastasia slid her hand into her pocket and wrapped Earth

Mother in her hand. She knew what she had to do. She had to go back to the trailer. She had to talk to Ivan, to tell him about Louis, to convince him to come back with her to help Henrietta with her brother.

First, though, she would fix breakfast for her own brother.

Twenty-Three

Louis looked away from his ruined house, across the field to the chateau. The giant pig-faced Gestapo had taken Isabella there.

Then he peered down at his mother lying on the steps. Her eyes dull and her mouth open, as if to say, "Oh!" but the upper story and the roof had fallen on her so suddenly the single syllable did not have time to be said.

The pig-faced German had killed his mother and father and taken his sister. He had destroyed the Defonce farmhouse. He had destroyed the Defonce family.

The Pig had taken Isabella. Louis knew what he intended to do to her. Rage as hot as a fire with a blacksmith pumping his bellows boiled up inside Louis. He would kill the Pig. He had to kill him before he could … take Isabella.

The German Papa had killed was Gestapo, not a rifleman. He carried a luger in a holster. Louis took it. It had a full clip. He'd never fired one, but Jacques had given him instruction on how to handle a number of rifles and pistols.

He considered what to do. Get in the truck and drive to the

chateau and charge in the door and shoot anyone who got in his way. How many Germans were in the chateau? He did not know. He did not know where the pig-faced sergeant came from. There might be a lot of Germans. No. He could not just burst into the place. They might even shoot him as he drove up to the place.

No.

The escape tunnel. He would enter the chateau that way. He would find the Pig and kill him. He would save Isabella. They would get away through the spy passageways and the tunnel. She would love him for saving her.

From the lower level spy passageway, Louis found Isabella in one of the dungeon cells in the chateau basement. She was stretched out on the dirt floor, her arms above her head with ropes binding her to an iron ring in the wall and other ropes on her legs. Isabella was naked.

Louis pressed his eye to the hole. So many nights he lay in bed and yearned for sleep, but yearned more to see her just as she was, but his mind lacked the imaginative power to create such a divine image. So many nights. But now, here she was. The ropes held her there so she could not get away. She could not get away until he had enough of looking at her.

I will never have enough of looking at her.

Voices speaking German and boots clumping on wooden steps came to Louis. The clumping stopped and the voices grew nearer.

"You promised, Otto. I can have the older one, right?"

"You can have her."

"Sometimes, your promises—"

"You can have her!"

The Pig and a smaller man, the one who'd driven the half-track away from the farm, entered the dungeon.

"Bah! You lied again. Where is she?"

"She got away. Find her."

"You find her. I will stay here with the young one."

For such a huge man, the Pig moved fast. He backhanded the

smaller man across the face, and he spun and dropped to his hands and knees.

"Get up."

The smaller man pushed himself to his feet and wiped blood trickling from his split lip. He looked at the blood on his hand, glared at the Pig, and dropped his hand to the holster flap securing his pistol.

"Heinrich." The Pig smiled. "You don't want to be dead."

It was as if Heinrich's anger mask melted exposing his true face, which wore pure fear.

"Maybe we should get out of here, Otto. All I found in the garages was a sedan. We need to find a truck. What if that girl brings someone? Resistance maybe."

"I tell you this only once more. Find that girl. Do what you want to with her, but then you kill her. Do not take all day or I will leave you here. Now find her."

Heinrich backed out of the dungeon and disappeared from Louis's view.

The Pig leered down at Isabella. She leaned her head back as if looking at the ceiling, then craned farther back. Her eyes met Louis's one at the spy hole.

The Pig fell on top of Isabella completely covering her. His trousers were down around his knees. A moment of surprise flitted through Louis. No pigtail sprouted from the German's tailbone.

Louis pulled back from the spy hole, shook his head, then looked again.

The Pig stood up and pulled up his trousers. "I like it better when you cry."

Isabella stared at the ceiling. Louis did not know if she was alive or dead.

"Otto," Heinrich entered the dungeon again. He stared at Isabella.

"Did you find the girl?"

The Pig grabbed Heinrich and spun him around. "Did you find her?"

"No. There was an open door at the end of the building. She got away into the forest. We won't find her in there." Heinrich looked down at the girl again. "I will have her, then we need to get out of here."

In a flash of motion, the Pig pulled a knife from his belt, bent and slashed Isabella's throat.

"Pig!" Heinrich fumbled with the flap over his pistol.

The Pig jabbed his knife into Heinrich's belly. He squealed.

"That sounded like a pig squealing, Heinrich."

The Pig ripped the blade up and Heinrich fell to the dirt floor.

Louis stared at Isabella, at the puddle of her blood growing larger. Rage blinded him, and he tore through the spy passageway, out into the basement, and down the corridor.

The Pig picked up Isabella's dress and wiped the blood from his hands.

"Turn around," Louis said. "Let's hear you squeal."

The Pig slashed the knife. Louis jerked back and fired the luger. A line of fire burned on Louis's jaw. His hand came away bloody. Then he looked at the Pig.

The Pig had his hands over his crotch. The hands leaked blood. The Pig bared his teeth, grimacing against the pain. He raised his head, and the beady black eyes gored Louis with bolts of hate fire that burned black.

The hair on the back of Louis's neck prickled. He came close to turning away and running like hell, but he flicked his eyes to Isabella lying on the dirt. Her splayed raven hair melded into the black blood puddle on the dirt.

With the luger hanging at his side in his right hand, his left holding his jaw, Louis's fear morphed into anger and further into rage. He turned back as the Pig launched toward him with outstretched bloody hands. Louis started raising the pistol. The Pig almost had him. He fired. Louis jerked away to his left. The Pig howled and fell to the right.

The huge German was on his side on the ground holding his right knee. The howling ceased. The Pig raised his face, and surprise flitted across the ugly visage. He fears me, Louis thought. He aimed the gun and fired twice into big man's left knee. Louis's ears rang from the gunshots reverberating in the stone walled dungeon, but he heard the German's howl. And now Louis was sure. The German feared him. At that moment, Louis lusted after one thing: to see more and a more powerful fear on the hated face.

The German was propped on his hands, arms extended straight. Louis kicked him on the shoulder and he rolled onto his back. There was fear aplenty, but hate alternated in waves behind the black eyes. Louis fired the gun into the Pig's belly. The fear, he was pleased to see, had intensified. Louis watched him and saw the hate begin to form again, and again, he fired another bullet into the bloody splotch on the Gestapo uniform.

The German's body twitched. Two bleeding bullet holes appeared over his heart. Then the head jerked as a black hole punched into the pig-face just above the snout.

Louis spun around. He found Jacques beside him. Jacques grabbed Louis's arm, took the gun away from him, and led him upstairs and into the foyer. The other two members of the cell, Eric and Claude, were there watching out the windows beside the front door.

Jacques sent Eric out to the half-track parked in the circle for a first-aid kit.

As Jacques wrapped enough gauze around Louis's head to garb a mummy, he asked, "You made the run to Louvain this morning?"

"Oui."

"What did they say?"

Jacques stopped wrapping.

"They said don't do anything. The Germans are retreating, running for home. If you interfere with them, they will strike out and retaliate. They insisted, 'Don't interfere with the German retreat.'"

Jacques laughed. "A little late for that." Then he related what he and the others had done that morning.

They'd hidden in the garage next to German staff car waiting for the two soldiers to go on their search for a truck. Before the soldiers came out of the chateau, a half- track army truck passed through the garages and stopped in the circle. The Gestapo lieutenant and his soldiers came out and stood on the top step. A tall sergeant stepped down from the truck. He saluted.

"Who are you? Where are you coming from? What are your orders?"

"I am sergeant Otto Klein, Herr Lieutenant."

The two soldiers next to the officer snickered.

"Silence!"

The soldiers snapped to attention.

"A giant called small. You must hear jokes about that all the time."

The giant nodded. "All the time, Herr Lieutenant."

"Your orders?"

"We are coming from Normandy, sir, with orders to return to Berlin."

"What's in your truck?"

"Weapons, sir, and food for the journey."

The lieutenant gestured for one of the soldiers to check the back of the vehicle. The giant sergeant pulled a pistol from his belt and shot the lieutenant who tumbled down the steps.

The two soldiers stopped at the foot of the steps and raised their hands.

"You work for me, now," the sergeant said.

One nodded and said, "I work for you, Herr Sergeant."

The other nodded and parroted the first's sentence.

The sergeant told them to lower their hands. Then he questioned them.

They had no orders, but the lieutenant intended pulling out anyway. There were a number of valuable paintings they had in the chateau they intended taking back to Germany with them. The lieutenant thought it would be better to take their treasure in a civilian vehicle on the run to the homeland. Sometimes American fighter planes patrolled the highways.

"The farm there," one of the soldiers pointed east, "might have a truck. And there is a village, Toussaint, close by. They might have one."

The sergeant ordered one of his men to accompany the lieutenant's former soldier to the village to find a truck. He ordered the other one to drive the halftrack to the neighboring farm, where they would also look for a suitable civilian vehicle.

The halftrack roared down the lane between the garages and the remaining two soldiers hustled toward the garage. Jacques and his men surprised the Germans, killed them, and loaded them into the staff car. They drove a kilometer to the west and left in the woods to hide it. Then they hustled back to the chateau. Along the way they found Henrietta clutching her torn clothing in front of her. Jacques left Eric to bring her along. He and Claude entered the chateau through the open door on the ground floor at the west end and crept along the corridor to the foyer door. Jacques jerked it open. A sentry began to swing up a rifle. Jacques shot him twice. Just then gunshots boomed from the basement.

"So, there you are, Louis," Jacques said, as he tied off the gauze. "That's how we spent our morning. What happened at your farm?"

"Jacques!" Claude rushed in from outside. "The back of the army truck is filled with bags of gold and silver coins, cases of brandy, and weapons."

The rest of it went by like a video tape running at high speed.

Eric brought Henrietta into the foyer. She wore a torn dress and clutched a jacket closed in front of her breasts. Eric put his sister in Louis's arms. Jacques and Claude unloaded the treasure from the army vehicle and hid them behind the escape tunnel entrance in the basement. Eric was sent to the Defonce farm to return with the delivery truck.

The rear of the halftrack was empty. The delivery truck was parked behind it.

"Now we will bury the Germans and girl in the dungeon," Jacques said. "Thank you, god, for the dirt floor."

"No!" Louis shouted. "You will not bury Isabella with the Pig."

Someone was shaking him. He opened his eyes and light stabbed in. He peeked out.

Henrietta leaned over him. But she was old.

He began to push himself upright. She helped him. The world eddied about him. His head hurt. He was thirsty. There was a bottle beside his leg. *Bah! Empty.*

"Where am I?"

"In the hayloft."

Louis wrinkled his nose. "What stinks?"

"You do."

Twenty-Four

BILL MARSHALL SAT AT THE DINING ROOM TABLE WITH KATE TO his right. Back in the states, Bill made his own breakfast and ate it alone. There Kate could enjoy an extra hour of sleep before work and the children's school drove her out from under the covers. In Belgium, however, she always woke when he did and prepared breakfast while he was in the bathroom.

Bill pinched off a piece of croissant, stuck it in his mouth, and wiped the butter off his fingers with his napkin. "Good," he said, "even if the Belgiques would be horrified that we'd eat these a day old. But the bakery shop in Toussaint doesn't open until six, by which time I'm at work."

Kate stole a pinch of Bill's pastry.

"You're getting the hang of life here," Bill said.

"I was fighting it, I guess, trying to force them to do things the American way. It took me a while to figure out what I was doing, and when I decided I wasn't surrendering my soul to them, well, life turned more pleasant."

"Good. And it's good to see some happiness shining in your eyes, Katie Girl."

When she turned those green eyes on him, and she loved him, it was as if he sank into them, in one sense. In another, it was as if the eyes poured something warm and buttery inside him and it melted what was inside his chest. And it invariably stirred desire.

"You, Bill Marshall, are a dirty old man."

"That's not true. I'm not old." He waggled his eyebrows like a leering Groucho Marx.

Then, what was in her eyes took them out of the moment of banter and beyond it, and he saw that she loved him, deeply, thoroughly, and forever, and that the betrayal had been stuffed into a chest and stored in the attic. And he saw that she knew he loved her just that way, too.

Kate knew Bill would never be able to put the betrayal behind them, the way she had. Perhaps that was another reason to so helplessly love him.

She touched his hand, knowing what a touch would do in such a moment of spiritual and emotional intimacy.

"Stay home," she said. "Until the school bus comes for the children."

"Katie Girl—"

"You have to go to work to save the free world from the godless Commie hordes, right?"

"Um—"

A phone in the living room rang.

JR burst into the dining room. "It's the Bat phone, Dad."

General Sampson's office had installed a special phone line into the chateau along with a secure phone. Bill wore a key on a chain around his neck. By inserting the key into the phone and turning it, the call would be encrypted. JR insisted on calling it the Bat phone. It had never rung before.

Bill got up to answer it as it rang again. JR dogged his father's heels.

"Stay."

"Aw, Mom."

"The cereal is on the counter in the kitchen. Eat your breakfast."

JR moped off.

Bill had left the doors to the dining and front rooms open.

"Cap'n Marshall, sir."

A short pause.

"General Sampson. Good morning, Sir."

A long pause.

Bill said, "Thank you very much, Sir."

Bill returned to the dining room, stood behind his chair, and placed his hands on the back. He shook his head, looked at Kate, and shook his head again. A tiny grin curled up the corners of his lips. Then he screwed up his face as if he were lifting two hundred pounds, and he pumped his arms and legs up and down as if he were running in place.

"What in the world has come over you?" Kate asked.

Bill stopped dancing, grabbed Kate by the arms, and pulled her to her feet. Her chair went over backward and crashed to the floor. He embraced her so tightly it squeezed the breath out of her. He let her go, grabbed her around the waist, and spun her around.

"Katie Girl, I made admiral."

"What? I thought you said—"

"That it would never happen. I know. It's what I thought. But General Sampson told me the Chief of Naval of Naval Operations called and said my name is on the promotion list."

Now Kate shook her head. They had believed he had had his last promotion as captain. It had become dogma, like the things in the catechism. *Bill made admiral.* It would be as easy to believe the pope was Protestant.

No. The pope was Catholic. And Bill had been promoted. It was real. She kissed him hard.

The Bat phone rang again.

Kate heard, "Hello, sir, this is JR. Mom is kissing Dad. I'll break it up and get him."

Bill pulled onto the autoroute and f loored the accelerator of his BMW. When the speedometer blew past one hundred fifty kilometers per hour, he backed off. The speed limit was one twenty here, but, god, how he'd wanted to keep flying.

He'd been so sure admiral was an impossibility. It seemed so strange to feel euphoric over what was impossible. So many things he'd told himself. His favorites:

Admirals are politicians, not warriors.

I don't want to be an admiral.

I, Bill Marshall, am a warrior.

However, he admitted to himself, he'd acted as giddy as a teeny-bopper in the first row of an Elvis concert.

He'd gotten up this morning, and making admiral would not and could not happen. And here he was, 0730, and he was on his way to meet the tailor at the base exchange. The second call had been from Herb Lange. "General Sampson is going to frock you at 1000. Hustle out to the base exchange. The tailor will put the admiral stripe on your blues. And your wife and kids are invited to the ceremony."

"Herb," Bill said, "How the hell did this happen?' "Captain, when you have the word *supreme* in your job title, lots of things are possible mere mortal officers could never dream of doing."

When he'd told Kate he was going to be frocked, she asked, "That means you get to wear an admiral's stripe on your uniform, but you don't get the pay raise until the promotion list runs its way through the mill, that right?"

"Who cares about the money?"

"Well when is this frocking?"

"This morning at ten."

"What? What will I wear?"

"Leave the curlers in your hair and wear a bathrobe"

She'd slapped him on the shoulder.

"Oh. Sorry, Katie Girl. I wasn't thinking. Fifty-one percent of this promotion is yours. Come on. Let's go look at your closet. We'll find something supremely elegant."

Bill turned off the autoroute for the road to the exchange.

Holy crap! Admiral Bill Marshall.

⸺⁓⁓⊙⊙⁓⊙⊙⁓⊙⊙⁓⁓⸺

At 1000, General Sampson's exec entered the auditorium and announced, "Ladies and Gentlemen, the Supreme Commander."

The assembly of European and American officers and about fifteen wives, including Mrs. Sampson, got to their feet. General Sampson walked to the podium and said, "Seats."

After the rustling subsided, the general told his audience how, after the wall came down, initial efforts to craft a new strategy for NATO military forces fell short of what was required. Many in Europe thought the collapse of the wall, and of the USSR as well, harbingered a period of peace. In this glorious new future, military forces, especially NATO military forces would not be needed.

"One thing I have learned," General Sampson said, "is that the enemies of democracy abhor a vacuum. And I knew something out there would solidify out of seeming nothingness to challenge us in new and unanticipated ways."

He called, he said, friends from all the US military service branches, and explained he was looking for someone to help craft a new strategy, and explained what he was looking for.

"I need a colonel level man who has served in more than one command, and further, he has to be a real horse's—" The general paused and some in the audience snickered. "Well, let me put it this way. He has to be worried about getting the job done no matter what people think of him or how he gets it done."

More snickering.

"My navy friend offered Bill as the answer to my prayers. And he has been. He has unique powers of perception. Where others have seen the disintegration of threat, he sees the seeds of the new threat. Perhaps not in specifics, but in strategic terms. Once he saw the threat and articulated it, we had the beginnings of our new strategy."

It always surprised Kate to sit through laudatory comments about Bill at ceremonies like this. He had made so many enemies among senior navy officers, but they still found it necessary to give him medals. And, it seemed, the officer pinning the new medal on was Bill's boss, and he had *I don't want to give this horse's ass a medal* written in bold and all caps on his face. Bill explained that a number of things he had been involved in were important to officers senior to his bosses. They were the ones insisting on the medal, and Bill's boss had to present the medal or be guilty of the same thing the boss was mad at Bill about. Trying to make sense of it was something she'd given up on.

This ceremony was different, however. General Sampson seemed genuinely appreciative of Bill and what he had done. *Funny. It takes an army general to appreciate a navy guy.*

"So, Captain Marshall, Mrs. Marshall, will you join me up here at the podium please."

The general's aide called the room to attention and read the orders appointing Bill to the rank of rear admiral.

"Take your coat off, Captain Marshall." The aide stepped over and took Bill's coat festooned with captain stripes, and he handed Kate the one with the admiral stripe. She helped him on with it.

"Ladies and gentlemen," General Sampson said. "Admiral Bill Marshall."

There was applause and a round of "Hip, hip," from the Brits.

"Have a seat please," General Sampson invited. "I have a question, Bill. When I called you this morning, you didn't seem at all surprised. You acted so cool. Did you know your name was on the list? Did Admiral Early call you?"

"Can I answer your question, General Sampson?" Kate asked.

"Mom rolled her eyes before she said that, Dad," JR piped from the front row of seats.

After the laughter subsided, General Sampson invited Kate to the microphone.

"He did not know, General. I am absolutely certain of that. He went into our front room to answer the phone. After he talked to you and hung up, he came back into our dining room with a stunned look on his face. The reason he acted the way he did on the phone with you is US Navy fighter pilots learn how to be cool in all stressful situations. If he was flying and surrounded by MiGs and they were all firing missiles at him, he would say to his wingman, 'Goose, this is Maverick. We are surrounded by MiGs. They are all firing missiles at us. We have them right where we want them.' So he acted cool on the phone with you, General, but let me tell what he did one minute after he finished speaking with you.

"He got this look on his face like he was lifting a heavy weight and all of a sudden he started dancing and pumping his arms up and down. Like this."

Kate demonstrated. She'd worn flats, just in case she had the opportunity.

"Oh, he was cool all right, General."

Which brought the house down.

Later, after she'd dropped the children off at school, and she was driving home, she wondered if she'd just had another best day of her life.

Twenty-Five

"**I**VAN, I AM SORRY FOR troubling you."

Anastasia poured coffee for him at their table in the trailer.

"Thank you, Sister. And I am sorry I did not listen to you, to understand how important it was for you to see that Rene and Henrietta were safe."

Anastasia poured a cup for herself and sat.

Ivan pushed his empty oatmeal bowl away and ate a slice of apple.

"We both know something dangerous is about to happen, Ivan. You faced it the way you know how."

"What I know, and forgot, was when we face danger, we face it together. I won't forget again, and, Sister, it is good there is no longer animosity between us. This is a great blessing from God of All People."

"You are a blessing from Him, Ivan. I will never forget again."

After they washed the dishes, Ivan drove them to Toussaint. He took the van to a garage for carburetor repair. Anastasia visited a shop that sold the embroidered blouses and tablecloths she made.

Once the van was repaired, they drove to the Defonce farm.

Henrietta invited them to have lunch with her and Rene. Anastasia tried to refuse but Henrietta insisted.

Roast beef, potatoes, string beans.

They ate, then Henrietta served coffee and lemonade for Rene.

"Louis?" Anastasia asked.

"He was a mess this morning. I threw his clothes away. I think it was two days since he ate anything. He hadn't slept. So, I got him in the bathtub, then fed him, and he is sleeping soundly now."

"I have known you and Louis for twenty years," Ivan said. "It is not like him to be this way."

"I think it is the Second War. He was with the resistance, you know. The German who abused me, Louis killed him, and was almost killed himself."

"Huh," Ivan said. "He never mentioned that to me. He told me he never did any fighting. He just carried messages."

"He doesn't talk about it, to anyone. What I know I learned from one of his friends."

She sent Rene to watch television. Then Henrietta told them about August of 1944, about escaping from the chateau, being found in the forest by a man from Louis's resistance cell.

"Mama and Papa did not know Louis was involved with them. Neither did I, but it was good he was. They saved us. After Mama and Papa were killed, after what happened to me, and to my brother, I don't see how Louis and I would have survived without them.

"In the chateau, I found Louis with bandages covering his head, except for the eyes. I expected his face to be horribly disfigured. As it turned out, he had only a knife scar on his jaw. *Only.* I do know that if the knife had sliced a centimeter lower, it would have cut his neck and he'd have bled to death. He hides the scar under the beard."

Anastasia reached across the table and clasped Henrietta's hands. The two women poured pain and compassion into each other's eyes.

"One of his resistance friends, Jacque, had wrapped an entire roll of gauze around Louis's head. I guess all of us were excited and not thinking clearly that day.

"Jacque told Eric to drive Louis and me to Louvain. The resistance there would take care of us, he said. He and Claude would bury the two dead Germans and Isabella in the basement.

"But Louis would not allow Isabella to be buried with the German animals. He left me with Eric, went to the basement, wrapped Isabella in a blanket, and carried her out of the chateau.

"Louis told Jacque he would bury Isabella. So, Jacque and Claude buried the two Germans in the basement of the chateau, and Louis and Eric dug a grave for Isabella next to the house in our backyard. Near the spot where Isabella loved to sit and eat her lunch.

"There is a stone there with her birth and death dates on it."

"I have seen the stone, but I did not know this story," Anastasia said.

"That time is hard to talk about. To talk about it, I have to think about it."

"Henrietta," Ivan began.

"No, no. Perhaps I need to say these things now. To you. Louis and I have never been able to. And perhaps I should have seen before how terrible it was for my brother. But all I have been able to think about is how terrible it was for me."

"Rene," Ivan said. "Louis told me his father was a resistance fighter from Louvain who was killed in the Second War."

"That is the story he told everyone."

"Henrietta, Anastasia, the things that happened during the Second War were terrible for us, too. With the help of God of All People, we have managed to survive. It seems that what happened to Louis back then is destroying him now. He has had terrible things bottled up and stored deep inside. Now they are bursting out and poisoning him. He needs our help."

"Anastasia found him in the hay loft last night. Drunk. Passed out. This morning, I got him cleaned up and in bed. I think that was all anyone could have done for him at that point. When he wakes up, we will have to see what shape he is in, and what help he needs. But this is my family's problem. I don't want to burden you with it."

"Anastasia considers you and Rene to be part of our Clan. I do, too. There is nothing more important to us than to help Louis get through this time of ancient trouble infecting his spirit. Wewill help Louis."

Henrietta smiled thanks across the table and squeezed Anastasia's hand.

"We will get through this," Ivan said. "Together."

Louis woke. He was in bed. In his room. A line of daylight sliced under the thick curtains.

He had been sleeping. Deeply. Something had awakened him. He lay still and roved his eyes around the room and saw nothing. He listened. Intently. Voices. From the kitchen. Women's voices. Henrietta and someone else. Then a man. *Ivan? Ivan.* The little man had a deep voice.

" … help Louis …" floated up from below.

Another thought took shape: *The pig had taken Isabella from him. But, a new Isabella was in the chateau. At this moment, she was there.*

From below: "We will get through this," Ivan said. "Together." *Together! No!*

Louis swung his feet out from under the covers and stood. Dizziness swarmed through his head. He grabbed the headboard, but it was the urgency of his quest that steadied him. He got clean clothes from the closet and dressed. Carrying his boots, he walked carefully down the steps, staying close to the wall, so the boards wouldn't creak.

In the hallway, he heard water running and silverware clinking on plates. From the front room, the TV whispered lines of dialogue. Sometimes, when Rene watched by himself, he had the sound turned low, or even off. The door to the front room was closed. Louis hurried down the hallway, opened the front door, slipped out, and eased the door shut again.

He jammed his feet into his boots, tied the laces, and hurried to the east side of his house. This side the Germans had not been able to knock down with their infernal war machine. This side still stood strong, as it had for two-hundred years. First Louis Defonce had built the house well, and he was proud to be named for him. Today, however, there was no time to dawdle in the past. Today, the present ignited Louis's passion.

He sidled along the house and around the barn and crossed his field to the tunnel entrance. Inside, he lifted the lid off the top crate of Calvados, pulled out a bottle, and replaced the lid. As usual, the corkscrew on his pocket knife broke the brittle cork into pieces. He removed the chunks from the bottle neck with the blade and took a healthy swallow of brandy and small floaters. The first drink, as always, went down rough. He coughed and spat out bits of cork. Then he took another drink. As usual, after that first fierce flush down the chute, the second slug slid down smooth and warm and welcome.

He took the scabbarded dagger the Frenchman always wore and stuck it in his belt. There were slots inside the sides of the chimneys in the basement room and upper bedroom, which, when the dagger was inserted, triggered the opening to the escape tunnel.

He was about to start down the tunnel when he paused at the crates next to the brandy. In the next stack, the bottom box held American M-1 rifles and ammo clips. The next box, with the lid lying loose atop it, held lugers. Louis pulled one out of the crate, ejected the clip, checked that it was full and reinserted it. He set the safety and stuck the gun in his belt.

He hurried through the tunnel and into the chateau. There he checked the ground floor and upper one from the spy corridors. No one was home. It was disappointing. Then he noticed a wall clock in the dining room. Noon.

Stupid.

He should have checked the time. The Americans' children would be in school.

How could I be so stupid. Not even check the time. Merde!
Maybe not so stupid.

He would go into the chateau and hide in an upper- floor bedroom on the west end. The Americans did not use those rooms. He'd seen that on his last visit.

He lifted the bottle and swallowed a slug. A toast to his new plan. And he had the pistol. The American, Bill, would not be able to stop him. If it came to that.

Isabella. Taken from him so long ago, and now, as if by a miracle, here again. He could not lose her again. The age difference, sixteen and nine, *bah*, that was nothing.

He entered the basement through the servant bedroom and closed the tunnel door. He listened, then started down the central corridor. As he passed the dungeon cell where Jacques had killed the Pig, he stopped and looked at the dirt floor. The floor had soaked up so much blood that day. The Pig's. The other German's, Heinrich's. And Isabella's. But only the two Germans were buried here.

Blood didn't matter. Blood was just red water. Bodies mattered. A man's spirit lived in his body, not his blood.

"Are you down there, Pig?" Louis asked.

Louis drank and entered the dungeon chamber. "No answer?"

He walked to the center of the room, unzipped his pants, and urinated. He hoped Heinrich was buried on the bottom so the Pig got the undiluted insult.

Suddenly, Louis's head felt as if thousands of old-time flails adorned with razor blades beat at the inside of his skull. He fell to the dirt floor and raised his hands to the sides of his head as if to hold it together. His heart thundered.

Abruptly, the pain in his head ceased. He was on his side. Dust was in the air. He coughed. Lying on the dirt floor, he waited for his heart rate to coast down.

"*Vas gibst?*"

He recognized the room he was in. *The dark-haired girl, where was she?*

He pushed himself up. He staggered. Inside his head, the world swirled, like he was the sun, and the earth had moved very close and spun about him very fast.

Drunk, he thought. *Not the first time, eh Otto?*

A bottle of brandy lay on the dirt floor. Almost empty. Spilled. He picked it up and drained it. He smiled. There was more and he knew where.

Twenty-Six

Thoughts of Bill's promotion ceremony, and her performance at it, romped with pleasure through Kate's thoughts. Just in time, she remembered the speed trap at the edge of Toussaint, and slowed down. In time.

As she passed the stake-mounted camera, she thought, *Not this time!*

Maybe she had, as Bill suggested, begun to figure out how to get along with Belgium and *Belgiques*. But there was the saying about Rome being built. It seemed to fit. No, she could not let down her guard regarding *these people*. For all her ability to read Americans for jury selection purposes, reading these *foreigners* was a whole different kettle of fish.

I have taken a baby step forward in a journey of a thousand miles.

She allowed herself that as she turned off George the Tall and pulled up in the circle in front of … *her home?*

Perhaps. But that was still a stretch, too, but not as much a one as it had been.

Baby steps, Katey Girl.

Her father's voice elicited a weensy smile.

She entered the foyer, and stood still with her hand on the doorknob, the door still open. She looked up at the upper floor west end hallway door. Closed. She listened. For a long moment. Then she closed the front door and went in to the kitchen and took frozen chicken breasts out of the freezer for dinner. She thought about calling Claire in San Diego, but decided it was too early. She'd wait a couple of hours then call.

The tart dish. Her neighbor. Henrietta. Defonce. She would return the dish and call Claire after she returned.

Kate took the dish and a box of chocolates. Neuhaus. A Belgian chocolate Bill said.

"Nuehaus seems like a German name," she'd said.

"Kate, Europe is about the size of Texas, maybe, or—"

"Wyoming, Dad?"

"No, JR. Wyoming and Montana." To Kate: "At any rate, Europe is small and over the centuries, there have been all kinds of social forces driving people from one place to settle in another."

Bill's argument made sense, still, it seemed to Kate, as persnickety as she found the Belgiques, there should be more national purity to the place, especially, if, as Bill said, the Belgians were known for the quality of Neuhaus chocolate, and according to him, most Belgians preferred Neuhaus to Godiva chocolate. She tried to picture the women she'd encountered in the bakery shops in Toussaint if she offered them a chocolate with a German name. And Henrietta's brother, Louis, had had such a strong reaction to German beer. But it said *fabrique en Belge* on the box.

"That means 'made in Belgium,' Mom," JR'd said.

She considered driving back to Toussaint and buying a pastry to take to her neighbor, but Henrietta had given her a homemade tart. A purchased similar product just was not appropriate. Neuhaus chocolate is what she had. Maybe Louis would not be there.

Kate slipped her coat on, locked the chateau, and, with the Neuhaus riding atop the tart plate on the passenger seat, drove to her neighbor's house.

A white panel van was parked next to the two-story stone structure. Kate parked behind it. As she got out of the car, she studied the stone wall of the Defonce's dwelling. A good bit of the wall facing the driveway appeared to be newer stone than the base of the structure. A storm perhaps, or a fire had destroyed some of the original building? The stones at the base appeared to be fairly old. Older than the stones forming the base and walls of parts of the Marshall family house back in Wyoming. Parts of that house dated from the 1890s. This was older.

Kate entered the open gate in the fence around part of the backyard. She was about to mount the steps to knock, when she noticed what appeared to be a grave marker near the rear wall of the house. One grave marker next to the house? So it wasn't like a family burial plot, like some farms in Wyoming had. She stepped over to read it.

ISABELLA
N. 7 APRIL 1935
D. 23 AUG. 1944

August 23, 1944. That was her birthday. And April 7th, that was Sally's.

Kate almost dropped the tart plate. She'd begun to feel she was getting used to this strange country. This was certainly strange. Stranger than the things that had happened in the chateau.

Isabella. Henrietta had mentioned an Isabella during her visit. Henrietta's behavior had been ... well, strange during the visit. Sally looked like Isabella, and it deeply affected Henrietta. It was like seeing a ghost. Henrietta's friend had explained it that way.

Katey girl! Her father's voice invited her to get a grip, to cease probing for exotic meanings in a simple coincidence.

Kate took a breath and let it out.

Yes, Daddy. She saw him frown at her. He wanted her to call him "Da," as children did back home, where he came from. But to Kate, even as a kindergartner, it seemed wrong. Her friends called their fathers "daddy." Daddy felt right. Da was just wrong.

Sorry. Daddy.

Kate climbed the three steps and knocked.

Footsteps across a wooden floor. The door opened.

Henrietta Defonce frowned, puzzled. For a moment.

"Ah, Madame Marshall. *Bien venue!* You come in, yes?"

"Yes, for a moment, if I am not intruding?"

"No, no. You come in."

Kate stepped into a large kitchen, as large as her dining room. Refrigerator, a closed door to front-of-the- house rooms apparently, a large counter with a double sink in the middle, and an appliance— dishwasher maybe— filled one wall. A tall hutch with interesting carvings adorning the front sat next to the window looking out toward Toussaint. A large stove against that wall. And an oval shaped table. The dark-haired woman who'd accompanied Henrietta and her son when Henrietta gave her the apricot tart sat at the table.

"*Bon jour, Madame,*" Dark-hair said.

"*Bone jure,*" Kate said, with a nod and a smile.

"My friend, Anastasia, you remember, yes?"

"Yes. Of course." She hadn't remembered the name, but she did remember her blouse. Crisp white cloth adorned with vivid red, green, blue, and yellow embroidered flowers. She wore one like it today. "And I remember your beautiful blouse."

"Anastasia *faire des broderie, les chemises,* um ... tablecloths, other things. She sells. In shop in Toussaint. *Tres belle,* no?"

It was like work, paying attention intently to the words, then translating them, or trying to find a meaning in English. *Broderie.* Embroidery. *Chemise* was easy. Reaching understanding was like fighting a talented opponent in tennis, and finally scoring the point after a protracted volley.

"Very beautiful. The colors are so brilliant."

Anastasia lowered her dark eyes, as if the praise for her embroidery made her feel uncomfortable.

"You will sit?" Henrietta asked. "Please?"

"Your son, Rene," Kate said. "Is he here? My daughter, Sally, and he seemed to … be drawn to each other."

"Rene has, as I think you say, the heart of gold," Anastasia said. "I have known him for twenty years. I just meet your Sally, but she is like Rene. Very special. With nothing but good in her heart."

Kate faced Anastasia. The woman's words, comparing Sally to a Down's syndrome person, could be taken as an insult. Kate was sure Anastasia did not intend it that way. Rather, she had in fact complimented both Rene and Sally for their unique goodness. Still, there had been times when Kate had worried about her daughter, her mental development. As Kate looked into the Anastasia's dark eyes, she felt a sense of communication between them that was deeper than words could convey. Anastasia, Kate thought, knew her thoughts.

And I can read some of hers!

Henrietta placed a cup and saucer in front of Kate and poured coffee. "Rene is not here in the house. He is with Ivan, Anastasia's brother. They are out tending the animals."

Kate poured milk from a pitcher and stirred. She sipped and replaced the cup. And noticed the table. Oak. The surface glowed with a reddish, orange, golden patina. Old. This table was older than the one in her dining room. The end toward the stove had burn marks on the top.

"The other evening, when your brother stopped by our house," Kate said, "he noticed my dining room table. It's not as old as yours, I'm sure." Kate paused to choose her words. Louis Defonce's behavior that evening had been a bit strange, but she did not want to offend Henrietta. "I bought our table from an antique dealer. I asked but the man didn't know the history of the table, or the family who had owned it."

"On Sundays, Louis sits here and I think he sees all the good times our family had seated here." Henrietta caressed the top. "I have seen my brother rub his hand across the top, and I am sure he is seeing Mama and Papa, our grandparents, uncles, aunts, cousins." Henrietta's eyes met Kate's, then flitted away to the burn marks.

The conversation, the table elicited some heavy and painful memories for Henrietta. Then Kate saw determination gel on her face. After shoving the memories aside, she smiled, and told the story of her grandfather building the table and the hutch.

"The carvings on the front of the hutch, the lion's heads, the angels, the young girls, grandpapa said he wasn't sure if grandmamma was the most beautiful girl on earth or an angel, so he carved both. The lion, the king of beasts, that's how grandpapa saw himself married to grandmamma. He was king of everything that had any value to him."

Kate felt a twinge of envy spark like a pea-sized ember uncovered in a fireplace bed of ashes. Bill, as did most navy fighter pilots, acted like he was king over all the earth, but it was because he flew jets above the planet. And up in the sky, he was master of all who dared enter his realm.

A new Shakespeare should write a play about Henrietta's grandparents as the epitomic love story.

"So many good times at this table," Henrietta said, and Kate imagined an aura of happiness glowing like the northern lights above this piece of family history. "Before the Second War." The mention of which, snuffed the aura.

Some words of sympathy were called for, but Kate struggled to find appropriate one. Finally, "I'm sorry. The Germans—"

"Here, it was the Germans. But during the Second War, the whole world was overrun by evil."

Kate had forgotten the dark-haired woman as she had listened to Henrietta.

"Anastasia is a wise woman," Henrietta said. "I have not been two hundred kilometers from this farm. She and her brother have seen much of Europe."

"I think Madame Marshall has seen much more of the world than I have," Anastasia said. "And in twenty years, I have not been farther away than Mons."

"I have *seen* Japan, Singapore, and the Philippines," Kate replied. "But I do not know those places. Being here in Belgium, I see that I was an alien there, as I am here."

"Do you hear the wisdom in Madame's words, Henrietta?"

"I do. Sometimes I think if it weren't for women, there would be no wisdom at all."

"There is one wisdom," Anastasia said. "And I believe it is easier for a woman to see it than a man. Wisdom is trusting in God of All People."

"You would care for more coffee, Madame?" Henrietta asked.

"Oh. No, thank you. The children will be home from school soon. I wanted to return your plate, and to give you this." Kate handed over the box of chocolates. "We enjoyed the tart very much. It was delicious."

"My boy baked it. He loves the baking. And he loves the chocolate. Thank you, Madame."

"Please, call me Kate."

Kate took her leave. As she drove home, she thought about Anastasia's name for Him. God of All People. Across the planet, different people had different names for the Supreme Being. God of all People seemed so very appropriate. She stuck her hand in her pocket and felt the rosary beads. The rosary was, in one way, a prayer to the Mother of God, to ask her to intercede, on the supplicant's behalf, to her son. God of All People. That name seemed to go with a prayer aimed directly at the Almighty, like the Our Father.

She thought about the creed, or creeds forming part of her faith. There were, in effect, two forms. One began, "I believe." The other, "We believe." To Kate, God of All People embraced both forms of the creed. It was at one time, both an individual and a communal prayer.

God of All People. What an extraordinarily appropriate name for Him. After all, was there a different devil for Americans and for Belgians?

Thank You, God of All People, for the blessings of this day, for wise women to talk to.

Kate turned into her driveway and stopped between the garages and checked the windows of the chateau for signs of someone looking out.

Seeing nothing, she drove up to the house.

Oh foot! I wanted to ask about the Isabella headstone. Oh well. Next time.

Twenty-Seven

THE MAN CRAWLED OUT OF the escape tunnel and closed the hatch. Holding the bottle of brandy so it wouldn't spill, he pushed himself upright, staggered, took a step, and smacked his face against the trunk of a tree. He staggered back and shook his head.

He felt like he'd just woken. But he'd been awake.

Awaker now, he told himself and smirked at his joke.

An ache in his head pushed the humor out. He felt his forehead and found blood on his hand.

Where am I going? The answer to that was more important than an ache and blood.

Through the foliage, he saw the tin roof of a large structure. A barn. He started his leaden feet moving in that direction. At the edge of the forest, he saw a barn, a machine shed, and a two-story farmhouse. Away to his right, several kilometers of fields and pastures.

The farmhouse. He could use the barn to screen his approach. He set off. At a wooden-slats-nailed-to-posts fence, he considered ripping down boards, but he did not want to set the brandy bottle down. He climbed over without spilling a drop. In the pasture, he drank and found a few horses and two dozen cows looking at him.

"Why you look at me like that?" he growled. He pulled the pistol from his belt and brandished it at the beasts. "Later I come back and shoot one of you. And eat you." He laughed. "No. I shoot one horse and one cow. I eat you both."

The animals began moving away from him.

That made him feel better. He felt a lot better and strode across the pasture to the rear of the barn. He heard voices from inside.

When school let out, her father was there to give Sally and her siblings a ride home. Back home in the States, that happened rarely. When it did, it usually meant something bad had happened.

"Is something wrong, Dad?" Heather asked.

"No. General Sampson told me to come home early and celebrate my promotion."

As they piled into the car, JR asked, "Do I have to call you Admiral Dad?"

"No, Son."

JR settled onto the rear seat. "Admiral Dad. It sounds cool. That's what I'm going to call you."

"Goose," Heather said from the front passenger seat.

"You're a goose," JR shot back. "And you can call me Admiral JR."

"Why would I call you that?"

"Because Admiral Dad said so at the ceremony. He said his promotion was for Mom and all of us. He said we earned it even more than he did."

"Goose," Heather said.

Sally sat listening to the banter, sensing the two parts of the dialogue. There was love and fondness riding side- by-side—as she was with her brother—with an intent to hurt. The intent was to hurt in a very small way. Still, it was something to wonder about, that love and wounding on purpose could be so close together in the words her brother and sister spoke with each other.

As her father drove, Heather and JR continued their dialogue, picking at each other. As she'd seen chickens do at Uncle Norman's ranch. And as if they were the only ones in the car.

Heather and JR, she saw, took such delight from poking, or pecking, at each other. But, too, Sally had seen her sister and her brother rush to the aid of the other. During recess that day at school, JR had been bragging about his father's promotion. Students were not supposed to talk about their fathers, their ranks, their work. But JR had been so excited he'd forgotten, and he wound up in a shoving match with a boy whose father was in the army. Heather had run to the boys and pulled them apart. Others might have thought Heather had acted impartially, but she hadn't. Sally knew Heather was protecting her brother from a larger boy.

The car turned off the autoroute and entered the village of Toussaint. JR spoke with Father about the Halloween party, still some weeks away. Things like the party got JR so … enthusiastic. Sally sensed that his enthusiasm inspired Heather to peck at him. Inside herself, JR's *getting so fired up about everything,* as Uncle Norman described him once, made Sally smile. In way, JR getting fired up got her fired up, too. At least a little.

As the car sped up after leaving the village, Father said, "Do your homework right away when we get home. After dinner, we can all watch a movie. Which one do you want?"

"My name is Inigmo Montoya. You killed my father. Prepare to die!" JR said.

From Heather, "Not *Princess Bride.* Again!"

Father: "If JR hadn't suggested it, that's what you'd have picked, Heather."

The car turned onto their driveway.

"What would you like to watch, Sally?" Father asked.

"Star Wars."

"The first one," JR piped in.

"Princess Bride," Heather demanded.

"Why is it you three can never agree on anything? You are outvoted, Heather."

Sally was pleased. She liked the parts where Jedi knights exercised mind control. If she could learn to do that, maybe she could stop people from fighting with each other.

Father parked the car. Heather bolted out the door with JR racing to catch her. Easily inside the house first, Heather slammed the door. And locked it. JR banged on it.

Father sighed and moved the seat forward for Sally to get out of the car.

At the top step, Father said, "Heather!"

The lock clicked and JR pushed through the door. Inside, Heather was stomping up the stairs. JR chased after.

"Homework," Father said. "Now. Before dinner."

The feet stomped.

"Homework!"

That elicited responses: "Yes, Dad," and, "Yes, Father."

Sally's father looked at her, shook his head, engaging her in the business of condemning her siblings' childish behavior.

Father walked into the house. She followed.

Immediately, she sensed the difference. The Menace.

The Menace was no longer there. Always before, upon entering the chateau, she'd sensed it. The Menace. Present. But not as a present threat. As something to worry about. Tomorrow.

Today, though, the Menace was gone. Gone. As thoroughly gone as if it had never been there.

She took no comfort in that fact. She worried about the sense she had. She knew it was different from what other people had. But, was it reliable? Did she understand it? Did she know what it was she was … sensing?

No!

She did not understand. She only knew that she felt things. Some of the times, she trusted those sensations. Sometimes, they confused her.

"I'm on the phone," Mother hollered from the kitchen.

Father went toward the kitchen.

Go to the basement, the voice said.

Sophia? Sally wondered.

By way of the west wing. It was Sophia.

Sally entered the west wing, closed the door behind her, traversed the length of the hallway, and descended to the basement. At the center point of the corridor, Sally stopped and entered the dungeon cell. JR's favorite room in the entire chateau. There was a dark spot in the center of the dirt floor. The scent of urine, like at Uncle Norman's ranch—when a horse urinated—filled the air.

He was here, but now Evil is gone.

Sophia's voice said, *Go back up.*

Sally retraced her steps down the length of the basement, up the stairs, along the west wing, and into the foyer. She heard voices. Mother and Father.

In the kitchen, Mother hung up the phone.

"So, how, exactly," Father said, "did Claire know I made admiral?"

"From Admiral Early," Mother said. "He called just after I got home. He asked me to convey to you that you are to be congratulated and cautioned."

"Cautioned?" Father asked.

"Cautioned," Mother said. "You made so many navy admirals mad at you, it took a very important army general to make you one of the navy's lowest admirals. Clarie said that Admiral Early told her to say to you, 'You will have to kiss a lot of asses to make a second star. Admiral Early does not expect your lips to have it in them. But, he wants you to know, he congratulates you. Most heartily.'"

"Thank you, I think," Father said and laughed.

Sally walked into the kitchen.

"Kate," Father said. "I invited General Sampson to dinner next Friday. I should have asked you first. I hope you don't mind I've added to the endless list of sins I committed against our marriage vows."

"Admiral Husband," Mother said, "If that's the worst thing you do to me the rest of our lives together, I will die pleased."

Sally was pleased at the love she saw pass from one to the other.

"For the dinner," Father said, "there will be the general and his wife, Brigadier General Hastings and his wife—he is the general's executive assistant, remember?—Warrant Officer Herb Lang and his wife—and Herb is—"

"Warrant Officer Lang runs Europe. That's what you told me. You also told me it's his fault we live in this monstrosity."

"Um. There will also be Colonel L'Herault and his wife. He's the Belgian liaison to General Sampson's headquarters."

"The children?" Kate asked.

Sally knew sometimes she and her siblings sat at table with guests at a dinner like the one Father was talking about. At other times, they were not in attendance. At such times, they were not to be heard from. Which, considering Heather and JR, was expecting the extraordinary.

"We can set up a card table in the corner of the dining room for them," Father said.

"We could get the children at the table with us. It would be a little crowded. But we can arrange the chairs so that only the children are packed together."

"Well," Father said. "There's also Louis Defonce. And his sister. I know General Sampson would like to talk to Louis about resistance activities in World War II."

"Wait," Mother said. "You've already invited—Mother counted them up—five couples, plus you and me. And the children. And you didn't ask? You just invited them!"

"Well," Father said. "Louis Defonce, and his sister, them I haven't asked. Yet. But I was going to drive over and do that right now."

Tell him to call, Sophie said inside Sally's head.

"Call, Father," Sally said. "To see if he's home."

Mother and Father turned toward Sally. They were clearly surprised to see her there.

"You should call Mr. Defonce," Sally said. "To make sure he's there."

"His number is by the alarm panel," Mother said.

Father nodded, retrieved the sticky note, returned to the kitchen, and dialed the number.

Sally heard it ring. And ring.

Father hung up the phone. "I'll call again after dinner."

This is good? Sally asked Sophia.

This is good, Sophia responded.

As she left the dining room, she heard Father say, "What's come over Sally? This pushiness. Is this the way she's going to be now? I kind of expected her to revert to … what she was."

"Perhaps she's just growing up," Mother said. "Being sandwiched between Heather and JR, she needs to be somewhat assertive to hold her own."

He peeked through the slit at the edge of the barn door. A man, with his back turned, pitchforked straw into a stall.

From the hayloft, "Watch out, Rene. I'm tossing down another bale."

A bale tumbled through a hole in the loft floor. Then a short, slender, sprig of a man climbed down the ladder. At the floor of the barn, the small man turned. The watcher at the barn door noted his swarthy complexion and knew him for what he was. A gypsy. The taller man moved to the bale to push it along the floor. The mark of Down's syndrome on this one's face.

Two of the sub-human types. No different than *Juden.* The man drew his luger from his belt and entered the barn.

"Louis, are you all right?" the Gypsy asked, in French.

The man raised his pistol.

The child-man, with the pitchfork in his hands, moved in front of the Gypsy. "No, Uncle. Don't hurt Ivan."

The man snorted. "You will attack me with a pitchfork? I will kill you both with one bullet."

The Gypsy grabbed the pitchfork from the other's hands and

tossed it aside. "No one will attack you, Louis." This time he spoke German. "We only want to help you."

Pain contorted the child-man's face. He clutched his hands over his chest and fell to his knees. The grimace softened and melted to smile. Then he toppled forward onto his face. And lay still.

"Louis, you killed him!"

Ach, French again. *I killed him, the Gypsy said. Did I? Without firing a shot.* The man drank from the bottle. He smiled at the notion of killing the child-man without wasting a bullet.

The Gypsy knelt, rolled the child-man onto his back, brushed dirt and straw from his face, and closed his eyes. "Ah, Rene," he said, "I failed you." Then he stood. "God of All People," he said, in German, "Please help Louis. Only You can save him."

The prayer enraged the man, and he pointed the pistol again. Then he lowered it. The pitchfork. There was no need to waste a bullet on the Gypsy.

Anastasia dried dishes. Henrietta washed them.

"I have been thinking about Madame Marshall," Anastasia said. "I do not think I have met an American before. Have you?"

"A few. Since the NATO headquarters moved to Mons, there have been Americans here." Henrietta rinsed a plate and leaned it in the second sink. "Louis doesn't like them. He says they destroy peoples' cultures with their McDonalds and Disneyland. Our history books, though, spoke highly of what they did after the Second War. Instead of punishing the war's loser, as we did after the First, the Americans rebuilt Europe, including Germany."

"Ivan says they are a rich country, and that some people consider them to arrogant. But Ivan says they are generous. Especially when there's an earthquake or a hurricane. They are the first to bring aid."

"I suppose they are like the rest of us," Henrietta said. "We are complicated creatures. We all have some good and some bad in us."

That brought to mind her defying Ivan. It was a bad thing. Even though it was for, as she saw it, a good purpose, it could not erase the face that she had hurt her brother with what she had done. Hurting Ivan could never be considered anything but bad.

"Madame Marshall seemed to be an uncommonly good woman."

Henrietta nodded. "When we called on her, I was too worried about visiting the chateau to see it. But with her sitting at the table with us, well, yes, I liked the woman very much. I hope we get to know her better."

Anastasia dropped a dish and it shattered on the floor.

"What is it?" Henrietta asked.

"The evil. It has come."

Anastasia looked toward the backyard.

"Did you hear something?"

Anastasia had never told her about the gift. She nodded.

"It is near," Anastasia said.

Henrietta hurried up the stairs to wake Louis. From the upper floor, she said, "He's gone."

Anastasia took the statuette of Earth Mother from her pocket. It warmed her palm.

She put her mind on God of All People. She sighed out the icy fear and the thorns of anxiety needling the inside of her. Then she went to face the evil.

Twenty-Eight

S ally did as Sophie directed.

Leaving Mother and Father talking in the kitchen, she went to her room to get a flashlight, then returned to the ground floor. She entered the west wing corridor and eased the door closed. In the first bedroom on the rear side of the chateau, she knelt in front of Father's cruise box. A metal box as long as a yardstick. Half a yardstick wide. And knee high. Two combination locks secured the top.

By following Sophie's instructions, Sally opened the locks. Inside there were swords and knives and one pistol. Father collected these items at *brocantes* he called them. Mother said they were junk markets.

Sally selected what Father had explained to JR was a German bayonet from World War I. The locks were to keep her brother from getting at the fascinating collection. She closed the lid and snapped the locks in place.

Clutching the scabbarded bayonet in one hand, the flashlight in the other, she hurried down the hallway to the west end and descended to the basement. At the foot of the stairs, the light switch lit half the corridor.

Sophie: *Don't be afraid.*

Sally set off down the passageway. Inside her, the place where fear lived sometimes, was empty now.

Stopping at the opening into the dungeon, she played the flashlight over the space. She wanted to make sure the evil had not returned. She wrinkled her nose at the pee smell.

You must hurry.

At the foot of the stairs up to the kitchen, Sally turned on the switch lighting the other half of the basement corridor. She entered the last room to her right. The single bulb in the ceiling turned the room from dark night to evening. The room was furnished with a bed frame, a chest of drawers, and a straight-back wooden chair.

Sally placed the flashlight and bayonet on the floor and dragged the chair to the fireplace. With Sophie's voice directing her step by step, she placed the chair in the firebox and pushed it back against the rear wall. Then she turned on the flashlight and set it on end, on the floor of the firebox shining up the chimney. After pulling the bayonet from the scabbard, she climbed up onto the chair. As high as she could reach, she felt the slot.

Stick the knife in the slot.

Sally had to stand on tiptoe to get the bayonet inserted.

Push. Hard.

Something gave way. The bayonet moved a tiny bit. Something clicked.

Sally climbed down from the chair and dragged it back to its original spot.

The end of the brick fireplace had opened like a door onto a dark tunnel. She retrieved the scabbard and placed the bayonet in it. She retrieved the flashlight and shined it down the tunnel. The light didn't seem powerful enough to burn through the darkness.

Don't be afraid.

Sally stepped into the tunnel and looked at the blackness. If she played the light to the side of the brick- walled tunnel, it was as if the light worked better, as if she could see farther. If she shined the light at the middle of the tunnel, the blackness ate the light up.

You must hurry.

She hurried, feeling more like she was being carried than walking, or like she was in JR's red wagon and Father was pushing and JR was steering with the handle. Riding. Not having a thing to do with where, how, or why she was going. It was sort of like that, she decided.

After a time, the flashlight played on the end wall of the tunnel. Her light had been following the left wall. To her right, the light found three stacks of wooden boxes. Three boxes in one stack, two in the middle stack, and a single box.

As Sophie directed, Sally lifted off the lid on top of the three-box stack. Inside, the box was partitioned to hold twelve bottles of liquor, but it held only three. She removed two of the bottles and set them on the floor. Then she removed the straw-like packing material from the rear side of the remaining bottle and stuck it in her pocket.

The single box stack contained pistols. And hand grenades.

You must be very careful now. You must do exactly as I say.

With her mouth open wide, she stuck the base of the flashlight in, and, almost, took it out again. She was afraid she couldn't breathe.

Don't be afraid.

Breathing was easier, without the fear.

Sally followed Sophie's instructions, replaced the lids on the two boxes she'd opened. Then, tucking the light under her arm, she picked up the two bottles from the floor, and returned to the chateau. Just before exiting back into basement, she placed the two bottles on the floor of the tunnel and emptied her pocket of the packing material. Then she stepped into the basement and pushed the hidden door closed until it clicked.

Anastasia descended the steps and into the fenced backyard and stopped. Ivan. She knew his spirit had returned to God of All People. Rene. His spirit, too. Gone. And now, the evil was coming for her. It was near, looming dark and hard, like a monstrous storm cloud, with so much hate inside it couldn't contain it all, and some or it arced and sparked.

She closed her eyes.

"Thank You, God of All People, for the blessings of this day. Thank You for a long life, so many days, and not one of them without some blessing.

"We sought to know Your will, to serve Your purpose. The Clan when confronting Evil, never fought back. Even to save our lives. We would not add to the violence rampaging over the earth in the hearts of the Other People.

"Thank You for the opportunity to speak with You, this last time."

Some other people would have to be the repository of good and innocent spirits to counter ubiquitous evil. Madame Marshall appeared in her mind. A good woman. And her mysterious youngest daughter. With the altered spirit. Had the evil corrupted her? Then she wondered how a person came to be an Innocent. Were they born that way? Did some miraculous spiritual transformation occur at some point in a person's development?

There was no answer to the questions, but Anastasia felt as if a heavy load had lifted from her heart.

I lift up the girl, Sally, to You, God of All People. Thank You.

"Gypsy!"

She opened her eyes at the gruff voice. "Louis." He stood in the gate, glowering at her. Hate, loathing contorted his face.

Anastasia felt only compassion for him. That, she saw, only enraged him more.

He lunged for her, grabbed her neck with powerful hands and squeezed. Her vision registered only the color gray. Then even the gray collapsed from the sides into darkness. She did not feel her last breath, but she knew she could not draw another. She did feel her body exhale her spirit.

The man flung the gypsy ragdoll near the base of the rear wall of the house and mounted the steps. He ripped open the door and saw her. The one who had gotten away from him. He'd tied her up in the basement of the chateau. She'd gotten loose. But he found her. She would not get away this time.

She was standing by the stove. Holding a fork.

Cooking sausages in a skillet.

Good. After he killed her, he would eat her food.

"Louis," she said. In French.

He saw surprise. Then worry. Then fear.

That's what he'd been looking for. Fear. He started toward her.

"Louis, what has come over you? What are you doing?"

The fear was big in her now. The fear pleased him. It aroused him.

"Where is Rene?" she asked.

Suddenly, the fear disappeared. Disappointing, but as soon as he got his hands on her, it would return. He started toward her slowly, expecting his approach to frighten her.

She stepped to the side of the stove, grabbed the handle of the iron skillet, and flung its contents into his face.

The searing pain staggered him. For a moment. Then revenge and hate pushed the pain aside. It didn't matter. Getting his hands on the woman mattered. He could only see out of his right eye. Didn't matter. He could see her. That was all that mattered. He clubbed the woman on the side of her head with his fist. She fell to the floor. He picked up the skillet.

"May God have mercy on your soul."

Why wasn't she afraid?

He smashed the skillet against her face. With the second blow, he heard bones snap, which inflamed his passion, and he beat her harder. Until his arms grew tired.

He stood up, dropped the skillet, and saw the sausage on the f loor. He picked up a piece. Dirty. Only half cooked. No matter. Eating her food mattered. He bit off a mouthful, chewed it twice and swallowed. Brandy. *Where did I leave it?*

The barn. He left the house. Outside the backyard fence, his face hurt. Seeing with one eye annoyed him. Half way across the lot, he saw the elevated fuel tank between the barn and the machine shed. She had burned him.

The man diverted to the machine shed and found two dirt-brown gas cans. The kind the damned Yanks used. He filled them from the gravity flow tank and carried them back to the house.

One burner on the stove was still burning. He turned that off, then doused the woman's body with diesel and splashed some around the kitchen.

The stove was gas.

He went behind the stove, found the gas line, and tore it from the rear of the appliance. He smiled at the slight hiss. In one of the kitchen cabinets, he found a box of matches. Then he left the house leaving a trail of fuel all the way to the barn.

He decided to wait a few minutes for further gas build up in the house. As he waited, however, the burned side of his face ached. He gritted his teeth. His hissed a curse, knelt, and held a match to the wet trail of fuel leading to the house. The flame progressed in fits and jerks but steadily.

The man turned away. He had one more thing to do. The black-haired girl. He passed through the barn and between the Gypsy with the pitchfork stuck in his belly and the child-man. Just beyond them, his brandy bottle lay on its side. Still a swallow left. He killed it and threw it aside. As he exited the barn, a *whomp* sounded behind him.

Concussive pressure pressed on his ear drums. He wondered how much of the house was still standing. Perhaps he would come back and see after he found the other girl. The black-haired girl made him smile. That the smile made his face hurt didn't matter.

Suddenly, rocks and bits of lumber began raining around him. The man ran back inside the barn.

Bill Marshall popped the cork from the champagne over the sink in the kitchen. An unnecessary precaution, as it turned out. He filled two flutes, brought them back to the dining room table, and set one in front of Kate.

She raised her glass. "To the admiral."

They clinked and drank.

Bill raised his. "To you, Katey girl. I thank the good Lord every day that you forgave me and made our family whole again. Thank you. That is so much more important than the promotion."

Clink.

Kate sipped, wrinkled her nose, and looked at the bottle. "*Dom Perignon.* Expensive stuff, right?"

"I don't know if it's the most expensive champagne or not, but it is expensive."

"The good stuff is wasted on me. I wouldn't know the difference between this and $4.95 California bubbly."

"I'm glad General Sampson can't hear you speaking this sparkling wine heresy."

"Well, it was incredibly generous of him to give such an expensive gift. After the promotion ceremony, he did tell me one of the smartest things he did was to shanghai you away from the navy. I know he meant it. He was pleased and proud of the work you've done for him."

With former Yugoslavia falling apart and Saddam Hussein's invasion of Kuwait to deal with, the mainframe of the new NATO strategy had come together just in time. Bill didn't tell her that. That would become obvious to her soon enough. Right now, it was time to savor this unexpected blessing. This miracle, almost.

"Dance with me, Katey girl," he said.

He took her hand. She stood.

Then he and she clenched their teeth as if fighting to contain ecstasy, and they pumped their hands and feet up and down. They stopped and looked into each other's eyes.

Bill took her in his arms and kissed her. "Oh my, Katey girl. You taste wonderful." Another kiss. "You taste sinfully expensive." Another kiss.

"Later, Romeo."

"Perhaps you'd like another glass of champagne, my Dear."

"See the master *seductor* at work."

"The word is seducer, my Dear."

"The answer is still later."

Whomp!

The windows rattled. An explosion. A big one. From the east.

Bill ran to and opened the east end door. The roof of the Defonce farmhouse was missing. Red and orange flames fed a billowing cloud of rising black smoke. He ran back to the kitchen and jerked the phone from wall mount.

While Bill struggled to pull up enough French to report the fire, Kate stood in the open doorway and watched the cloud of thick black smoke rise higher and bend away toward the village of Toussaint.

She had been in the kitchen of the house not more than a couple of hours ago. The faces of Henrietta, her friend Anastasia, and of Louis and Rene materialized in her head.

"Please, God!" she said, with her hand on her rosary beads.

"Heather. JR," she said, and raced back through the kitchen.

Bill grabbed her arm. "I'm going over there."

"The children," she said.

He nodded and followed her up to the upper floor. They found Heather and JR standing at the window at the east end of the hallway.

"They're okay," Bill said. "I'm going to see if I can help the Defonces."

Kate ran the length of the hallway and embraced her children. Relief flooded through her. There should have been no reason to worry. They were in their rooms doing homework. Still, when something like this happened, she had to put eyes on her—

"Sally!"

Sally stuck her head out of the children's bathroom.

"Come," Kate said.

After Sally joined them, Kate said, "We'll say a prayer for the Defonce's."

JR said, "I see Father's car."

Which delayed the prayer a moment.

"For the Defonces, their friends, and Father," Sally said. "Our Father," she began, and Heather and JR left the window, joined hands, and joined the prayer."

Twenty-Nine

T HE RATTLE OF DEBRIS ON the tin barn roof ceased. The man stepped out the door and turned his good eye upward. He did not like waiting, but when it was raining bricks, a man, unless he was stupid, waited in shelter.

Safe now.

He set out across the pasture, anxious to get to the dark-haired girl. And brandy. He needed another bottle.

Inside the forest, he stooped to grab the handle hidden in the brush to release the trap door. *How did I know where the handle was?* appeared at the front of his brain. *Doesn't matter. The girl matters.*

Inside he found the flashlight atop the stack of crates of brandy bottles, turned it on, and set it on its base on the tunnel floor. He took the lid off the top crate. Only one bottle remained. *Only one?* He was sure there should be more than one. The light was dim. Only one eye functioned. He shined the light directly in the box. One bottle remained.

"*Dummkopf!*" he muttered. It didn't matter. Besides the one bottle, there were two cases below the empty. He would take the brandy. Then he would take the girl.

He placed the flashlight back on the floor and pulled out his pocketknife with the corkscrew. Then he lifted the bottle out of the comparted box.

Click.

The sound worried him. He grabbed the light and shined it in the box once more. There, at the bottom of the tiny compartment that held the bottle. An American hand grenade. The handle lay beside it.

The damned resistance had booby trapped his brandy. The booby trap would kill him.

Rage boiled through him. He would not be able to find those bastards and get his revenge. The rage gave him enough strength to bust out of the concrete tunnel.

But then, a thought blossomed and filled his head. He did not believe in heaven or hell, but in that instant, he knew it for a fact, with utter certainty.

There was a hell!

Fear, much more powerful than the almighty rage he'd felt a half-second before, blasted a scream from the man's lungs. The scream lasted one second.

Kate stood with a hand on JR's shoulder, Heather close in front of her, and holding Sally's hand. Peering out the east end upper floor window, she couldn't see what Bill was doing a kilometer away at the burning farmhouse. They'd seen him pull off Rue George the Tall and park his car, but then, the line of trees at the edge of the edge of the chateau property blocked sight of him.

They'd been standing there a while.

"Come with me," Kate said. "Your father will find the Defonces. They have lost their house. We'll have to give them supper. You can help me."

"No, Mother," Sally said. "We can't go. Not yet."

Tears streamed down her daughter's cheeks.

"What's the matter, Sally?" Kate asked.

"Rene," her daughter said.

Kate wondered how a nine-year old could pack such profound sorrow into one word.

"A fire truck," JR said.

Indeed, one was coming from the direction of Toussaint. A gendarme car preceded it. The curious ululating siren grew in intensity until the car pulled off the road and parked next to Bill's car but pointed in the opposite direction. Then the warning warble ceased. Silence ensued.

A sudden scream, muted by distance and barely audible, but high-pitched and terror-filled, startled Kate. Heather and JR did not react. Beside her, Sally did. Then Kate heard a tiny thump, and felt a small tremor as if someone somewhere in the house had dropped something heavy.

Sally withdrew her hand from her mother's. She opened her hands, gazing down at them. In a courtroom once, a witness on trial for killing his wife, had looked at his hands just as Sally was. Kate thought the man was wondering how his hands could have strangled anyone, much less the woman he had married. She remembered thinking at the time, the defendant was not putting on act, one scripted and rehearsed. Scripts, rehearsals, acts, those sorts of things happened. In that case, though, if she was any judge of character, the man was genuinely puzzled by what his hands had done. And how could Sally wear that killer's look on her little-girl face?

"Dad's coming back," JR said.

Bill's car was no longer parked next to the gendarme's.

"He's coming really fast," Heather reported.

"Come with me. We'll wait for your father in the foyer."

"I want to stay here, Mom."

"I want all of us together. Come along. Now."

"Aw, Mom!"

As they descended the stairs, a car roared up outside. Brakes screeched. Kate stopped the children. The front door jerked open. Bill charged in and hollered, "Kate!"

"Bill."

He looked up, and pure relief flooded over his face. "Oh, thank God!" he said and ran up the stairs to them. JR he lifted onto his left arm. He hugged Kate, then Heather, then picked up Sally.

Descending the stairs, he told Kate to stay with the children in the front room. He had to make a phone call. Then he'd tell them what was going on.

Kate sat on the sofa with JR on her lap and a daughter to each side. Maintaining physical contact with each one felt so very important.

Bill returned from his phone call in the kitchen. He knelt in front of the sofa and put his arms around his family. Kate felt him suck in a couple of ragged breaths.

He leaned back and said, "Remember when you thought you saw a man in the upstairs window? Hondo and the gendarmes came and searched. They found no real evidence that a man had been here. I think you did. I think a man was here in this house. I think you saw him."

She remembered that day. A man had been in the house. A tiny ice cube passed through her heart. *At least*, she thought, *the children weren't with me. Thank You, Father, God.*

Then she saw how frightened Bill was. Bill and frightened did not go together. He was the world's greatest fighter pilot. Nothing scared him. Not even fear of wrecking his career.

"When you thought you saw a man in the window, and we all looked but then gaffed it off. You really did see someone, Kate. I should have trusted you."

It was ironic. A few days ago, she thought she might have seen a man in an upstairs window. Hondo and his security team and gendarmes came. They investigated, and although they told her she had done the right thing to sound the alarm, Kate knew they judged her to be a hysterical woman, out of her element in a foreign land, and she had imagined the whole thing. She had thought about it and concluded they had been right. She'd imagined seeing the man. Now they, Bill, Hondo, and the gendarmes, were convinced she really had seen a man. But she, herself, still was not sure about it.

But this man, if he had invaded her house, he had not harmed her, but, this same man, probably, had rampaged murder and destruction on her neighbors. Kate thanked God for saving her children from encountering this killer. For saving Bill, too. Bill. Alpha male silverback gorilla, Wyoming cowboy, world's greatest fighter pilot. He'd have gone after the intruder with a pocket knife and been shot to death.

And for saving me, she appended to her prayer.

Hondo and the gendarmes returned. They swept the whole mansion inside, again, while armed soldiers searched the forest behind it. Other than finding a tiny, ancient house trailer, they discovered nothing of note in the woods.

At bedtime, Heather went up. JR wanted to stay with the adults. Too many extraordinary things were going on. Sally took his hand, led him up, and slept beside him in his bed.

Hondo returned from a visit to the Defonce farm at 2200. Searchers had discovered another body. A gypsy woman. Buried under rubble in the backyard. People in Toussaint knew her as Anastasia. Bill had discovered her brother, Ivan, and Rene Defonce in the barn. There was no sign of Henrietta and Louis. The rubble was still hot in the remains of the farmhouse. Searching the burnt-out structure would wait until morning.

Hondo left two of his security men in the chateau when he departed for the night. Bill had argued that it wasn't necessary.

"Admiral Marshall," Hondo said. "Across Europe, there are ancient and eternal animosities. Greeks and Turks. Spanish and Portuguese. French and Brits. There is one new hatred. Of American officers. The more senior the better. A number of attempts have been made on four stars, colonels, and navy captains. Once even a lieutenant colonel was wounded on a Turkish Army base. We have contingency plans. We are just executing one. So, Admiral, sir, shut the hell up, and accept the protection."

"We accept. With gratitude," Kate said.

When they were in bed, Bill rolled onto his side.

"Kate. When I found the gypsy, Ivan, with a pitchfork stuck in his belly, I just knew you really had seen a man in our house. I knew he was the one who killed Ivan and the Defonce boy. He was in our house and could have done the same thing to you and the children. It hit like a ton of bricks. I betrayed you. I dragged you to Europe, and I almost got you—"

She smothered the rest with a hard and lasting kiss, and when she let him catch a breath, she shucked off her nightgown.

"The security guys," he whispered.

"Is there a security camera in here?"

"I, uh, don't think so."

"I'll be able to tell in the morning," she said, "by the look on their faces."

"Kate."

She shut him up again.

Later, when Bill was zonked, a word he used for deep sleep, she prayed a decade of the rosary.

Sometimes, the measure of the goodness of a man was in how much and how deeply he felt guilt. Sins, she mused, *were easy to forgive. Guilt was another matter. Once it got smeared on a person's soul, there was no forgiving it off.*

But, thank you, God, there were ways to push guilt far, far away. For a while.

⁕⁕⁕

Neither Louis Defonce nor his body were found. Fireman arson investigators did discover the badly burned remains of his sister in the basement, where the burned through wooden kitchen floor had dumped her.

The gendarmes and US intelligence sources, Bill Marshall knew, had considered the involvement of known radical anti-military organizations, but could come up with no reasonable supposition for any of these groups to target the Defonce family. The investigations had revealed Louis's involvement with the resistance during World War II. But it had also revealed the involvement of a number of his neighbors, who, according to the investigations, had done much more than Louis. Louis couriered messages. The others blew up trains and trucks and killed Germans. Why would the radical right target a messenger, when others had done much more to warrant vengeance?

The gendarmes and intelligence agents had also considered the burgeoning middle-eastern immigrant segment of the population of Brussels. This group of foreigners was of major concern, but, still, why would such people target Louis Defonce? Especially after it now appeared certain that, whomever the perpetrator had been, he had invaded the home of a senior American naval officer, and done nothing.

That nothing made no sense. Neither did anything else about the case.

Except for one thing. Gypsies. Two of the victims had been gypsies. What if there had been a falling out among … well, some of those people. The pitchfork in the belly of Ivan Zukov certainly spoke of some hyper animosity. And gypsies were known to be hot blooded, were they not?

One other thing came from the investigation. Louis had money. He did not borrow to rebuild his farm after the Second World War. He didn't borrow money to buy the best farm machinery. He didn't borrow money to modernize his house with electricity and plumbing. Those two Kukov gypsies, they were around the Defonces frequently. They must have figured out that Louis had money hidden someplace. It was common knowledge he had little money in the bank in Mons. The Kukovs must have enlisted the aid of others of their sort to get their hands on that money. But Louis must have fought back. Perhaps he grabbed the only weapon to hand to kill Ivan. But then Ivan's cohorts took Louis to torture him into revealing the whereabouts of his money.

But why burn the house down? Who killed Anastasia Kukov? And why?

Rene was easier to explain. Heart attack, the autopsy said.

Perhaps, one supposition went, after Louis killed Ivan, the gypsies went berserk and killed Henrietta and set the house afire.

Anastasia had been strangled. Who'd done that?

If the gendarmes could just find the right gypsies, they were sure they'd have the answers to all their questions.

Bill did not like mysteries with no resolutions. In this case, however, he and Kate had never been closer, never been more in love. She was … affectionate. Aggressively so.

He and his family were, however, going to have to leave Chateau du Chasse and move into an "admiral's house" in Mons. A smaller mansion. Easier to clear and protect. Closer to base and security. Kate was pleased to be moving out of the boonies. Heather was pleased to be within walking distance of the base and school and school activities. Sally was, well, who knew? JR had questions: "Is the new house a castle? Does it have a dungeon? Is it haunted?"

"We can take one ghost with us," Sally answered JR's last question.

"But a real one. Right?"

"A real one," she assured JR. "But it is a girl ghost. Is that okay?"

"Sure, if she's a real ghost."

"She has been a real ghost for two hundred years."

JR's face lit up brighter than the sun over midday Wyoming in July.

Extraordinary things had happened to all them since coming to Belgium, but the changes this European nation had effected on Sally were the second most profound.

Most profound was when he told General Sampson he was going to have to delay the dinner he'd invited him, and his wife, to, until they got settled in their new place.

"Balderdash, Sailor," General Sampson said as he jumped to his feet behind his Eisenhower desk. The general was five-foot ten and slender. If he hadn't been a four-star general, he'd have been skinny. "You are hosting the dinner. With a few modifications. Now, get the hell out of here and send my aide in."

There were modifications to the modest dinner he and, initially reluctant, Kate had planned. The general's staff moved the dining room table and twenty chairs from his residence to the chateau, which the chateau's dining room accommodated nicely.

The general's kitchen staff would prepare and serve the meal, Bill was informed. General Sampson modified the guest list and determined the seating arrangements.

Bill and Kate occupied the ends of the table. General Sampson and his wife sat across from each other at the center. The Marshall children sat next to the Sampsons. The other guests included Princess Lisle of the Belgian royal family and her husband, Warrant Officer Lang and Brigadier General Hastings from General Sampson's staff and their wives, a German Army general and his wife, the Belgian Army liaison to SHAPE and his wife, and Professor and Mrs. Robineau from Lousain. The professor was a wealth of knowledge about World War II Belgian resistance activities.

The last of the dinner guests to leave *Chateau du Chasse* were General Sampson and his wife Hermione.

Bill and Kate stood on the front steps until the general's driver pulled away. In the foyer, Bill put his arms around his wife and pressed her to him.

"That, Mrs. Admiral, was one heck of a dinner party you threw."

"I didn't throw anything. General Sampson brought his table and chairs, his china and silverware, his cooks and serving people, and his people brought the food, cooked it and served it."

"The general told me he knew we wanted the dinner to be a thank you to him for the promotion. He wanted the tribute, and the thank you, to go in the other direction. He knew what he'd cost us by bringing us to Europe. And he wanted us, and especially you, to know how much he appreciated the job I've done for him. And how much all this cost you."

"Well, Mr. Admiral, I am impressed that the general would do this for us. And I am very proud of you."

"Shall we go up while I tell you how proud I am of you?"

"By all means. Let us ascend to our chambers from the *pomme de terre*."

She took his arm and hiked up the hem of her floor length, and they started up.

"*Pomme de terre* means potato, Silly."

"So what do these people call the ground floor?"

"Katey girl, you know what they call it. You are a raven-haired beauty, not a ditz-head blonde."

They crossed over the level part above the front door. "This was an incredible evening," Kate said. "I will remember it the rest of my life."

"Yes. All the men in tuxes, the women in gowns, and JR asked the princess why she wasn't wearing a crown or a tiara or something. Before the princess could respond, one of General Sampson's young soldiers said he had taken her tiara along with her coat and put them in the closet. He would get it. In less than five minutes he returned with a crown made from a clothes hanger and aluminum foil. Mrs. Sampson donates a hairpin to hold it in place. The princess proudly wore the tiara all evening. So, we are all formally attired, which pretty well pointed out the social levels. Royal family. Four star American and German generals. A professor. And us commoners. But JR's intervention wound up making all of us so comfortable with each other."

They checked on the children, and as they hung up their clothes, Kate said, "When the professor spoke about what happened to Henrietta, and her son, and all the members of Louis's resistance cell being killed, I watched the German general. He listened attentively to all that was said, like all of us did."

"The professor did a good job of packaging his dissertation with the children in mind," Bill said.

"Then *herr* general said, 'We humans do terrible things to each other. War gives us an excuse to commit the greatest evils. The world has, in effect, forgiven Germany for the sins we committed against humanity. But no one can forgive the guilt we carry. And I hope we Germans never forget that we carry it.'

"I thought he put that quite well."

"Yes, and both the professor and General Klaus said nice things about the Defonces."

They went in to brush their teeth.

"How did General Sampson know I donated headstones for the Kukovs and for Henrietta and Rene?" Kate asked.

"The Belgian gendarmes think gypsies killed the Defonces. They wanted the Kukovs buried as paupers, not with a headstone like you bought them. The Belgian liaison officer went to General Sampson and told him how the Belgians felt. General Sampson told them Admiral Marshall's wife considered Anastasia Kukov to be a good woman. If Kate Marshall wanted to mark her grave in a respectful way, he, SACEUR, would consider it a personal favor if she were permitted to do so."

"General Sampson had to intervene?"

Bill nodded. They brushed and climbed into bed.

"The princess," Kate said, "she managed to be both royal and down to earth at the same time."

"She said the chateau was happier than it had ever been. Then Sally said, 'It is happy now.' Apparently, we are not done being surprised by Sally."

"But Sally's right," Kate said. "When we first moved in, the place seemed spooky to me. Now, well, I think JR's castle is a happy place. I am sorry we have to leave it tomorrow. Almost."

They were quiet for a moment.

"Good," Kate said. "At last we're done talking."

Thirty

Sally waited in the hallway outside her parent's room. Toward the east end of the chateau, sconce lights on either side melted a glow hole in the middle of the long rectangle of dark.

With her back to the wall, she cocked her head. Quiet. No more talking. She turned around. Inside, she sensed brightness, like just before the sun came up.

It is time. Sophie.

Sally opened her senses. The security man was in the foyer, she thought. Sophie confirmed it. Sally walked down the hallway to the east end and descended the staircase to the mudroom behind the kitchen. The key was in the lock. She opened the door carefully and stepped out and closed it again without making a sound.

Sally started walking toward the Defonce farmhouse.

Don't be afraid.

"I am not afraid," she whispered. "You are with me."

Don't be afraid because God is with you.

"God is with me? Isn't He with us?"

God is with you. You don't have to whisper, you know. Just think the words.

"It's easier to think the words if I say them."

Sophie remained silent as Sally crossed the field.

Not much of the house remained. The stone front still stood two stories tall. Most of the sidewalls had been blown out. No wall at all stood in the back.

Sally looked down. A flat polished stone, a few inches tall, sat above the dirt near the foundation of the house. She'd seen stones like it in a cemetery and asked why the stones were so much smaller than the others. Mother said the small stones marked the grave of an infant. There was enough light to see an inscription but not enough to read it.

Kneel.

She knelt.

A pain in her knee woke her. She pushed herself upright. Sophie was to her right. She hadn't been able to see her since that first night.

Clear the rubble between the edge of the headstone and the house.

Sally cleared it and found a tiny stone statue. Of a woman. She picked it up. It barely covered her palm. It felt warm.

Follow me.

She took a step, stopped, and raised a hand to her head.

"I feel sick."

It will be better soon. Follow me.

Sophie moved toward home. Not exactly. Home was there. To the right. She was leading them to the forest. She did feel better. Sophie moved faster. Sally kept up. At the edge of the dark forest, Sally stopped.

Follow me. There is enough light.

There was. After a time, Sophie told her to stop. She did by a clump of bushes. She sensed the evil from the chateau. Very close. From under the bushes.

Don't be afraid. Stand still. I am behind you. Look forward.

Say this prayer: Father, God, ruler of heaven, earth, and hell.

She repeated the line.

Remove this evil spirit from the earth. If it be Your will.

"Remove this evil spirit. If it be Your will."

A noise like train whistle sounded from beneath the ground.

Don't be afraid.

The noise grew louder and louder, then a wisp of air, like from a fan, touched her face. The noise ceased abruptly.

The prince of devils loved this evil spirit he created. He kept it here on earth for a long time. It lived in three different bodies. But your prayer made it leave, made it go to hell, where it belongs.

I know you are tired, but we have more work to do.

Sophie led her deeper into the forest. Sally did not have a sense of how far or how long she walked. Sophie stopped.

Mother is buried here.

"There's no stone?"

No stone. Her body was thrown in a hole here to hide it. Not to bury it.

The spirits of those touched at death by truly evil spirits can be trapped on earth. A last cruelty inflicted on an innocent soul. A prayer to Our Father, God, however, can release them.

"Then they can go to heaven?"

They can go to where Our Father, God, sends them.

Mother was killed by a truly evil-spirited man. That evil spirit tries to torment her, but Mother has tormented herself more powerfully than the evil spirit ever could.

Say the prayer I taught you.

Sally said it. This time, instead of a train whistle, she heard a whimper, as a sad child might make. It made her feel sad. Tears coursed down her cheeks.

What you heard was the spirit of Mother breathing out the last of her shame and sorrow. Pray this: Father, God, lift the sorrow from the soul, if it be Thy will.

Sally prayed and felt happiness enter her heart.

Thank Him. Be ever thankful.

"Thank You, Father God."

We have one more chore.

Sophie led Sally back to the chateau and through the east-end door. Inside, she turned the key. The lock click was loud in the deep of night stillness. Sally opened her senses. The security man was at the opposite end of the house. Moving.

Sophie led Sally down to the basement and to the dungeon room, the one smelling of pee.

At the doorway to the dungeon, Sophie told Sally to say the prayer. She did and felt two souls whisper past her, almost like a sleeping baby exhaling.

Sally felt ashamed.

Ask Him.

"Father, God, lift this bad thing from my heart, if it be Thy will."

Sophie cocked her head to the side, like a teacher waiting for a student to come up with the proper reply to her question, a reply that was obvious, if only the student would *think*.

Sally said thanks, *to Father God*. Then Sophie told her she could go to bed, and then disappeared. Sally opened her senses and found the security man, again, in the foyer. She went up to her room by the east-end staircase.

As she ascended, she remembered the princess at the dinner they had. The princess said the chateau was happier than she ever knew it to be. The next time the princess visited, Sally knew she'd find the royal mansion happier still. Sally's already happy heart, it, too, became happier still.

The next day, movers transported the Marshall family's belongings to their new residence. Kate had supervised moves by herself any number of times before. This time, the move was the easiest ever. The movers strapped dresser drawers closed and carted them down to the truck and set them up in the new place, ready to operate with no unpacking necessary.

Kate loved her *tiny* new home. Five bedrooms. The dining room only accommodated twelve. And it was in the town of Mons, not out in the boonies.

The government put a large crew to work at relocating the family. By late afternoon, all the furniture had been placed in the rooms, and the kitchen dishes and cookware were stowed in the cabinets. General Sampson's wife brought dinner.

Bill worked late, occupied, as the SHAPE headquarters was those days, with Operation Desert Shield, dealing with Iraq's invasion of Kuwait, but he returned home in time to put the children to bed.

When he came back downstairs, Kate had dinner warmed up for him.

"Funniest thing," Bill said. "I listened to JR pray the Our Father. He began the prayer with, 'Father God, who art in heaven.' I waited for him to finish and asked him why he said the words that way. He shrugged, you know, like little boys do in the way that says, 'I don't know.'

"Then, when Sally began her prayer with, 'Father God, who art in heaven.' When she finished, I asked her why she changed the words. Didn't she know Jesus, Himself, gave us the words another way.

"She knew Jesus gave us the words, 'But, father,' she said. 'He gave those words to the apostles when they asked Him how to pray. They didn't know how to. I do know how to pray.' That, from our nine-year old! And we worried about her, you know, about her development.

"I went to Heather's room. We knelt beside the bed and said the prayer. I kissed her good night, and as I left, I thought, you know, finally, one of the kids said it the quote, right way. But as I walked down the steps, I had another thought. Saying the prayer with Heather, kneeling side by side, it was the perfect way to say it. There were two of us. Our fit.

"I feel like I have had the most profound theological teaching at the hands of our children."

"Eat, before it gets cold."

Bill bowed. "Thank You, Our Father who art in heaven for this bounty You set for us on earth to nourish our bodies."

He took a bite.

"You know," he said, I'm Bill Marshall, a Wyoming cowboy and

Navy fighter pilot. I'm not sure I'm worthy to be the father of three angels."

"Husband dearest, I profess to God above, that I have, with my own eyes, witnessed your servant Bill behave in ways that I say were halfway close to sort of decent."

He swallowed and smiled. He asked in and from his heart, *Father God, is it okay for man to be this happy on earth?*

The two looked into each other's eyes. They shared an intimacy, not as one flesh, rather, as one spirit. Together they knew that in that time and in that space, their children were up in their beds, sleeping peacefully, and no evil could touch them.

Together they prayed, *Our Father, we thank You for this blessed moment of freedom from worry about our children.*

It was the tiniest of moments. Then they rejoined the world, and the ever-present niggle of worry for the safety of their offspring rejoined their minds and souls.

That night in bed, Kate began their decade of the rosary with, "God of All People, who art in heaven."

Before the ten Hail Marys started, Bill said, "Why am I not surprised Saint Kate, mother of angels on earth, has her unique way to pray, too?"

In the passing years, they remembered that night as the one their children and a gypsy woman taught them to pray. And they remembered that one blessed moment, when Father God lifted the omnipresent worry parents have for their children, and the blessed feeling of that freedom from it. They remembered when the worry returned after momentary absence, and saw it as a blessing, too. They never questioned the validity of these memories. They were grounded, they believed, in laws of physics governing the spiritual realm with the same iron- handed inviolability as the laws governing the physical world.

www.ingramcontent.com/pod-product-compliance
Lightning Source LLC
Chambersburg PA
CBHW060929190726
48286CB00002B/692